The Match of the Day Murders

Also by Patrick C. Walsh

The Mac Maguire detective mysteries

The Body in the Boot

The Dead Squirrel

The Weeping Women

The Blackness

23 Cold Cases

Two Dogs

The Chancer

The Tiger's Back

The Eight Bench Walk

Stories of the supernatural

13 Ghosts of Winter

The Black Vaults Experiment

All available in Amazon Books

Patrick C. Walsh

The Match of the Day Murders

The seventh Mac Maguire mystery

Garden City Ink

A Garden City Ink ebook
www.gardencityink.com

First published in Great Britain in 2018
All rights reserved
Copyright © 2018, 2020 Patrick C. Walsh

A CIP record for this title is available from the British
Library

Cover art © Seamus Maguire 2018
Garden City Ink Design

'Some people think football is a matter of life and death. I assure you, it's much more serious than that.'
Bill Shankley, Liverpool Manager

For my footballing hero Peter McParland

Note for American readers – Football, as mentioned throughout this book, refers to the version of the game you may know better as 'soccer'. *Match of the Day* is a long running and very popular football TV highlights show on the BBC. It is broadcast on Saturday evenings in the UK and is the author's favourite show.

Five years before...

He'd seen her in the pub and he found that he couldn't take his eyes off her. She was beautiful. Her eyes, her smile, even her habit of flicking her hair out of her eyes all resonated with him in a special way. He didn't do anything about it though apart from having another drink. When she and her friends left, he finished his drink and went home. He came back out again a few minutes later but he had no idea why. He'd felt a sort of dark restlessness inside him that night and the drink had only made it worse.

He was driving aimlessly around Baldock when he saw her again. She was walking on the grass verge holding her shoes in her hands. He pulled up and spoke to her. She told him that she'd broken the heel on one of her shoes so she was looking for a taxi home. He offered her a lift. She asked if he'd been drinking so he lied.

He wasn't drunk, not even near it, he told himself.

He asked her if he could show her something before he dropped her home, something that had been important to him once. He was surprised when she said that she would.

There was no one waiting for her at home, she told him, so why not?

He parked the car on the street and led her out onto the football field.

Is this it? she'd asked as she looked around.

He could see that she was disappointed.

He told her why it had been so important to him. When he'd been a kid, he'd scored a goal on this pitch, a goal in a very important game. The other kids in the team didn't seem to like him much and so he didn't often get a game. That day four of the team had been ill and so they had to put him in the side. He'd played well but it was the goal

1

that he'd scored in the eighty fifth minute that had made all the difference. It had won them the game.

He showed her exactly how it happened. He received the ball in his own half and then dribbled past three players and shot from distance. The ball flew straight as an arrow right into the top corner of the net. Of course, he hadn't meant it. He'd been afraid of the posse of defenders coming at him and he'd just thrown his foot at the ball to get rid of it. He honestly hadn't known that he had a shot like that in him. She laughed as he described the goal and, at that moment, she looked so incredibly sexy.

He felt strangely disconnected as though he was in a weird dream. All he knew was that he desperately wanted her. He needed to touch her, to feel himself inside her. He forcibly kissed her and grabbed her crotch.

She pulled away, slapped his face and shouted at him. She called him an animal.

His lust was replaced by an unthinking red rage. She turned to go but he grabbed her scarf and pulled her backwards. She fell onto her knees and tried to shout but nothing came out. He pulled hard on the scarf as the rage coursed through his brain.

He'd show her, he told himself.

Then it was as if a switch had been thrown and he came back to consciousness. His first thought was, 'Show her what?' as he let the scarf slip through his fingers.

He suddenly felt dizzy and nauseous and turned away. His thoughts were in a turmoil. Then, the memory what had just happened surfaced in his brain. It seemed so unreal that he was sure it must have been some sort of drink-fuelled delusion. He fearfully turned and looked down.

She lay there unmoving. Her dead eyes staring up at him.

He wanted to run off but he stopped himself. He grabbed the scarf and pulled off her panties as carefully as he could. He adjusted her skirt and then he ran off as fast as he could. Before he left the football field he looked back. She was still lying there.

He ran on still hoping that he might wake up soon and find that it just a bad dream after all.

The 'Wedding of the Century'

Mac couldn't help but go back for seconds. The goat curry with rice and peas was as good as anything he'd ever tasted. While he waited in the food queue, he looked out over the assembled crowd. His gaze first fell on his colleague Jo Thibonais. This was no surprise as she was resplendent in her long white beaded wedding dress and surrounded by a scrum of guests all waiting to speak to her. She was rightfully the centre of all attention.

No, I'm wrong there, Mac thought. She's Jo Thibonais-Dugdale now, isn't she?

He wondered at the plethora of double-barrelled names that were around these days. When he was young, if you had two surnames separated by a hyphen, then it normally meant that you had a landed estate, pronounced 'house' as 'hice' and went grouse shooting every August.

He looked over at her new husband Gerry who was wearing a smart grey suit, a blue tie and the widest of smiles. He too was looking at Jo and his love for her could be clearly seen on his face.

The church hall was fairly crowded but everyone seemed to be mixing together well. The music certainly helped in that respect. A live band was bashing out some old soul and reggae tracks that seemed to be pleasing just about everyone. This definitely included Dan Carter and his wife who were dancing away like teenagers. The head of the Major Crime Unit was shaved and slightly less rumpled than normal while his wife was dressed in a stylish blue frock. Mac guessed that the music must have reminded them of their younger selves.

Behind them he could see that some of the team from the Major Crime Unit were seated together at a table. Young Leigh Marston was looking quite fetching in a little black dress and he was quite surprised that she still had no young man in tow as yet. Chris Skorupski was dressed very sharply and he was accompanied by his young wife who was very pregnant with their first child. They looked happy together. Andy Reid and his wife looked happy too. They'd been married for quite a while now but they still hadn't stopped holding hands.

Even Martina McEwan and her partner had turned up. Mac had asked her how she'd been getting on at the Rape Unit. She'd said that it was hard work but she was finding it rewarding. He'd wished her luck. He felt that she hadn't exactly gone for the easy option when she'd left the team.

Mac thought back to the ceremony. It couldn't have gone any better and certainly the music would stay with him for some time. It's not often you get to hear a full gospel choir giving it all they had. Jo and Gerry had decided to have the ceremony at the church in Stevenage that she and her family had attended for some years.

Jo had arranged it so that Mac and her police colleagues were seated on the groom's side as her side of the church was jam packed with all her relatives. Mac discovered that Jo had four sisters and two brothers while her mother had even more; six sisters and two brothers. On her father's side he had just the two sisters and two brothers. All the resultant uncles, aunts, cousins, nephews and nieces plus friends made for quite a crowd. As Mac looked at Jo's family, he had to admit that, although he knew that they were mostly devout Christians, they certainly knew how to have a good time.

On Gerry's side his brother and sister had turned up as had his ex-wife and her partner. Gerry's two children were there too, indeed his grown-up son was acting as his best man. They all looked to be enjoying themselves too. He thought it was a wonderful thing when families could still pull together and get on with each other even after something as traumatic as a divorce.

'Mr. Maguire, what can I get you?' a voice asked.

Mac turned to see that he had reached the head of the queue. A large lady in her sixties was waiting for his order. She was wearing a bright yellow dress that was partly covered up by a white apron. She had a white hat precariously perched on her head that looked as if it had been sculpted out of meringue. This was Jo's mother, a woman who didn't believe in taking it easy even when you were the mother of the bride.

'Oh, Mrs. Thibonais. I was hoping for a little more of your wonderful goat curry if you have any left,' Mac said.

'Oh, you liked my curry, did you?' she asked with a wide smile.

'I certainly did,' Mac replied.

'I'm sorry,' she said, 'I'm afraid it's all gone but if you want to wait a minute, my sister's goat curry is nearly ready. It's not as good as mine but it will do, I suppose.'

Mac thought that he could detect a hint of sibling rivalry going on.

'It's all gone really well today, hasn't it?' Mac said making some small talk while he waited.

'Oh, it's been more than lovely, Mr. Maguire. I must admit that I was just about to give up on Jo ever getting married but then life always surprises you, doesn't it? He's a nice man too and he knows who wears the trousers in the house, Jo of course, which is a good thing in my book. Yes, I think she definitely fell on her feet there.'

Behind her a lady of a similar size dressed in a bright orange dress and an apron emerged from the kitchen. She had a massive metal pot in her hands that was steaming with some luscious aromas. The lady smiled at him and went back into the kitchen.

'Here you go, Mr. Maguire,' Mrs. Thibonais said as she handed him a plate with a healthy helping of curry on one side and rice and red beans on the other. 'Tell me what you think and be honest now!'

Mac took a small sample of the curry.

'Oh it's…er…nice but you're right it's not quite the same as yours.'

'See I told you,' she said with a wide smile. 'Thank you, you're obviously a man who really knows his food.'

Mac smiled and nodded and then headed for his table. He couldn't wait to tuck into the curry. He hadn't lied but he hadn't exactly told the truth either. While Mrs. Thibonais' curry had been wonderful, her sister's curry was simply beyond compare.

'You won't need to eat for a week after this,' his friend Tim said as he returned with some drinks.

'You might be right there but it's not often I get the chance to eat such wonderful food. Are you enjoying yourself?'

'Oh yes, I'm really glad I came,' Tim replied. 'It looks like your daughter is too.'

Bridget and her boyfriend Tommy were also up on the dance floor and they were both laughing at something Bridget had said.

'You wouldn't think that they'd only just come back from their holidays late yesterday evening now, would you? I don't know where they get the energy from,' Tim said. 'By the way how did they like the flat?'

'They were very impressed,' Mac replied. 'Tommy had picked all the colours before he went but even he was surprised at how good it looked. The decorator did an excellent job. He moved all the furniture around himself and everything. When they left for Cyprus the flat was a bit dingy but you could really see the difference once it was all finished. It was so much lighter and the rooms actually looked larger, if you can believe that.'

'I'd bet that Bridget shed a tear or two, am I right?' Tim asked.

'Yes, she did. It was a nice surprise for her.'

'Well, you're a good dad in paying for it all.'

'Not really. In fact, it was the least I could do after all the time that she and Tommy had spent looking after me when I was bedbound,' Mac replied.

'Oh look, Kate's arrived,' Tim said as he stood up and waved.

Mac turned and saw Kate wave back at them. However, she first went over to Jo and then Gerry and had a few words with each of them before she went over to the table where her colleagues were sitting. After a short chat with Dan she eventually made her way through the crowd over to Mac and Tim.

'God, what do I have to do to get a drink around here?' Kate exclaimed with only half a smile as she sat down.

Mac thought that she looked more than a bit frazzled.

'A large red?' Tim asked.

Kate nodded her gratitude and Tim went off to get her a glass of wine.

'I'm so sorry that I missed the ceremony but something came up,' Kate said.

'Nothing serious, I hope?' Mac asked.

She didn't say anything for a moment.

'My father was involved in a car accident late last night.'

'I'm sorry to hear that. Is he okay?' Mac asked.

'Unfortunately, yes. I got a message early this morning and it sounded as if he was at death's door. So, I rushed out to the hospital in London, a private one of course, and when I got there he was sitting up, drinking coffee and reading the Financial Times.'

'Well, I suppose that's better than finding him seriously injured, isn't it?' Mac said trying to be positive.

'Is it? For some reason I'm not too sure about that. Anyway, he was lucky, as usual. The police turned up to interview him and I had a word with them first. He was over the limit they said and he took a corner too fast. He probably had a few too many of those single malts that he likes so much. Well, whatever it was he ended up wrapping his McLaren sports car around a tree. They showed me the photos. Thankfully the tree didn't look too badly damaged but the car was totalled. For God's sake, the man's in his sixties! What's he doing driving around in a high-powered sports car anyway, never mind the alcohol. It's like he thinks he's still a bloody teenager or something.'

Mac could clearly hear the exasperation in her voice.

'To top it all, when I got there all he could say was something about it taking a quarter of a million pounds of wrecked car to get me to visit him. He said that it was worth it too, the sarcastic sod. Oh, thanks Tim,' she said as a glass of wine appeared in front of her.

As a father himself Mac couldn't help thinking that those words might not have been as sarcastic as she took them to be.

'Anyway, enough about him, how did the wedding go?' she asked.

'It was fantastic,' Mac said. 'They had a full gospel choir singing too. I normally find weddings a bit boring, the ceremonial bit anyway, but this was fun.'

'I'm glad it went well. Who caught the bouquet?' she asked.

It had become something of a competition within the police station and some had even started practising for it as though it were an athletics event of some sort.

'It was Toni, Toni Woodgate,' Mac answered.

'I had a go at catching the bouquet too but that Toni beat me to it. I'm sorry to report that there was clearly some Illegal use of the elbows going on,' Tim said as he tried to keep a straight face.

This got a real belly laugh from Kate.

'Toni? Is she still here?' she asked once she'd stopped laughing.

Mac observed her closely as she looked around the room. Her pale skin had flushed slightly and her breathing had speeded up.

9

'No, unfortunately she had to go,' Mac said. 'She got a phone call from one of her team. I believe that there was some new information about a case she's working on.'

'Oh,' was all Kate said.

Mac could clearly read the disappointment on her face. He briefly wondered if there was anything he could do but he immediately dismissed the idea.

If it's meant to happen it will happen, he thought.

Bridget and Tommy came over and said hello to Kate. While they were talking Mac felt a tap on his shoulder. He turned around to see a woman. She was in her late forties and had blonde hair cut fairly short. She wore a light blue dress with matching shoes.

She looked somewhat unsure of herself, Mac thought.

'I'm sorry to interrupt you but I've been told that you're a private detective, is that right?' she asked.

'Yes, yes I am. Can I help you?' he asked.

She was going to say something and then hesitated. She had a sudden change of mind.

'No, it's okay. It's nothing really,' she said as she turned to go.

'No, please wait,' Mac said.

He quickly got a card from his wallet and put it in her hand.

'In case you change your mind,' he said.

She gave him a fleeting smile and disappeared into the crowd. He sat down and wondered what that might have been about.

'Oh, come on Mac,' Tim pleaded. 'Back me up here. Bridget and Kate are ganging up on me. Who would you sooner have in mid-field, Roy Keane or Patrick Viera?'

Chapter One

Kate had woken up that Tuesday morning with a distinct hangover. She found this strange as she hadn't been drinking the night before. She felt tired and bleary and all she wanted to do was to roll over and go back to sleep. She had to force herself to get out of bed and into the shower.

As she let the water wash some of the tiredness away, she started wondering about the new case that her boss Dan Carter had lined up for her. It had been really slow lately which she thought was just as well as they were quite short-handed. Jo and Gerry were still sunning themselves on their honeymoon in Jamaica while Jo's partner, Leigh Marston, had decided to take some leave as well. After all the problems he'd had with the press on their last case, she'd have thought that Dan would have been happy to have a bit of a lull. However, it just seemed to make him even more grumpy than usual.

She was still thinking about this as she dressed. She checked herself in the mirror and a pale skinned face framed with flame red hair looked back at her. Other people found her slightly strange looking and she wasn't surprised. She thought she looked strange too at times. She'd watched a documentary the evening before about the Elizabethans. The women back then used to whiten their skin with lead and even bleed themselves to look a little paler. They'd have loved her.

She quickly drank a glass of orange juice and then checked herself once more in the mirror. She was ready to go. She'd stopped having breakfast in her flat months ago, eating by herself just made her feel even more lonely and desperate. She'd grab something at the station. She was just about to open the door when her doorbell rang. No-one ever rang that bell. She hesitated for a moment while she tried to think who it might be before giving up and opening up the door.

A slim man in his late twenties stood there with a bulging backpack in one hand. He had fair hair and his normally pale skin had been turned to bronze by the sun. He was wearing khaki coloured chinos and a black T shirt that read 'Save the Rhino'.

'My God, Magnus!' Kate shouted with surprise.

'Hello, sis. How have you been?'

They hugged each other fiercely for some time. When they let go of each other Kate stared at her brother as though she still couldn't quite believe her eyes.

'I can't believe it! Why didn't you tell me you were coming?'

'I left a message on your phone last night and about an hour ago too,' Magnus replied.

Kate pulled out her phone and checked it.

'God, I'm so sorry. I was tired and went to bed early last night and I must have turned my phone off. How long are you staying for?'

'Just for a couple of days or so. I have to be back in Johannesburg for an important meeting on Friday.'

'Where's Nobomi? Is she with you?' Kate asked.

Nobomi was Magnus' wife. She was a Xhosa girl who he'd met in South Africa and who he'd fallen in love with.

'She's still at home. I didn't want to stress her out by dragging her all the way here. She's expecting Kate. We only had it confirmed just before I left.'

'Wow, my little brother's going to be a dad!' she said with a look of surprise. 'My God, that means that I'll be an aunt. I'm afraid that it will take me a while to get my head around that one.'

Somehow the word 'aunt' always made her think of someone frowsy and getting on a bit. She felt as though time was tapping her on the shoulder.

'Anyway, the circumstances being what they were with dad, I didn't think it would be such a good idea to bring her along.'

'What circumstances?' Kate asked.

'You know, what's happening with dad,' he replied with a shrug of the shoulders.

'Oh him, he just wrapped his car round a tree that's all, there wasn't even a scratch on him. You haven't come all this way just because of that, have you?'

'He hasn't told you then?' Magnus said looking puzzled. 'Why would he not do that?'

'Told me what?'

'Sit down and I'll tell you.'

Kate sat down. She could tell from her brother's face that she wasn't going to like what he was about to say.

'Kate, dad's dying.'

She gave him a sceptical look.

'No, I find that hard to believe. It's just one of his little stunts to make us come running that's all.'

'Not this time I'm afraid,' Magnus said. 'I had a word with his doctor and he sent me over his scan results. I showed them to a friend of mine who's a surgeon. He just shook his head. It's a brain tumour and it's inoperable.'

Kate gave this some thought.

'Did that have something to do with the crash? I know he was over the limit but he's never crashed his car before.'

'Almost certainly. His doctor said that part of his field of vision has gone. Even if he hadn't been over the limit he'd probably have crashed anyway.'

Kate's head was spinning, she just couldn't take it all in. Then she remembered that she was supposed to be on her way to work.

'What have you got planned for the day?' she asked.

'I was going to go to the hospital a bit later, that's all really,' Magnus replied.

13

'I've got to be at work today, we're starting on a new case. Can I meet you at the hospital this evening? I'll try and get off as early as I can.'

'That's fine with me. I'll go to the hospital and try and find out as much as I can about dad's condition in the meantime.'

'Where are you staying?' Kate asked.

'Well here, if you don't mind that is,' Magnus replied. 'I didn't really have time to book anywhere and your sofa looks really comfortable.'

'I was hoping you'd say that. It will be nice for us to spend some time together. Have you had any breakfast yet?'

'No just coffee.'

'Come on then. Let's treat ourselves to a Full English,' Kate suggested.

Magnus smiled.

'God, I haven't had one of those for ages. I hope they've got brown sauce too. It's just about impossible to get where I live. It's funny the things that you miss.'

As they walked to the pub they chatted about when they were children. They were close because all they really had was each other and their mother of course.

'Oh, look!' Kate said. 'I can't believe they're showing that again.'

She pointed at a poster for the cartoon version of *One Hundred and One Dalmatians*. It was showing at one of the local cinemas.

'God, I loved that film! I remember us both going to see that with mum. I must have been around seven at the time, I think. I remember booing Cruella DeVil with all the rest of the kids. It was only ever mum who took us anywhere, I never remember dad doing anything with us. Sad that, isn't it?'

She didn't notice that her brother was giving her a puzzled look.

Kate rang Tommy from the pub and told him that she was with her brother and asked him if he could let Dan know that she'd be slightly late.

'That was my partner. He's really sweet. He reminds me a bit of you, I suppose,' Kate said.

He raised his eyebrows.

'It sounds as if you really like him.'

'Oh, not in that way,' Kate quickly replied. 'Anyway, he's already got a girlfriend, one he's very happy with too. I'm still having trouble believing what you said about dad though. I honestly thought he'd outlast us all.'

'It's not going to be easy, is it?' Magnus said. 'For us, I mean. All of those things that we've pushed to the back of our minds will come crawling back out again. I just wanted to forget about it all and I almost had.'

Kate took his hand in hers.

'You're lucky, you're in such a better place now and you've got Nobomi to help you. Not only that but you'll be a dad soon and you'll have lots of other, much more important, things to think about.'

'What about you Kate? Is there anyone who'll be able to help you when you need it?'

'No, I've not met anyone and, if I'm honest, since the divorce I've not really been looking anyway.'

'I wish you could find someone Kate, I really do' Magnus said. 'I've got a feeling that this is going to be hard on the both of us. I don't know about you but, for all that he's arrogant and cold and an excuse for a human being, I still love him and that's the problem.'

Kate didn't say anything but Magnus was right. She loved her father too and that was the problem.

They hugged each other at the train station. Magnus was going into London while Kate was going in the opposite direction.

'Call me if there's any news. Otherwise, I'll try and get to the hospital around six or so,' Kate said.

She watched as her brother strode away. There was a confidence in the way he walked that she hadn't noticed before and she suddenly realised that he was a man now. For most of her life he'd always just been her little brother but, since she'd seen him last, he'd changed. He even looked like he'd grown a little. Had she changed? She doubted it. She felt as if she was stuck in a rut and she had no idea of how to get out of it.

She thought of her father as the train made its way northwards towards Letchworth. Magnus had been right. Things were already crawling out of the back of her mind. She thought of all the birthdays and school plays he'd missed and all the weak excuses he'd come up with but that wasn't what really hurt. If she ever wondered why she and Magnus had turned out even half sane, she knew that it was all down to her mother.

She had always been there when her children had needed her and she always seemed to be able to cheer them up. Her father treated her as if she were a fool. The way he tried to control her so that she had no life of her own and all the sly little digs making her out to be stupid and inadequate. Kate could never forgive him for that. Unfortunately, her mother stuck with him and it was his part in the Icelandic bank crash that had finished her off. She'd been ill anyway but Kate could see that she no longer wanted to live. She was obviously ashamed of her husband but he had no idea what shame was. He'd even made money out of betting that his own bank would crash.

With a start she realised that the sign outside said 'Letchworth'. She quickly jumped off the train and made her way up the steps. She felt weary and not really up to working. She knew that Dan would give her time off if she asked for it but what would be the point? All she'd do is sit around and think. That was the last thing she wanted to do right at this moment. She reminded herself that she'd be soon starting on a new case and that was good.

16

She knew that work was the only thing that might stop her thinking about her father for a while.

Chapter Two

She was later than she'd thought and so she ran the short distance to the police station. It had started raining heavily which prodded her into speeding up a little more. She arrived at the station damp and breathless. Once again, she lamented giving up playing football. She was really out of shape. Andy and Tommy looked up and waved at her as she walked in. Dan was sitting on a desk talking to Chris.

'Sorry, I'm a little late. Am I holding things up?' she asked breathlessly.

'No, we're still waiting for Adil. He should be along in a few minutes,' Dan said.

He gestured for Kate to follow him into his office.

'Tommy said that your brother is over from South Africa. Is that right?' Dan asked.

'Yes, he just turned up on my doorstep this morning,' Kate replied. 'I wasn't expecting him. It came as a bit of a shock I suppose.'

'Tommy also said that you've had some bad news about your father.'

Dan saying it made it even more real for some reason. Kate suddenly felt the tears welling up and it took some effort to stop herself from crying.

'Yes, he's got a brain tumour. I only just found out this morning. It's affecting his vision and that's why he crashed his car.'

'Look, if you need any time off please take it, take as long you need. I know myself how difficult it can be to try and carry on working during a situation like this.'

'Thanks Dan, really thanks but I'm okay for now. I'd sooner be working than just sitting around thinking about it. Later might be different, I suppose...'

She really didn't want to think about later just now.

'Okay, I understand,' Dan said. 'Just let me know if you need anything.'

'Thanks, Dan.'

They joined the rest of the team in the main office. Adil had now arrived.

'Okay,' Dan said, 'as you're all aware we seem to have more or less run out of work. All the villains have gone on holiday for a while so it looks as if we've only got two jobs on at the moment. Yesterday evening a robbery was reported over at Rushden. A Mr. Benson had just gotten out of his car after returning home from work when he was assaulted. The thief took his keys and made off with his car, a top of the range BMW. Mr. Benson had a contusion on his head and went to hospital for observation but it appears that, so far at least, he's okay. It's similar to a couple of unsolved cases we've had over the last few months, all of which involved the theft of some very expensive cars.'

'Do you think that they're stealing them to order?' Andy asked.

'If I had to guess then I'd say that it was likely,' Dan replied.

'And what's the other case?' Chris asked.

'A cold case, I'm afraid, but I promised the boss that I'd put someone on it for a few weeks as it's bound to feature in the press for a while. He wanted to be able to say that we had a team looking into it again.'

'The Match of the Day Murders, I take it,' Andy replied with a sigh.

'Yes, that's right,' Dan replied. 'It will be the fifth anniversary of the first murder in a week or so. It's technically still a live case as far as we're concerned but, as there haven't been any more murders, I don't think that anyone's looked at it for a while now.'

Dan could see that the prospect of getting involved in a case that had already been investigated to death didn't really appeal to any of them.

'I was on that case,' Andy said, 'and it was one of the most frustrating experiences of my life. Months and months of work and it was all for nothing. Talk about banging your head against a brick wall.'

'Fancy banging your head a bit more?' Dan asked.

Andy smiled as he said, 'Sure, I'd be happy to.'

'Okay, so perhaps if Chris, Adil and myself take the assault and robbery and that leaves Kate and Tommy to help Andy. Depending on how the cases go we can always swop resources around a little. Is that okay with everyone?' Dan asked.

They all nodded their heads.

'Okay, let's get on with it then,' Dan said.

Kate and Tommy turned to Andy.

'Okay, I think it would help if you both spent some time looking through the case files,' Andy said. 'There's quite a lot in there so it will take you a while. While you're doing that I'm going to see if I can get us some help.'

'He'll be in the Magnets at two,' Tommy said. 'Tim has to get up really early tomorrow as he's driving up to Newcastle for a furniture sale so they brought their drink forward a bit.'

'Say hello to Mac for me,' Kate said.

'Thanks, I will,' Andy said with a smile.

Chapter Three

It was early August and, supposedly, the height of the English summer. That being the case Mac should have been surprised when he got caught in a heavy shower of rain but he wasn't and he had his umbrella readily to hand. It had rained solidly for the last couple of days now and the unseasonal dampness had become the main topic of conversation.

Well at least the rain's warm, he thought.

He looked around for some shelter. Luckily, he'd been ambling along one of Letchworth's main shopping streets when the cloudburst had started and he found that he was only a short distance away from David's Bookshop. The thought of passing some time browsing through the crime section quite appealed to him. He still had a couple of hours to kill before his appointment at the Magnets for a drink with his best friend Tim.

The wonderful combined smell of book paper and coffee hit him as soon as he walked in the door. There was a large display of hardback books right in front of him. The centrepiece of the display was a large poster which read –

'The 'Match of the Day' Murders – The true story of the sensational unsolved crimes that rocked England – Revised and updated by the author for the fifth anniversary of the three horrific slayings.'

The poster displayed the photos of three girls all of whom were young and very pretty. He wandered over to the display and picked up a book. He turned it over and on the back was a picture of a woman in her fifties called Rebecca Ferrante. It had first been published a couple of months after the murders had taken place by a local journalist who had covered the story at the time. Mac tried to remember some of the details but found that he couldn't for some reason. He could remember his wife Nora commenting on the killings afterwards though.

She'd felt so sorry for the mothers of the murdered girls and had then thanked God that Bridget was away at medical school in London. This had made Mac smile as he remembered how worried Nora had been when their daughter had left sleepy Letchworth for the big bad city.

He then remembered why the murders hadn't left more of an impression on him. He'd been dealing with some murders of his own at the time, murders of a very sensitive nature. Only a little of the story had ever made it into the press but the death of several Russians, all of who had been hostile to the regime at the time, had caused something of a diplomatic storm. Mac and his team had ended up right in the middle of it all. He'd slept in his office for well over a week as the team realised that they were in something of a race to find the murderers. They all knew that it was probably only a matter of time before the 'men in suits' from MI5 or one of the other intelligence agencies stepped in.

Unfortunately, they hadn't managed to find the killers although they had gotten very close. Mac later guessed that this was probably why the cases had been shut down so quickly. He'd later been told by a friend from one of the agencies that they'd been under immense pressure from Downing Street to end the investigation. They were told by the Prime Minister's office that there could be no diplomatic 'unpleasantness' as an important state visit by the Russian President was in the process of being arranged. Mac's team had also been quite forcibly reminded at the time that they had all signed the Official Secrets Act and that they should say nothing about the case unless they wanted to get banged up themselves. And that was basically that.

He found that it still annoyed him. Even so, he was still somewhat surprised that he hadn't remembered a bit more about the girls' murders. He was curious and bought a copy of the book. He wandered into the coffee shop where he bought himself a large cappuccino and found a table next to the window. The rain was falling even harder now and people were sheltering under the awnings of shops and in doorways, looking up to the sky now and then in the hope that it might soon stop. From where Mac was sitting, he could see that there was a raft of black clouds coming their way. It wasn't going to stop any time soon.

Mac smiled as he pictured his dog Terry. Right now, he'd be waiting by the front door for Amanda Drinkwater to come and take him for his daily walk. Amanda was a neighbour of Mac's who, some six months before, had told him about a squirrel that she'd found dead in her garden. It had led to him becoming involved in the case that had become universally known as 'The Letchworth Poisoner'.

Amanda took her dog for a long walk every day and she had volunteered to take Terry along too. It was an arrangement that suited Mac as he couldn't walk for any distance these days due to his back problems. Unfortunately for Terry it looked like he'd have to wait for a little while longer for his walk.

His nurse and housekeeper Amrit was holding the fort today and he knew that she'd be hoping that the rain would stop soon too. Although Mac was fairly certain that his dog couldn't tell the time, he was always at the front door just a few minutes before Amanda was due. He'd then sit down and whimper and look at you with soulful eyes until finally the doorbell rang. This would then be the cue for some frenzied barking and jumping up and down.

Mac hadn't had Terry for long but he was already finding him to be good company especially in the evenings and mornings when he was by himself. They had started to learn each other's little ways and were beginning to

23

get comfortable with each other. Mac wasn't used to being alone and it was really nice to have someone else around, even if it was just a dog.

He took a sip of his coffee and hoped that the rain would soon stop if only for Amrit's sake. As it was, he was glad that he was tucked away somewhere nice and dry and not out there trying to walk between the raindrops.

He opened the book.

It started with a graphic description of the first murder which he found quite compelling. There was no doubt that the book was well written. Mac stopped reading after a while and looked outside. The rain was still falling and people were still sheltering and hoping for a respite from the seemingly endless downpour. He thought about what he'd read.

Chloe Alexander had been just eighteen when she'd disappeared on a Saturday night in August some five years before. As it had been a warm evening, Chloe had only been wearing a short black dress with a bright red silk scarf draped around her neck. She'd been out with a group of friends in Baldock celebrating a friend's birthday when she'd disappeared somewhere between two pubs. A few of her friends went back to the first pub they'd visited to look for her but she was nowhere to be seen. They guessed that she must have met someone she knew and gone off with them.

She certainly had met someone and that someone had strangled her to death. Her body had been found the morning afterwards when a team of ten-year olds had turned up for their regular Sunday morning football match at a school's playing fields. One of the parents had gone over when she saw a group of children standing still and looking at something near one of the goals. She could see that there was something on the ground and she thought that someone must have dumped a bag of rubbish on the field. It had happened before.

As she came closer, she could see that someone was lying on the ground, a young woman. She wondered if there had been an accident of some sort. She ran over but the woman lay there unmoving. She felt for a pulse but there was none. The woman's skin was ice cold. Her eyes were a whitish blue and she could see that there was no life in them. They reminded her of the eyes of dead fish. Afterwards, when the nightmares came, those eyes would always be in them somewhere. She rushed the children away and rang for the police.

They arrived within minutes and a forensics team turned up not long afterwards. Despite all their best endeavours they found very little. There was lots of DNA evidence found at the crime scene but once it was analysed at the lab nothing definitive was found. Sex hadn't taken place and Chloe hadn't managed to scratch her attacker. They found out later that there had been masses of contact DNA but, as she had just spent quite a few hours in pubs that had been packed on a Saturday night, then this might have been expected.

It looked like sexual assault might have been the motive as her panties were missing yet sex hadn't seemingly even been attempted. She was strangled with some sort of ligature and, as her silk scarf was missing too, it was thought that this had most likely been used to kill her. She had no other injuries apart from some slight bruising in the middle of her back where it was thought that her attacker might had placed a knee to give him leverage as he pulled on both ends of the scarf while he strangled her.

The two items that had disappeared, the scarf and the panties, might have been taken as trophies but it was also thought that it might be because that was where most of the murderer's DNA might have been found. If true this showed either prior planning or quick thinking on the part of the murderer.

No-one had come forward to say that they'd seen Chloe at any point after she'd disappeared so how she'd made it the two miles or more from Baldock to the school playing fields was a complete mystery. Forensics said that they felt she was most likely murdered on the spot that her body had been found. However, they couldn't totally rule out the possibility of her being killed somewhere else and her body dumped on the football field if it had been done carefully.

Mac had been involved in a few cases like this before. With most murders, if you put the hard work in, then something will break sooner or later. It might just be a minor detail that had been previously overlooked or a question that just hadn't been asked before. Sometimes looking at the case from a different perspective could also help to put you on the right path and often it was just pure luck that led to a murderer being caught. Then there were those cases that stubbornly refused to reveal their secrets and, no matter how hard you tried, you just kept ending up at the same dead end.

Mac hated those cases. He read on.

A week later and the police were no closer to finding Chloe's killer when the second murder was reported.

Nineteen year old Ana Tomas disappeared while she was on her way home from an evening shift as a receptionist at a hotel in Welwyn Garden City. It happened on a Saturday night exactly one week after Chloe had been killed. Ana's walk home normally took her around fifteen minutes and she should have gotten home well before eleven thirty. When she hadn't arrived by midnight her father went out looking for her. He took the same route that she would have taken going home. There was no sign of her. At the hotel they told him that she'd finished work at eleven and had just the one drink in the pub next door before leaving. That was the last time that anyone saw her alive. At one o'clock her father phoned the police.

She wasn't found until the following day by some early morning runners. Her body was spotted lying in the goalmouth of a football pitch at a sports centre that was no more than a couple of hundred yards from the hotel she worked at. The football pitch had a running track laid around it and this was what the runners had been planning to make use of.

Ana had also been strangled but this time she hadn't been wearing a scarf so the killer must have brought the ligature with him. Again, her panties were missing and again sex hadn't taken place. There were multiple DNA contact traces but nothing stood out as being significant except for the fact that traces of Chloe's DNA were found on Ana's neck. It looked as if the same scarf had been used in both murders. No-one saw Ana after she left the hotel. Yet another dead end.

Mac stopped and looked out of the window. It had finally stopped raining. He looked at his watch. He'd been reading for longer than he'd thought and it was nearly time to meet up with his best friend and to sink a few cold pints.

He was looking forward to both.

Someone came and sat opposite him. Mac looked up. With some surprise he recognised her from Jo's wedding. She was the woman that he'd given a card to.

'I'm sorry, I hope that I'm not intruding,' she said.

She was wearing a waterproof hooded coat that was bright yellow and similar coloured wellingtons.

Properly dressed for this summer, Mac thought.

'No, you're not intruding at all. I only came in to get out of the rain.'

'Yes, me too,' she said. 'I noticed you sitting here and, when I saw what you were reading, I thought that I'd come over.'

Mac looked at her closely. He could see that she was nervous and more than a bit upset.

'Did you know one of the girls who were murdered?' Mac asked gently.

She nodded but couldn't speak for a while.

'I should introduce myself. I'm Karen Alexander,' she said.

Chloe Alexander's mother!

'Mrs. Alexander, when you came over to me at the wedding, I take it that you wanted me to look into your daughter's case for you?' Mac asked.

She nodded.

'Yes, yes I do. Oh, and please call me Karen. It's hard to think that it's been five years now since Chloe left us and we're still no nearer knowing what happened. I think the police have given up on us although I can't say that I blame them. They've tried, I know that, but I just can't leave it like this. We've all been waiting five years for the other shoe to drop and it's been awful, absolutely bloody awful. I just want to know why my child died,' she said giving Mac a harrowed look.

Mac gave it some thought. He knew that if he said 'yes' it wouldn't be something he'd be able to drop if another case came along. It didn't take him long to reach a decision though.

'Of course. I'd be more than happy to look into it for you.'

'Could you start straight away?' she asked. 'Just spend as much time as you can on it, Mr. Maguire, and I'll pay you whatever the going rate is.'

Mac could see that she was desperate.

'There'll be no charge. To be honest I've nothing on right now and I was thinking of looking into it anyway.'

'Thank you so much, Mr. Maguire, you're so kind,' she said. 'You've given me some hope again.'

'I can't promise anything except that I'll do the best I can. By the way, I was just wondering how you knew Gerry Dugdale?' Mac asked.

'His ex-wife is my cousin. I've known Gerry for years. It was his idea that I should ask you. He said that if anyone could help then it would be you.'

She gave him her mobile number and Mac promised that he'd be in touch. He also fervently hoped that he could live up to her expectations.

Chapter Four

Mac could see his friend Tim as he walked down the road towards the pub. He'd managed to get their favourite table, number thirteen, right by the window. There were no drinks on the table so Mac went via the bar and ordered two lagers. He left one on the bar and made it back to Tim and handed him a pint. He then went back and got his own refreshment. He'd found out long ago that one of the major frustrations of using a crutch was having just the one hand free when it came to carrying drinks.

'So, what time do you have to be up at in the morning?' Mac asked as he sat down.

Tim took a long drink from his beer before answering.

'I'm sorry about that but I've been doing some sanding this morning and it always makes me thirsty. I'm getting up around three as the salerooms open at nine. I want to be there as soon as they open so I can have a good look around before the auction itself gets going. I'll stop for breakfast somewhere along the way.'

'I take it that it's a big sale then if you're going that far?'

'One of the biggest, so big that it lasts for two days,' Tim replied. 'I'll be hard at it for both days so I'm staying for two nights at the hotel and then I'll drive back the day afterwards.'

'You're really looking forward to it, aren't you?' Mac said.

'Oh, I am that. You know how much I love a bargain and there's usually loads going there if you know what to look for. It will be great fun. You should come along one of these days.'

'Yes, I might just take you up on that if I've got nothing on but Newcastle's a bit too far away for me. After four or five hours in a car, I don't think that I'd be able to straighten up enough to walk anywhere.'

'I know and that's why I didn't ask you this time around but there's a sale on in Cambridge in three or four weeks if you fancy it?' Tim asked.

'Sure, so long as I haven't got a case on.'

'What's the book? Is that to do with a case?'

Mac passed the book over.

'Yes, it's about a case, the Match of the Day Murders actually. You know it's only been a couple of days since the wedding and I'm bored stiff already so I thought that I might look into it.'

'That's all that gallivanting you did in France,' Tim said. 'They say that you're never the same again after you've visited Paris.'

'Well, I suppose that it was quite exciting, too exciting at times so I shouldn't really be moaning,' Mac said. 'Anyway, I saw the book on sale and I just thought I'd read up about the case. To be honest I don't remember that much about the murders as I was dealing with some of my own at the time.'

'I remember you not being around when it happened but it was a quite a big deal for Hertfordshire. Three murders in three weeks. All the bodies were found on football pitches and all the girls were killed at around the same time that 'Match of the Day' was being broadcast on TV. We've never seen anything like it before or since. I remember the fourth weekend all too well, all of us were waiting for news of another murder but it never happened, thank God,' Tim said.

'Yes, I remember that too. Nora got out of bed early that Sunday morning and went into the kitchen and turned the radio on. She was smiling when she came back and told me that there was nothing on the news.'

Mac gave Tim a sad look.

'It'll have been a year in a couple of weeks or so, won't it?' Tim asked gently.

Mac nodded. He'd somehow managed to get through it but he had to admit that it had been the worst year of his life by far.

'What are you going to do to mark it?' Tim asked.

'Bridget saw Father Pat yesterday and he's agreed to hold a little service of remembrance at the church. It'll be just family, oh and you're invited too of course.'

'I'll be there,' Tim said briefly touching Mac's hand with his.

Mac knew he would. His friend had always been there for him when the days had been at their darkest and his lightness of being and silly jokes had helped to light the way back towards some sort of sanity.

'Well, as I was saying, I'd just bought the book and I was sitting in David's when a woman came and sat opposite me,' Mac said. 'It was the woman that I gave a card to at Jo's wedding. Anyway, it turns out that she's the mother of the first girl who was murdered, Chloe Alexander, and she wanted me to look into the case for her. So, I said that I would as I haven't anything official on at the moment.'

'If I'm not mistaken you might have spoken too soon about that,' Tim said.

'What do you mean?' Mac asked with a puzzled smile.

'Because, from where I'm sitting, I can see young Andy Reid walking towards us and I'd be willing to bet that he has some work for you.'

Mac craned his neck and waved at Andy when he came into view. He came through the door and joined them at their table.

'What will you have to drink?' Tim asked as he stood up.

'Could I just have a coffee, please?' Andy replied.

While Tim was gone Andy turned the book around so he could read the title.

'I thought that's what it was!' he exclaimed in some surprise.

'Tim was guessing that you've got a case for me. Was he right?' Mac asked cutting to the chase.

'He was and that's the case right there,' Andy replied pointing towards the book.

'Now, that's a coincidence. I bought the book because I was curious and I thought that I might look into it a little if nothing else turned up. Then Mrs. Alexander asks me to look into it and now you. So, how come you've opened the investigation again?'

'Mrs. Alexander?'

'Yes, she was at Jo's wedding,' Mac said.

Andy screwed his face up as he tried to remember.

'Short blonde hair?' he eventually asked.

'Yes, that's her,' Mac said.

'You know, I thought that she looked familiar but I just couldn't place her. Her hair's very different to how it was five years ago. Anyway, it's not really that much of a coincidence as it will have been five years next week since Chloe was murdered, so there's bound to be a lot of interest in the case. Even more so now, I should think, as the book's been republished too.'

Tim came back with a coffee and handed Mac another pint.

'I take it that business is a bit on the slow side as well?' Mac asked.

'You've certainly got that right,' Andy replied. 'Dan's of the opinion that all the criminals are abroad sunning themselves on a beach somewhere. You'd think that he'd be happy about it but he's not.'

'He just likes to keep busy. There was one thing that made me wonder though. How come that none of these cases were in the cold case files that I was looking at when I was bedbound a while ago?'

Andy gave it some thought.

'Well, you could check with Martin but I'd guess that all the cases he sent you were all more or less officially parked. This one is still a live case. The last time it was followed up on was about a year ago when we chased up a rumour about a possible suspect. It was just another dead end unfortunately.'

'I suppose that makes sense,' Mac said. 'So, what do you want me to do?'

'I've got all the case files here,' Andy said as he pushed a memory stick towards Mac. 'Kate and Tommy are boning up on the case this afternoon so it would probably be best to leave it until tomorrow morning before we all meet up. If you're up for it that is?'

'Oh, I'm up for it alright,' Mac said with a smile. 'Tim here's going to be away for a few days so this couldn't have come at a better time as far as I'm concerned.'

And indeed, it couldn't have. With Tim away, Mac was afraid that he'd start thinking too much about Nora and the upcoming anniversary of her death. He knew that depression was a slippery slope into the darkness and he really didn't want to go down there again.

'That's great,' Andy said. 'By the way, have you got Mrs. Alexander's number?'

Mac did.

Andy entered it on his phone.

'I'll give her a ring and let her know that we're looking into the case officially and that you'll be helping us too.' He finished his coffee and said, 'I'll see you at the station at nine tomorrow then. I'll see you, Tim, and thanks for the coffee.'

They both watched Andy as he walked out.

'See, I told you that he had some work for you,' Tim said with a certain degree of smugness.

'Yes, and it's not just any work either. The Match of the Day Murders will keep me busy for quite a while I should think,' Mac said feeling relieved at the thought and then instantly feeling a little guilty about it.

They ended their drinks session at six and Mac phoned his favourite taxi driver Eileen to take him home. While they drove back, he asked her if she remembered the murders.

'Oh, I should say so,' she exclaimed in her light Irish accent. 'You know, I only mentioned to Sam the other day that the fifth anniversary of the murders was coming up and she could hardly believe it.'

'Did you know any of the Letchworth girl's friends or family?'

Mac knew that Eileen's friends were numerous and her acquaintances even more so.

'Yes, I used to pick up Chloe's cousin, Sondra, around that time. She was really cut up about it. I still see her from time to time but she's never brought up Chloe's murder once since it happened.'

He paid Eileen but, before he got out of the car, he got her to write down Sondra's address. It wouldn't hurt to have a word with her.

Terry scampered out of his box when he heard the key in the door and he was jumping around with joy as Mac opened the door. Anyone would have thought that he'd been left alone for days but Amrit had only gone an hour or so before Mac arrived. Terry's antics made Mac laugh out loud.

He made himself a pot of coffee and had a conversation with Terry who silently sat there watching his every move expectantly. Mac had eaten at the pub and he knew that Amrit would have fed Terry too but he had gotten into the habit of giving him a little treat in the evening. They were supposed to be good for him too but Mac would never tell him that.

He tossed Terry a treat which he caught in mid-air. He went and got his laptop and then made himself comfortable. Instead of seating himself in his armchair he sat on the sofa, in exactly the same spot that Nora used to sit. Terry climbed up onto the sofa and lay against Mac's thigh. He found the little dog's warmth quite comforting for some reason and, in between scrolling

35

down the pages of the case files, his hand moved down to give Terry a reassuring pat.

He was alone perhaps but not altogether.

As Mac was going through the case files, a few miles away a woman was looking anxiously at a calendar on her kitchen wall. The anniversary had been on her mind for some time and for good reason.

Five years ago, she'd driven her husband away from the very spot where Chloe Alexander's body had been found. He'd been drunk and asleep in his car when she found him. She'd wondered when she heard about the murder on the news the day after but she'd dismissed it. She knew that he could never have done anything like that.

Then she'd found the panties in his jacket pocket.

She told herself again and again that it couldn't be him, he just wasn't capable of murder. Yet, despite her inner protestations, the caustic acid of her suspicions had eaten away at their relationship until there was nothing left except the divorce papers. Yet she still hadn't told anyone. Every day that went by without them catching the girl's murderer made her feel even more unsure.

Maybe it was him after all.

Chapter Five

As usual the morning train was packed and Kate was lucky to get a place to stand near the window. She hated it when the train was like this. She'd never liked playing 'sardines' with strangers. Thankfully, some people near her got off at the next stop so she could at least breathe. She stared out at the scenery as it sped past and thought back to what had happened the evening before.

She'd been optimistic in thinking that she'd be able to make it to the hospital by six. She'd gotten so interested in the new case that she'd stayed longer at the police station than she'd planned. It had been nearer seven by the time she'd arrived. Magnus had got up to meet her as she stepped into the ward. She'd given her brother a hug and then looked over at her father. He was asleep, so she'd just sat by his bed for a while. He looked old, old and frail and somehow vulnerable.

If only he'd been a better man and father, she'd thought to herself. If only.

Even so, she took his hand in hers when Magnus had gone to talk with one of the doctors.

When he came back, he suggested that they might as well go back to Hatfield and find somewhere to eat. He'd been in the hospital for most of the day and he'd managed to have a long talk to her father's doctor and an even longer talk with her father.

Now he needed to talk to her.

They had steaks at a pub not far from Kate's flat and, while they ate their meal, they chatted about anything but their father. Magnus showed her a photo that Nobomi had sent him just a few hours before.

She looked even more beautiful, Kate had thought, and the word 'blossoming' came into her mind. Mother-hood looked like it would suit her.

Magnus had returned from the bar with two very large drinks. Kate had felt butterflies the size of crows in her stomach. She wasn't looking forward to this conversation.

She'd given her brother a half smile and said, 'Okay, tell me what the doctors said.'

'It's not good, I'm afraid. Apparently, dad's known about his condition for some time now,' Magnus replied.

'How long?'

'Nearly three months. He thought that he'd be okay driving for a while yet but the tests have shown that the tumour has increased rapidly in size and not only that but the cancer has spread into his lymph nodes. It's a lot more aggressive than they'd originally thought.'

'Christ,' was all Kate could mutter.

She'd felt dazed. Once, during an arrest, a suspect had punched her in the jaw and for a while she'd been groggy and not quite sure of where she was. That feeling was very similar to how she felt now. What she couldn't quite get her head around was why it was bothering her so much.

'How long?' she'd eventually asked.

'A month, weeks maybe.'

'Christ,' she'd muttered again.

She wasn't ready for this, dealing with all the shit from her past. She just wasn't ready. A lonely tear had fell down her cheek. She'd quickly wiped it away with her hand.

'So, what now? What do we do?' she'd asked.

'There's nothing that the doctors can do for him now so we just need to make him as comfortable as we can. I've arranged for him to be moved to a hospice near Hatfield, so that he can be close to you. I have to go back to South Africa soon but I'll come back in a week or so. I'll bring Nobomi with me and we'll stay until...'

Until he dies, Kate had thought, finishing her brother's sentence off in her head.

She'd felt such a rush of love for her brother in that moment. He wasn't going to leave her alone when it happened. She leant over and kissed him on the cheek.

'Thanks, Magnus,' she'd said.

'You don't need to thank me. I'm doing it as much for myself as for you,' he'd said as he squeezed her hand. 'I don't want there to be anything left unsaid when he goes.'

'You're probably right but the only problem is I don't know what I want to say to him. He was such a monster, wasn't he?'

'Is that what you really think?' Magnus had said giving her a puzzled look.

'Yes, why? Don't you?'

Magnus shook his head.

'Self-centred, egotistical and a bit cruel at times perhaps but no, he isn't a monster.'

'But what about what he did to mum? He seemed to delight in hurting her. You must have seen that,' she'd said with feeling.

'Yes, I did see that and yes, I thought for a time that dad was a monster too for doing that to mum but not anymore.'

'I don't understand,' she'd said. 'I really don't.'

'You say that you remember a lot about when we were kids but you've forgotten a lot too,' Magnus had said.

'Like what?'

Kate had no idea what her brother was getting at.

'Like that film you were talking about this morning,' he'd said.

'What? One Hundred and One Dalmatians?'

'Yes. You said we saw it with mum when you were seven. You were eight at the time and I was five but even so I remember that it was Mary that took us to see that film, not mum.'

Mary?

40

She'd thought for a moment. A face had flashed into her mind, the face of a young woman who was their nanny for a while. An oval, pretty face, a face framed by red hair. Not as red as hers but still red and she had loved her for it. She'd felt a little less alone. How had she forgotten about Mary?

'Yes, you're right, it was Mary. Why did I think that it was mum then?' she'd said giving her brother a puzzled look.

'I don't know but I remember that you used to miss mum terribly when she went away on her little trips.'

'Little trips? What do you mean?'

'Don't you remember that every month or so she'd disappear for two or three days and we'd be left alone with Mary? It always seemed to happen when dad was away on business somewhere,' Magnus had said.

She then gave her brother an incredulous look and shook her head. Another picture flashed into her mind.

The window.

There was a window in the front of their house that was on the upstairs landing and it had a little cushioned seat below it. From there she could sit and look down the drive to see if any cars were coming. She remembered that she'd sit there for hours and hours at a time anxiously waiting, endlessly waiting. But for what?

Another picture. Mum getting out of a taxi and Kate running down the stairs to meet her. Mum hugging her and telling her that everything was alright. And it was.

There was a question that was on the tip of her tongue. She'd decided not to ask it but it slipped out before she could stop it.

'Where did she go?'

Her brother took her hand in his. She could see a tear in the corner of his eye. She knew this was going to be bad and the food that she had just eaten started to revolve in her stomach.

'She had a lover,' he'd said.

41

'A lover!' Kate had almost shrieked.

She looked around. Luckily no-one had been nearby.

'Christ a lover? Really?' she'd said in a near whisper.

'That's what dad told me. It was someone she knew from before she married dad, a doctor. They'd been lovers for over two years but it all ended when he got married. It was an arranged marriage, the man was a Muslim, and mum was apparently heartbroken at the time. It seems as if she eventually resigned herself to it and married dad on the bounce. She knew that the man's family would never have accepted her anyway. So that was that. She met him again a year or so after I was born and they realised that they were both unhappy in their marriages and so they started seeing each other again. It apparently carried on until the man died a year or so before mum died herself.'

The words just wouldn't register properly; mum, affair, lover. They were words that just didn't go together.

'Did dad know?' she'd eventually asked.

'Yes, he knew. He'd suspected that something was going on and so he got a detective to follow her.'

Kate had violently shaken her head.

'No, no I don't believe it, any of it. If it was true then why did he stay with her? Why?'

'Because he loved her Kate, he loved her. He told me that even a part of her was better than nothing. He said that it got to him sometimes, especially when he drank, and he knew that he was often cruel to mum but there was a reason for it. He isn't a monster Kate, he's just human. He's just like the rest of us.'

She had been speechless. Her mum wasn't a saint and her dad wasn't a monster. She'd felt as though the bottom of her little world had fallen through and she was falling into darkness.

As she looked out of the window she felt as if she was still falling.

With a shock she came back from the events of the evening before to the present. They were announcing her station. She had to swim against the wave of people getting onto the train before she finally made it out into the fresh air. She pulled her umbrella out as it was raining again. She thought about the day ahead. She was looking forward to work, looking forward to not having to think about her dad. And mum come to that.

As she walked towards the station, she knew that she'd have to have a word with Andy.

She needed a favour.

Chapter Six

Mac had gone to bed early the evening before and, for once, he'd slept through the night. Because of that he was up early the next morning. He filled the bird feeder and drank his first cup of coffee as he watched the Coal Tits line up to get at the seed and fat balls he'd put out. They were mostly orderly but the odd squabble broke out leading to one of the birds getting knocked off the feeder and ending up at the back of the queue. He remembered his wife Nora buying the feeders many years ago and her saying that watching the birds was better than television. It still was.

As he walked into the living room he glanced at the calendar. He was forgetting that it was a patch change day. Every two days he had to change his pain medication. The little plastic patch was the only thing that kept him going. He went back into the kitchen and pulled out a small square pack from a box. The pack was flat and felt like it had nothing inside. He cut across the top of the pack and opened it up. Out of the foil lined interior he pulled out a small square transparent piece of plastic that had blue coloured lettering on it. He unbuttoned his shirt, located the old patch on his left shoulder and peeled it off. He stuck it to the outside of the empty pack. He then pulled one of the transparent plastic wings off the new patch and placed it on his thumb. He peeled off the other wing and expertly placed it on the other shoulder.

He patted down the patch, both to ensure that it adhered properly but also to warm it up a little. The Fentanyl that formed part of the glue worked on the heat of his skin. He looked at the old patch as he threw the pack into the bin. He still found it strange that something so small could make the difference between being productive or being wracked with constant pain. It didn't remove his pain, nothing could do that without taking his brain with it, but it definitely took the edge off. That was enough.

He then took his second cup of coffee into the living room and fired up his computer. He looked over at Terry's basket. His eyes were still shut but his tail was gently wagging. This made Mac smile.

He started looking at the case files from where he'd left off the evening before. He hadn't looked at anything in detail yet as there were thousands of documents in the files. All he was just trying to do was to get an idea about the basic facts surrounding the three cases for the team meeting later that morning. A movement caught his eye. Terry had wearily raised himself from his basket and was more or less sleepwalking towards Mac. He climbed up onto the sofa next to Mac, flopped down and instantly fell asleep again.

Mac looked down on him and smiled. His hand gently stroked Terry's head as he read on.

The third murder was that of a nineteen-year old girl called Ruth Avaloe. She had been found on a Sunday morning on a sports centre's five-a-side pitch at Fairfields Park in Stevenage exactly one week after the murder of Ana Tomas. She had been strangled with a ligature and left with no panties on. There was one major difference between this murder and the two previous ones, Ruth had had sex just before she was killed and, although there was no semen, the killer's DNA was all over her. The only problem was they hadn't been able to identify who the man was.

Anyone who might have remotely been a suspect was tested and no-one even came close to being a match. The evidence for the other two murders was re-examined and contact traces of the same DNA was found on both girls. This proved beyond any doubt to the investigators that all three murders were definitely linked.

Mac read on. Ruth Avaloe lived just five minutes walk away from where she was found dead. Her father was the vicar at a local evangelical church. He was a widower and Ruth had lived with him and served as his housekeeper and assistant. She was generally known to be a devoutly religious girl who had been highly praised by many of the congregation for the good work that she'd done in the parish. She had just the two friends and they both confirmed that she wasn't seeing anyone and had in fact never had a boyfriend. She'd apparently said more than once that she planned to stay a virgin until she married. No-one could think of any reason why she'd be anywhere near the sports centre or even why she might have left her room in the church that Saturday night.

Ruth had been the last of the Match of the Day Murders. There had been no murders with the same MO since. Mac felt that there could still be some urgency attached to solving the case. A gap of five years wasn't all that long when it came to serial killers. He remembered one in America where there had been a gap of fourteen years between two murder sprees. There was always a chance that the killer might start killing again.

With a start he looked up at the clock. It was nearly time to be at the station. Terry woke when Mac stood up and followed him into the kitchen. Mac made him his breakfast and then crept out of the front door while he was still eating. He didn't like shutting the door on Terry as he always let out this little heart-broken whine. It always made him feel immensely guilty.

He knew that Terry wouldn't be alone for long as Amrit was doing an extra day this week so as she could keep him company and then Amanda would be along at midday to take him for his usual walk. Tomorrow would be a problem as Amrit was doing something else. He'd have to have a think about that.

He made it to the car as fast as he could as it was raining again. He was slightly late and Andy, Kate and Tommy were all waiting for him when he arrived. No-one else was in the office.

'Good morning,' Mac said as cheerfully as he could. 'Where is everyone?'

'Morning, Mac,' Andy replied. 'Well Dan, Chris and Adil are all working on a robbery with violence, a BMW in this case, and they think it might have happened again late last night. An Audi was taken at knifepoint near Cambridge so they've gone to have a look. Leigh's taken some leave and Jo and Gerry are, of course, still in Jamaica where they might actually get a glimpse of the sun.'

'Yes, they definitely did the right thing there. I hope Leigh's gone abroad somewhere too. I pity anyone who's opted to holiday at home this summer,' Mac said.

'Okay, shall we start?' Andy said as he turned to face the team. 'I take it that you've all read the case files?'

'Well, I've sort of scanned it,' Mac said, 'but I'll try and have a more detailed read through as we go along.'

'Yes, there's quite a lot in those files so I don't expect you all to have read everything. Mac, I know all too well how often you've used detailed case reviews to crack cases in the past, so thanks for volunteering. So, we have three connected murders and a serial killer or killers who are still out there. I was part of the team that carried out the original investigation and we thought that we'd left no stone unturned. However, I'm now hoping that there might have been something we missed, something we can use to get the investigation going again. Our man is out there and it's possible that he could kill again. Dan's given us a couple of weeks to see what we can come up with so let's come up with something. I've decided that we should split into two teams to try and cover as much ground as possible. So, I'll work with Tommy and Kate will work with Mac. Is that okay?'

Mac noticed Kate flashing Andy a grateful smile and him then giving her an almost imperceptible nod. He wondered if she'd arranged it that way for some reason.

Andy went towards the whiteboard and said, 'Okay, so any ideas?'

There was silence for a while and Mac suddenly noticed that everyone was looking at him. He thought he might as well say something.

'Well, the one big advantage that we've got that the original team didn't have is time. Five years have passed since the murders took place and a lot could have happened since then. I take it that you're re-checking all DNA samples taken at the time against more recent samples in case our man or a relative might have been tested in the meantime?'

'Yes, Martin's facilitating that with the forensics lab,' Andy replied. 'He'll let us know if they come up with anything. He's also doing a search for any cases with similar MOs in both the UK and Europe in case our man hasn't stopped killing but simply moved somewhere else.'

'That's a good idea. Well, the only other thought I've had is about changing our perception of the case in some way,' Mac said.

'Changing our perception? What do you mean by that?' Andy asked.

'Have you ever seen any of those optical illusions that you can view in different ways?' Mac asked.

'Yes, there's one I remember that, depending on how you view it, could be either a young woman or an old crone,' Tommy volunteered.

'Yes, that's the type of thing I meant,' Mac said.

Kate had gotten something on her phone and passed it around. At first sight the picture just looked like a rabbit to Mac.

'Now, think of a duck,' Kate said.

Mac did and magically a duck appeared in place of the rabbit. He smiled.

'Thanks for that Kate, that's exactly what I'm talking about. So, if the original investigation had been looking

48

at this drawing and seeing a rabbit then, if we can think in a different way, then we might see the duck. I'm not explaining this too well but I hope you get my point,' Mac said.

'No, I think I see what you're getting at but how could we do that?' Andy asked.

'Well firstly, in everything I've read the team were looking for connections between the three murders and that is of course how we usually crack serial murder cases. But sometimes the connection may not be straight forward or even there at all and, if that is the case, then no matter what you do you won't make much headway. Investigations often fail because of the assumptions we make. Let's see if I can think of an example.'

Mac gave it some thought.

'Yes, this one might do. Around nine years ago we had a case where a woman had been anally raped and then killed. We had some DNA evidence but we got nowhere with it. We couldn't find any evidence of forced entry so it looked like she'd opened her door to whoever had done it. Due to this we felt that she must have known her killer. She was raped, probably at knifepoint as afterwards her throat had been cut. There was no semen but lots of contact DNA. There'd been a very similar case in the same area two years before and so we reasonably concluded that it might be the same murderer. We worked at it for weeks and got absolutely nowhere. Then late one night one of my team suggested that we try thinking about the case differently. We were desperate and we gave her idea a chance. Two days later we caught the killer.'

'What was the idea?' Kate asked.

'That the rapist might have been a woman,' Mac said. 'We found out that woman on woman rapes are far more common than you might think. In this case the murderer had used one of those strap-on dildos with a condom over it and that's why there was no semen.'

49

'Yes, I see what you mean,' Andy said, 'but wouldn't the DNA test have identified the killer as a woman?'

'Normally yes, but the killer wasn't normal and so she didn't fit into any of the assumptions we'd made. She looked like a woman and even had female genitals but her DNA was male.'

'I've never heard of that before,' Andy said.

'No neither had we but, while it's a fairly rare condition, it's something that the medical profession have known about for quite a while,' Mac said. 'I can't quite remember what they called it though...'

'Androgen Insensitivity Syndrome,' Kate said.

'Yes, that's right. How on earth did you know that?' Mac asked as he looked at Kate in wonder.

Kate smiled as she showed him her phone and the Google search results. Mac smiled too.

Andy gave this some thought.

'Well, there is something that's been bothering me for a while now. Throughout the investigation we've worked on the assumption that all three murders must be connected. After all that's what the evidence and the MO seemed to be telling us and so everything we did was based on that approach. However, there's only one thing that definitely connects all three murders and that's the contact DNA that was found when they retested the evidence from the first two murders after Ruth Avaloe was killed. We could try ruling that out and see where it leads us. If that's suspect then there's even a possibility that we might actually have two or even three different cases and not one as we originally thought.'

'You're thinking that the evidence might have become contaminated in the forensics lab?' Tommy asked.

'Yes, that happened in one of our cases a couple of years ago and it nearly led to a murderer getting away with it,' Andy said.

'You could well be right,' Mac said. 'I don't trust these labs as much as I used to when we ran them ourselves.

They're all privatised now and I've known them to cut quite a lot of corners at times.'

'So, why don't we take a case each and just try and concentrate on that one while forgetting about the other cases and see where it takes us? We might be able to work out what really connects them all later on, if there is a real connection that is,' Andy said.

'That sounds like a plan to me,' Mac said with a smile. 'A really good plan too.'

'So, which cases do you think we should work on?' Kate asked.

'Well the first, as it was the first, and the last perhaps as that seems a little different to the other two,' Andy said. 'Okay then Mac, as you came up with the perception idea in the first place, which case do you want?'

Chapter Seven

Mac looked out of the window as they drove towards Stevenage. Kate was driving the police car and for once Mac was enjoying being the passenger.

'So, why did you ask Andy if you could work with me?'

Kate's head snapped around.

'My God, you really are good!' she exclaimed. 'How did you spot that?'

'I saw you give Andy a smile when he said who the teams would be. When he nodded back, I guessed that you'd asked him for a favour. Do you mind telling me why?'

Kate looked a bit embarrassed.

'Well, I was going to try and slyly introduce the subject in conversation but it's about my dad. I'm sorry but I really need someone to talk to. I mean, I've got my brother but he's in the same hole that I am. I need some advice Mac. I feel as if everything around me is falling apart. It seems like everything in my life that I thought was true is turning out to be a lie.'

'Tell me,' Mac said gently.

And she did. She was still talking when they pulled up outside the sports centre in Stevenage. She was going to stop the story but Mac told her to carry on as another fifteen minutes or so wouldn't hurt the investigation.

'So, what do you think?' she asked when she'd finished.

'I've seen the sort of situation your parents were in quite a few times before as it can all too often end with murder,' Mac replied. 'Somehow that didn't happen and they made a sort of life together. I think that took some courage on both sides. They obviously loved you and your brother. Why else would they stay together?'

'I thought that mum was so angelic though and I thought that she loved dad too. It seems that I was wrong on both counts,' Kate said with a frown.

'Not necessarily. There are lots of different types of love and, while your mother obviously needed this other man, she must have loved your father in her own way. Why else would she have stuck with him for so long?'

'I just don't get that though, this 'needing'. Why would she need someone so much that she'd gamble with her marriage and her family?' Kate asked.

Mac looked at Kate for a while.

'You've never really been in love, have you?'

'I have, of course I have. I was married, wasn't I?' Kate said somewhat defensively.

'Marriage has nothing to do with it. Have you ever felt as if all the oxygen had left the room when someone walked out of it and then the mere sight of that same someone could light you up inside like a Christmas tree?'

'If I'm honest no, not really. I don't think I've never felt like that about anyone,' Kate replied with another frown.

Kate wondered if her ex-husband had thought about her in that way. She'd found out too late that he'd been having sex with as many women as he could, including some of her so-called friends. When she'd confronted him with this, she'd expected him to worm his way out of it but he didn't. He just said, 'You don't love me Kate. You've never loved me and, the worst of it is, I don't know how to make you love me.'

Perhaps he did love her after all. Unfortunately for him, she discovered too late that she couldn't love him back.

'Was it like that when you met your wife?' she asked.

'Yes, it was just like that with my Nora and it stayed like that until the very day she died,' Mac said.

He had a sad moment and it took him a few seconds to pull himself together.

'You were lucky, Mac. You may have lost her but you were still lucky to have found someone who could make you feel that way,' Kate said.

'Yes, someone else said that to me a while ago. I had thirty good years and I don't regret a second of it. You'll meet someone too. You never know but perhaps you've met them already and you don't know it yet,' Mac said with a smile.

A picture of DI Toni Woodgate came instantly into her mind. She'd only ever met her once and even that hadn't been a proper meeting, they'd just passed each other in a corridor at the police station. So, why was she thinking about her now?

'Anyway, this case won't investigate itself,' Mac said, 'but seriously Kate if you ever need to talk just ask. I know all too well what you'll be going through and please don't do what I did and try to deal with things by keeping them bottled up inside. I've found that approach doesn't work on any level. Talk really does help.'

'Thanks, Mac. I'll remember that.'

Indeed, she did feel some relief at having broached the subject with Mac. With some surprise she realised that, besides her brother, he was probably the person she trusted the most.

'At least it's stopped raining for a while,' Mac said as they walked towards the sports centre.

They went into the reception area and Mac showed his warrant card to a young woman dressed in a red track suit with the sports centre's name on it.

'It's about the murder, isn't it?' she asked giving him an excited look.

'Yes, that's right. We're looking into the case again.'

'They've all been talking about it around here for the last week or so. It sounds dreadful,' she said pulling a face. Her professional smile immediately returned as she brightly continued, 'My name's Carol. How can I help you?'

'How long have you worked here, Carol?' Mac asked.

'Only eighteen months or so,' she replied.

'Is there anyone who's still working here who was around at the time that Ruth Avaloe was killed?'

She gave this some thought.

'I think you'll need to speak to Jan. She's been here since the centre opened.'

'Is Jan working today?'

'Yes, I think she's looking after the Tennis Club people,' Carol replied. 'Shall I go and get her?'

'Yes please, but, before you go, is there anyone using the five-a-side pitches this morning?' Mac asked.

'No, I don't think anyone's going to be on them until later this afternoon.'

'I'd be grateful if you could take us there and then go and ask Jan to meet us as soon as she can,' Mac said.

'Yes, of course.'

Carol went and found someone to take over the reception desk for a while. She then picked up a bunch of keys and gestured to Mac and Kate to follow her. She led them outside and around to the back of the building. Behind a mesh fence that was at least twelve feet high, four small football pitches had been marked out side by side. At either end of each pitch there stood a miniature goal. Carol led them towards a mesh gate that was secured with a robust looking padlock. She opened the gate and gestured for them to go in.

'I'll go and get Jan then,' she said before disappearing.

Mac pulled his tablet out of his pocket and turned it on. He'd downloaded some of the images from the case files onto it but there were so many that it took him a while to find the particular photos he needed. When he did, he carefully studied the photos and then looked around.

'I think it's that pitch over there,' Mac said, 'the one at the far end.'

They walked to the end pitch and Mac positioned himself so that he was on the exact spot that the crime scene photographer must have stood. Nothing much had changed and, apart from the dead girl lying in the goalmouth, the photograph could have been taken a few minutes before. Mac gave the tablet to Kate and then looked around. He stopped and looked at the fence that ran down the long side of the pitch. Beyond it he could see the back of the sports centre's car park. He immediately found something that interested him.

'What are you looking at?' Kate asked.

'There's another gate in the fence there, like the one we've just come through.'

He walked over and looked at it closely. It had two large bolts fitted that were held in place by two chunky padlocks. The bolts were somewhat rusty and looked as if they hadn't been moved for quite a while. Mac wandered towards the other end of the enclosed space but found no other entrances that led beyond the high wire fencing.

'I'm wondering if the reason she died on this particular pitch was because they came in through that gate,' Mac said. 'If the killer had to coerce her somehow, say at knifepoint, then why go any further than the nearest pitch?'

'But wouldn't they have been visible from the car park?' Kate said.

'Well yes, but the murder took place around twelve midnight on a Saturday. I doubt if many people would have been around at that time,' Mac replied.

A woman on her fifties, dressed in a red track suit that was identical to the one Carol had worn, walked through the mesh gate.

'Well, perhaps Jan might be able to confirm that,' Mac said.

Mac showed Jan his warrant card and introduced himself and Kate.

'I've been hoping that you'd turn up. I take it that you're re-investigating the murder?' Jan asked.

'Yes, we're looking at all three murders again,' Mac replied.

'I'm glad, that was no way for a nice young girl like Ruth to die,' she said with a grim expression.

'Did you know Ruth Avaloe?' Mac asked.

'No, not really but I used to see her around the centre sometimes. She tried joining the judo classes for a while and she seemed to be enjoying it too, meeting other people and all that, but she had to stop.'

'Why was that?'

'I heard that it was her father, the vicar,' Jan replied. 'He had her working day and night at that church of his. I mean she was young but I don't think that he ever gave her any real chance to do what other young people do. She was quite shy as well which I suppose didn't help much either.'

'So, was it just judo that she tried?'

'No, she had a go at playing tennis too as she could do that a bit earlier in the day but that didn't last either. I didn't see her again after that until we found her dead right there,' Jan said pointing to the white semicircle that was marked out in front of the goal.

'You were there when she was found?' Mac said with some excitement.

'Yes, we always used to open up the centre first thing in the morning back then, me and my friend Sue. It was the two of us who found her.'

Mac had a think. He eventually remembered who had signed the two witness statements.

'So, you're Janice Smith and Sue is Susan Latteridge?'

'Yes, that's right. I remember that the two of us opened that gate there,' Jan said pointing to the gate that they'd come through, 'and as soon as we walked in, we noticed that there was something on the pitch. At first, we thought that it was just some rubbish that

57

someone had managed to throw over the fence but, as we came closer, I could see that it was a girl. Her eyes were wide open and I could swear that she was looking at us as we ran over to her. We checked for a pulse but it was no good, she was dead. Her skin was so cold, I'd never felt skin that was that cold before. I've never forgotten that morning, never. The poor girl was lying with the side of her face down on the pitch, she was on her knees and her skirt was hitched up around her waist so that her bare arse was visible to the whole world. It wasn't bad enough that he had to kill her but to leave her like that was really cruel. He could at least have covered her up.'

Jan shook her head and Mac could see tears forming in her eyes.

'How do you think that they might have gotten in?' Mac asked quickly.

'Oh, probably through that gate there I should think,' Jan said pointing to the gate that led into the car park.

'Wasn't that kept locked too?'

'Well, it was supposed to have been but no, not always. It's kept permanently locked now but back then there used to be some lazy bastards working here. It can only be locked from the inside so rather than locking it and then walking through the other gate and taking the long way around to the car park they used to just shut it behind them and leave it unlocked. That happened loads of times that did. I told the police about it at the time.'

Mac hadn't seen that fact in the file but he guessed that it was noted down somewhere. He felt that it was all the more reason for a really thorough review as small details like that can make all the difference.

'So, Ruth and whoever killed her would most likely have just walked in through an open gate?'

Jan nodded.

'Would there have been anyone around at the time that Ruth was killed?' Mac asked.

'What around midnight? No, the latest the centre would have been open back then was ten o'clock. It opens later now but it was definitely no later than ten in those days,' Jan replied.

'In all the times that you saw Ruth did you ever see her with anyone, a boy or a man perhaps?'

'No, never,' Jan said with a shake of the head. 'She was always alone, always. You could see that she wanted to make friends but as I said she was shy. I never saw her with anyone really, man or woman.'

'Tell me, is Sue working today?' Mac asked.

Again, he could see tears forming in her eyes.

'I'm sorry but you've come a bit too late to speak to Sue. She died two months ago, cancer,' Jan said.

'I'm sorry to hear that,' Mac said. 'Is there anything else you can remember?'

Jan slowly shook her head.

'Was there anything strange going on around that time? Anything at all, even if you don't think that it was connected to Ruth's murder,' Mac asked.

She thought for a while and then started to slowly shake her head. However, Mac could see that something had occurred to her.

'Well...,' she said hesitantly.

'Go on,' Mac prompted her.

'There was something funny going on in the park just there,' she said pointing to the hedge on the left side of the car park.

Mac remembered from the aerial photos he'd looked at that Fairfields Park lay just over the other side of the hedge.

'What do you mean by funny?'

'Well, there's a gap in the hedge that's been there for ages, it's still there now,' Jan said. 'People use it to get into the park and, if you live on the other side of the park, it's quite a handy short cut from here. Well, around the time of the murder when I was locking up, I used to see

59

men going into the park through that gap in the hedge quite late at night. I thought that they might be just walking home but a colleague of mine said that he'd seen men hanging around in that part of the park at night more than once. He thought that they might have been cottaging or something.'

'Cottaging' was a word that was used in a previous era to describe the homosexual practice of hanging around public toilets in parks and other public spaces when looking for sex. Mac hadn't heard that word used for quite a while.

'Do you still see men going into the park at night nowadays?' Mac asked.

'No, all that stopped after the murder for some reason. It was probably having all the police around that put an end to it, I should think.'

'Did you tell this to the police at the time?' Mac asked.

'Well, I'm not sure if I'm honest,' Jan replied. 'I mean no-one asked me and I just didn't think...well, I just wasn't thinking at all. I was quite upset at the time as you can guess.'

So, this might be a new fact then, Mac thought. Although whether it might be important or not was open to question.

'Is there anything else?' he asked.

Jan shook her head.

He thanked her and watched her as she made her way out. She stopped just before she stepped through the gate and turned around.

'Just catch the bastard, will you?' she said.

Then she turned and left.

'Easier said than done, unfortunately,' Mac muttered to himself.

He continued to slowly pace around the football pitch for a time only stopping to look at more photos on his tablet. He stood stock still for some time as if in some sort of trance. Kate eventually broke the silence.

'So, what do you think?'

It took a moment for her words to register.

'Oh, I'm sorry,' Mac said with an apologetic smile. 'I was just thinking that this murder somehow has a different feel to the other two and I was trying to figure out why that was. On the surface they all appear very much the same, don't they? I mean they were all carried out at around the same time, around midnight on a Saturday, and all the bodies ended up in the goalmouth of a football pitch. All of the girls were strangled with a ligature, probably a scarf, and all had their panties taken. Yet, if it really is the same person carrying out all the murders, then why would he change his MO for this one?'

It was Kate's turn to stand and think.

'So, the differences are that sex had taken place, leaving loads of DNA, and that she was left with the lower half of her body uncovered. The other two had their skirts pulled down even though their panties were taken.'

'Yes, it looks as if she was strangled to death during the sex act and she was then just left where she fell.'

'So, you think that they were doing it doggy style then?' Kate asked.

'Yes, that makes the most sense doesn't it? She's on her hands and knees while the killer is kneeling behind her with both ends of the scarf in his hands and that's slightly puzzling too. Usually, in these types of killings, the victim is usually killed either during or after ejaculation but this didn't seem to have happened here. Even if he'd been using a condom it's unlikely that there wouldn't be any traces at all either on her or on the ground. Did something go wrong? Did the murderer pull a bit harder on the scarf than he meant to?'

Mac was thoughtful again for a while.

'It's not just that though, is it?' Mac said. 'This is somewhere she knew, somewhere close to home, somewhere she'd visited before. From what I read they

61

couldn't find any direct connection between the other two girls and the places they were found in. I know in Ana Tomas's case it was just a stone's throw away from where she worked but it seemed that she'd never actually set foot inside that sports centre before. But there's something else about this one that seems a little strange.'

'What's that?' Kate asked.

'The other two girls were out and about when they disappeared. Chloe was out with friends and Ana was on her way back from work. However, Ruth was supposed to be tucked up in bed on that Saturday night like a good Christian girl and they never found any evidence to support the idea that she was abducted from where she lived. So, did she go out that Saturday night under her own steam and, if she did, why?' Mac asked. 'If we could answer that question then we might be a lot closer to finding her murderer.'

'So, what do we do next?' Kate asked.

'I've got his number here somewhere. So, let's go and see her father, the Reverend Pritchard Avaloe.'

Chapter Eight

Luckily, the Reverend Avaloe was still in residence at the church and he seemed more than happy to see them. Mac arranged to meet him inside the church at eleven thirty. He looked at his watch. It was just coming up to ten thirty so they had an hour to kill. He stood still for a moment while he looked towards the hedge.

'Come on, the rain's still holding off so let's go for a walk in the park,' he suggested.

The gap in the hedge was big enough to have allowed four people walking abreast through and it was obviously well used. A well beaten path ran across the grass from the gap to the nearest paved walkway. As they walked the sun came out from behind a cloud making the park look beautiful, fresh and even greener. The raindrops that were still gently falling from the leaves of the trees lining the path glittered in the sunlight. Mac smiled and noticed the same smile on quite a few of the other faces that passed them by.

'So, what are you thinking?' Kate asked as they slowly strolled towards the boating lake.

'I was thinking that a bit of sunshine can really cheer you up sometimes. I was also trying to remember what the case file said. I'll check when I get home but I haven't seen any mention of men being in the park so far.'

'Do you think that it might be important?'

Mac shrugged.

'Who knows, but we have to look closely at any new information we get. I was just wondering what we could do to find out a little more about what was going on in the park around the time of Ruth's murder. I've got an idea about that too.'

'What is it? What do think they were up to?' Kate asked.

'I'll not say too much as I might be totally on the wrong track but asphyxiation doesn't always have to have a victim, does it?'

Kate thought about this for a while.

'Wow! Is that what you're really thinking?'

'Well, it's just a thought at the moment but it's one that I'm fairly certain wasn't considered five years ago from what I've read. Let's see if we can get any evidence to back it up first.'

Mac pulled his phone from his pocket. He was going to ring Martin Selby, the team's computer specialist, for a favour.

By the time he finished his conversation they had reached the boating lake. In the short time that the sun had been out the park had suddenly become filled with people, mostly parents with young children. It was the school holidays and being penned up for days on end because of the rain must have been hard on the children. However, Mac thought that it was probably even harder on their parents.

'Come on, let's make our way back,' Mac said realising that he might have already walked too far.

Kate didn't say much on the way back as she was thinking about the implications of what Mac had just suggested. He'd talked about changing their perceptions of the case and the idea he'd just planted in her head certainly did that.

The church was only a few streets away. It was a modern building that stood behind a small shopping centre. If it wasn't for the cross on the roof it could have been easily have been mistaken for an office block or a warehouse.

They parked up outside and, just as they were about to leave the car, large drops of rain started hitting the windscreen.

'Come on, let's get inside before it starts properly,' Mac said.

They had only just made it inside the porch when the heavens opened and the rain started pounding the pavement. Mac thought of all those families with young children in the park and he felt sorry for them.

Inside the church was all beige walls and pale wooden office furniture. Even the large crucifix above the altar was nondescript being just two bits of pale wood stuck together with no other adornment. There were no pews and instead there were lines of generic stackable chairs on either side of a gangway. A black suited figure was on his knees in front of the simple pale wooden altar, hands clasped together and eyes tight shut.

Mac coughed but the figure didn't move. He coughed again but more loudly this time. The man opened his eyes and turned around. When he saw who it was, he climbed to his feet.

He was slightly taller than Mac but he was also much thinner, so thin that his black suit hung loosely from his frame and the Roman collar around his neck looked more than a few sizes too big. Mac knew that he was in his late forties but he looked much older than that. His hair was going grey and his face was lined with what seemed to be a permanent expression of suffering.

'Reverend Avaloe?' Mac asked.

'Yes, I take it that you're the police?' he asked in a slight Welsh accent.

Mac showed him his warrant card and introduced himself and Kate. The Reverend pointed to some chairs and Mac gratefully sat down on one. His back was aching now.

'I take it that you're looking into poor Ruth's murder again?' the Reverend asked as he gave them a sorrowful look.

'Yes, as well as the other murders,' Mac replied.

'So, how can I help?'

'We were just wondering if there was anything you could add to what you already told the police at the time of the murder. Has anything happened since your daughter's murder that might have given you any pause for thought?'

He thought for a moment and then slowly shook his head.

'No, I'm sorry. I told the police everything I knew at the time.'

'And nothing's occurred to you since, especially about why your daughter might have left her room that Saturday night?' Mac asked.

Again, that slow shake of the head.

'I can only say that she wouldn't have gone willingly,' the Reverend said. 'This church was her world. She rarely went anywhere else.'

'I thought that she had some friends. Didn't she ever go out with them?' Mac asked.

'No, she never went out. I warned her most strongly of the dangers of the outside world,' the Reverend said. Then leaning towards them he said in a near whisper, 'The temptations.'

He gave them a meaningful look before continuing.

'Anyway, the doors of the church and those of the house were always locked promptly at nine o'clock. However, Ruth had no wish for the outside world and she met with her friends here three or four times a week as they all ran the crèche together, looking after the little ones while their parents were at prayer.'

It looked as if Ruth hadn't exactly had an exciting lifestyle.

'Do either of her friends still come to church?' Mac asked.

'Well, one of them does, Tracey Altman. She attends regularly, in fact, she still runs the crèche.'

'And is Tracey still living at home?'

'Yes, I believe so,' the Reverend replied.

'And the other one? I think her name was Anne Foster. Does she still attend?' Mac asked.

Another slow sorrowful shake of the head.

'No, I'm afraid that she doesn't. She stopped coming to church shortly after Ruth left us.'

'Have you any idea why?'

'No, I'm sorry, I don't,' the Reverend replied. 'I never saw her again after the funeral.'

Mac thought for a moment.

'Would it be possible to see Ruth's bedroom?'

'Well, it's no longer her bedroom but yes, of course. Follow me.'

They followed the Reverend down a corridor and he opened the door into a small square room that was stuffed full of broken chairs and bric-a-brac. Mac could only just about squeeze inside the door.

'This is really where Ruth slept?' Mac asked in some disbelief.

Even a single bed would have taken up most of the space inside.

'Oh yes, she said that she liked being near the altar in case she felt the need to pray. Anyway, I only have the two rooms upstairs and I need to use one of those as an office,' he said giving them a sad smile.

The room had just one window. It was square, about three feet across and was filled with frosted glass. In front of the window a sturdy set of iron bars were screwed into the wall.

'Were these bars fitted when Ruth used to sleep here?' Mac asked.

'Oh no, we fitted those bars after the break-ins,' the Reverend replied. 'We moved Ruth's things out of this room after she left us. It didn't take long as she didn't have much. Like me, she lived very frugally. We then started to use it as a storeroom. Not long after that we had a series of burglaries. At first it was just some small amounts of money that were stolen but I drew the line when some of the sacramental silver went missing. I asked a friend who's a security expert to have a look

67

around the building and the only thing he spotted that might have been a problem was that window. The catch had been loosened so that, even though the window looked as if it was securely locked, it could still be quite easily opened from the outside. So, I had the catch fixed and I also fitted those bars as he advised.'

'Have you had any more burglaries since?' Mac asked.

'No, none at all.'

'So, when did all this happen?'

The Reverend gave this some thought.

'Now, how long after Ruth went was it? I can't quite remember whether it was two or three...'

Mac thought that two or three years was a long time to have left the room untouched but, then again, he supposed it was a mark of respect for his daughter.

'No, it was definitely two weeks,' the Reverend said.

'Two whole weeks?' Mac said as he stared at the Reverend in some amazement.

It took him a while to think about his next question.

'Did you tell the police about the window and the burglaries?'

'Of course. I told the local community policeman all about it. He even came and had a look for himself, much good did it do us though.'

'But did you say anything to the detectives who were investigating your daughter's murder?'

The Reverend gave Mac a puzzled look.

'No, it never occurred to me to do that. Why on earth would they be interested in a burglary?'

Mac and Kate exchanged looks. Mac shook his head and then nodded towards the door. As they walked back the Reverend told them of his deep feelings about his daughter's murder.

'You know, it's been very hard on me since Ruth left us, I've really missed her,' he said giving them both another deeply sorrowful look. 'I've had to employ a housekeeper and someone to act as an assistant too, so it's been very inconvenient, but the Lord's work must go on, mustn't it?'

Mac was more than happy to say goodbye to the Reverend. They stopped in the lobby for a few moments watching the raindrops hitting the pavement outside with some force. Kate breathed in deeply.

'Inconvenient! My God and I thought that my dad was a monster. Even so, I'm fairly certain that he wouldn't have put me in a bedroom literally not big enough to swing a very small cat in and then clear all my things out more or less straight after the funeral. Did you hear him when he said he missed her? He missed his little slave was more like it.'

She looked at Mac who was deep in thought.

'I'm sorry, Mac,' she said.

'Sorry for what?'

'For my little rant,' she replied. 'I'm still feeling a bit on edge unfortunately.'

'Oh, don't worry about that,' Mac said. 'I can't say I blame you really. He's obviously one of those religious people who wear their faith like a hair shirt and who are only too happy to show everyone how much they suffer for it. Anyway, it certainly gave us an insight into what Ruth's life with her father was like. She was young and she must have had dreams of some sort for her life. Living here she must have felt trapped, as if she was living in a cage.'

'So, what do you think then?'

'I think that I might have the beginning of a theory,' Mac said. 'What he said about the window catch was, in my opinion, crucial. The only problem we have is, can we find any evidence to back it up after all this time?'

'So, what do you want to do now?' Kate asked.

'Let's see if we can find Anne Foster. I'd be interested in knowing why she stopped going to church.' Mac said. 'Come on, the rain's not so bad now. Let's make a dash for the car.'

Chapter Nine

They drove to the last known address of Anne Foster but they drew a blank. It turned out to be shared house with four tenants all renting a single room each. Only one of the tenants was in and his English was very limited. After some failed attempts at sign language the man finally understood what they wanted and came back with a card that had the landlord's name and phone number on it.

Mac rang the number and got an office assistant. Fortunately, the assistant knew what she was doing and within minutes she was able to confirm that Anne Foster had left the house just two months after Ruth Avaloe's death. She had left no forwarding address.

'So, what now?' Kate asked.

'Another little job for Martin, I'm afraid. If Anne Foster's working then it shouldn't be too much of a problem to track her down,' Mac replied. 'Come on, let's try Tracey Altman then.'

They pulled up outside a fairly modern terraced house, a two up and two down. Mac thought that the rooms must be quite small and wondered at the current trend for miniaturising houses. His ancient pre-fab would be considered incredibly spacious compared to most modern houses.

A woman in her early fifties opened the door. She was grey-haired, round faced and wore glasses with strong lenses in them that made her eyes look unnaturally big. She was, however, quite small and so the house must have seemed exactly the right size to her. Mac guessed that she was Tracey's mother. He guessed right. Mac showed her his warrant card.

'Please, come in,' she said as she held the door open for them. 'This is about poor Ruth, isn't it? I've been expecting a visit, well, hoping for one anyway.'

'Is Tracey in at the moment?' Mac asked.

'No, I'm sorry, she's at work. She won't be back until five,' she replied in an accent that Mac had been more used to hearing in the East End of London. 'I could give her a ring, if you like? She doesn't work too far away and I know that she'd like to talk to you.'

'Yes, I'd be very grateful if you could do that. Do you mind if we ask you a few questions while we wait?'

She showed them into a spotlessly clean living room and pointed towards a black leather sofa. She offered them tea and they both gladly accepted. She came back with a tray with three cups and a plate of biscuits. She sat down in an armchair and took a sip of her tea.

'I've just rang Tracey and she said that she'll be along in a while. I take it that it's because of the anniversary that you're looking into Ruth's murder again?' she asked.

'Yes, we're reviewing her case and those of the other girls who were murdered too,' Mac replied.

'To think that it was only five years ago, somehow it seems a lot longer than that. You know, I sometimes think about Ruth and the murder and I wonder if I dreamt it or something. It all seems so unlikely, even now.'

'How did Tracey get to become friends with Ruth?'

'Oh, they were all at school together, Tracey, Ruth and Annie. They'd known each other since they were five or so, right through primary and then secondary school.'

'So, they were close friends?' Mac asked.

'Oh yes, they were always together. It was much better when Ruth's mum was alive though, at least she got to go out and have a bit of fun. After that her father more or less kept her locked up in that church of his.'

'Is that why Tracey and Annie helped with the crèche, so that they could see Ruth?'

'Yes, at first it was but I'm afraid that Tracey got the bug and she became all religious on us. I really don't know where she got that from, certainly not from me or

71

her dad. Anyway, she joined the church and started going there virtually every evening. She met her boyfriend there, so at least one good thing came out of that, he's a lovely lad. They're getting married in a couple of months or so. She was only talking about it the other day, how she'd always planned to have Ruth and Annie as her bridesmaids when she married. Now she's lost both of them.'

'What happened to Annie then?' Mac asked.

'She just disappeared,' Mrs. Altman said as she shook her head in disbelief. 'It was a couple of months or so after it happened and Tracey hadn't seen Annie for a couple of days. So, she went around to that shared house she lived in and they said that she'd gone, no forwarding address or anything. She never heard a word from Annie after that. It was almost as if she died as well, if you know what I mean. They were such lovely kids. I can still remember the three of them holding hands as they walked to school...'

She stopped speaking as a single tear rolled down her left cheek. She pulled out a paper hankie and blew her nose.

'I'm sorry,' she apologised, 'but it still gets to me at times.'

Mac gave her a moment before continuing.

'Why was Annie living in a shared house and not at home?'

'Tracey can probably tell you more about that than I can. All I know is that she had a massive fight with her mother when she was about seventeen or so. I don't know what it was about but Annie left that night and, as far as I know, she never set foot in her mother's house again. She was training to be a hairdresser at the time and she was really good at it too. She even did my hair once or twice and I must admit that it was the best cut that I'd ever had. She was making good money for her age with tips and that so I suppose that she could afford to move out.'

'And what was Annie like?'

'Annie? She was the quiet one,' Mrs. Altman replied. 'You know that old saying about still waters running deep? I never really knew what that meant until I got to know Annie. She didn't say much but she took everything in if you know what I mean. She really loved Ruth though. When she was a kid, she used to follow her everywhere.'

'What was Ruth like?' Mac asked.

'Well, she was definitely the leader when they were all young. You know suggesting the games they should play and so on but she was never a bossy-boots though. She was very creative too and I always thought she could have been an actress or a writer or something, if she'd been given half a chance that is. After her mother died it was like something went out in her. I'm sorry, I can't explain it any better but she was never quite the same again. Her father didn't help much either. God, what an overbearing man he was! Always ordering her around, Ruth do this, Ruth do that. The poor girl was run off her feet. She never went out, she wasn't allowed. She didn't even have a key to her own front door. Can you believe that?'

Having met Ruth's father Mac could.

They were interrupted by the sound of the front door opening.

'That'll be our Tracey now,' Mrs. Altman said with a smile.

Although they'd only left each other a couple of hours ago Tracey and her mum gave each other a hug and a kiss. Tracey wasn't anything like the girl he'd been expecting. He thought that she'd be a fairly plain girl who'd wear old fashioned clothes and no make-up. She was small, like her mother, but she was very attractive and stylishly dressed. She definitely wore make-up but it

73

was subtle and enhanced her features without being too noticeable.

'I've been hoping that someone from the police would call,' Tracey said as she sat on the arm of the chair her mother was sitting in.

She took her mother's hand and held it in both of hers.

Mac thought it was more to comfort herself than than her mother. She was obviously a little scared of opening up a five year old can of worms but, scared or not, she still looked quite determined.

'Have you found anything new yet? Is there any chance of catching him?' Tracey asked.

'Well, we've got some new evidence but we've only just started investigating so we've no idea whether it's of any value yet. Is there anything that you can tell us that you didn't tell the police five years ago?' Mac asked.

Tracey and her mum exchanged looks. Then she thought for a moment.

'I've thought of little else since Ruth died and I've gone over it again and again in my mind but I've never got any closer to understanding what happened that night,' Tracey said.

'Have you any idea why Ruth might have left the church that Saturday evening?'

'No, but I'd guess that she wouldn't have left of her own will. If I'm honest, I think that she became something of an agoraphobic after her mother died. Because of that I can only think that she must have been threatened in some way. Perhaps her murderer hid in her room when the church was open and then, when she went to bed, he surprised her and forced her to go with him,' Tracey said excitedly.

'That's what you think?' Mac asked.

'I don't know but it might explain why she left the church and ended up in the park.'

'Perhaps,' Mac said. 'Did Ruth ever have a boyfriend or someone that she said she liked?'

'No,' Tracey replied with a shake of her head. 'She said that she'd only settle for someone special and she'd know him when they met. She was determined to stay a virgin until then. She was still waiting for him when she died.'

'Did Ruth say or do anything that was out of the normal in the days before she was murdered?'

'I've gone through every conversation we had in my head again and again but no. She was just Ruth, the same as ever.'

'What about Annie? What happened with her?' Mac asked.

'I've no idea,' Tracey replied. 'Just like me she was dreadfully cut up about Ruth's murder. We used to meet up three or four times a week after that and then one day she just didn't turn up. I went to where she lived and they said that she'd moved out the day before. She left no forwarding address and they had no idea where she'd gone. I hoped for months afterwards that she'd contact me but she never did.'

'So, it wasn't because you fell out or anything like that?' Mac asked.

'No, absolutely not. We both needed each other after Ruth died or at least I thought we did. Perhaps, in truth, I needed her more,' Tracey said as she squeezed her mother's hand even tighter.

'What do you mean by that?' Mac asked.

'Well, Annie always liked Ruth more than me. It's just the way it was I suppose. It's been that way since we first met each other in primary school.'

'Did Annie say anything to you, anything that might give us a clue as to why she left so suddenly?'

'Not really, apart from the time that she said that Stevenage was getting her down a bit,' Tracey replied. 'She said that everything here reminded her of Ruth.'

'When did she say this?' Mac asked.

'I'm not sure. A couple of weeks before she left, I think.'

Maybe Annie was thinking of a change of scenery, Mac thought.

'Why did Annie leave home?'

'Oh, that!' Tracey said as she looked up to the ceiling. 'Annie and her mum never got on that well. Even when we were kids, she always used to come here or to Ruth's house. We never went to hers, not ever. It all came to a head when Annie was seventeen and her mum's latest boyfriend had left her. Her mum got really drunk and then accused Annie of driving him away. She called her a slut and said that she'd been having sex with him behind her back.'

'And had she?' Mac asked.

'No way! I mean he was over forty. Annie told me that he'd tried it on with her once and she'd told him where to go. So, her mum accusing her like that was just the last straw.'

'So, what happened?'

Tracey looked at her mum who nodded.

'Well, Annie totally blew her top and she found herself holding her mum up against the wall with a kitchen knife at her throat. She came to her senses though and dropped the knife but that night she packed her bags and left home. She never went back there again.'

Mac asked if either Tracey or her mum had anything to add. They hadn't. Kate gave them a card and they left.

Mac was silent as they walked back to the car and said nothing when he sat down.

Kate gave him a few minutes before she finally broke the silence.

'What do you think?'

Mac looked over at her in some surprise.

'Oh, I'm sorry I was miles away.'

'Did you get any ideas from what they told you?' Kate asked.

'If I'm honest, not really, but I always find this sort of background information really interesting. It helps to paint a more complete picture of the victim and the people who knew her.'

'So, what's next then?'

Mac looked at his watch. It was now past two o'clock.

'Well, I've had a thought but first let's get a coffee and a sandwich somewhere and then we'll have a chat.'

She looked at the news on her computer and noticed the snippet about the police opening up the investigation into the 'Match of the Day Murders' straight away. She'd been expecting something like this but it didn't worry her in the slightest. Five years ago, they'd spent months looking at the murders and had gotten exactly nowhere. She'd made sure of that.

She knew that this latest investigation was probably just a sop to the families of the victims and the press. They'd put a small team on it for a couple of weeks, just to make it look like they were doing something, and then it would be quietly put on the back burner and once again forgotten.

Even if they found something, it wouldn't necessarily be the end of the world. She smiled. Whatever happened he was safe and she regretted nothing. She'd done what needed doing.

She'd do it all again if she had to.

Chapter Ten

Mac had been hungrier than he'd thought and he wolfed down his cheese and ham sandwich. Kate was digging into a plastic bowl of salad while they watched the shoppers parading up and down the aisles with their shopping trolleys. The supermarket had been the first place they saw on their way back into the centre of Stevenage. Mac had suggested that they eat at the café there. He thought that this was a good idea as it was also close to the railway station but he hadn't said anything about that to Kate. Not yet anyway.

Kate must have been hungry too as she didn't say a word until she'd eaten the last strand of grated carrot and the last salad leaf.

'That wasn't too bad,' she said as she sipped at her coffee. 'So, what's your idea then? Have you come up with something new?'

Mac looked again at his watch. It was nearly a quarter to three.

'If I'm being absolutely honest, I haven't got a clue what we should do next. However, I do think that you need to go and see your father so my thought was that I should drop you off at the train station as soon as you've finished your coffee.'

Kate didn't exactly look thrilled at Mac's idea. In truth, she was hoping to put off seeing her dad for as long as possible. However, she knew that he was right.

'And what are you going to do?' she asked.

'I'm going to go home and get the case file out and do a proper case review. So, take some time and be with your dad. It's going to take me until lunchtime tomorrow at least but I'll need to be home until then anyway.'

'Why is that?' Kate asked.

'I'll be dog sitting. I don't want to leave Terry by himself all day. So, I'll pick you up at Letchworth station around mid-day tomorrow, if that's alright. I'm hoping that I'll have some clues as to what we should do next by then.'

'Are you going to update Andy?' she asked.

'Yes, I'll call him as soon as I get home,' Mac replied.

Kate stood up.

'Okay then, let's go,' she said with determination.

Mac almost felt a little guilty as he dropped her off at the station. He could see that she was nervous about what lay ahead but he also knew that it was important that she came to some sort of understanding with her father before it was too late.

Terry gave him his usual welcome home and Amrit looked glad to see him too. She was grateful to be able to get off a little earlier than usual as she had some shopping to do.

Mac made himself a pot of coffee and then got himself comfortable on the sofa. Terry climbed up, took his usual position next to him and promptly fell asleep. He guessed that the long walk he'd had with Amanda had worn him out a bit. While his computer was firing up, he rang Andy and told him of what little progress they'd made.

'Well, I'd guess that you're lucky in that Ruth Avaloe only had a few friends. Chloe Alexander had loads of them. She was a very popular girl and it's going to take us quite a while to get around them all,' Andy said. 'How was Kate today?'

'She was okay, I think. We talked about her father and I made sure that she got off early so she'd be able to spend some time with him. I said that I'll pick her up tomorrow mid-day as I'm planning on going through the case file in some detail. We came across some useful information today and it's given me a few ideas but I need to know if it there's anything in the files that might back it up.'

'Okay then. We can meet up at five or so tomorrow at the station and have a catch up then, if that's okay with you?' Andy suggested.

'That's fine with me. I just hope we've got something to catch up about,' Mac said before saying goodbye.

He patted Terry, opened the file on his laptop and dove in. He remembered that not many of his colleagues had liked doing case reviews. They saw it as looking for a needle in a haystack and something of a waste of time when they could be out there, running around interviewing people and looking for clues. Mac was looking forward to it though. At times doing a case review was almost pleasurable for him but only if he felt that there was a chance that the needle was actually in there somewhere. He could only hope.

Kate phoned Magnus on her way into London and they arranged to meet in the hospital café. As she walked towards him, she was surprised that he actually looked okay and he even managed to give her a genuine smile.

'I won't be staying long if that's okay. I've told Nobomi that I'll give her a call this evening so I was going to go back to your flat and Skype her on my laptop,' Magnus said.

'Yes sure, of course,' Kate replied hesitantly.

'Look sis, I'm not abandoning you and I really do need to have a long chat with my wife, but the main reason I'm doing it is because you and dad need to talk, to really talk. I've been speaking to him for most of the day and, well, it's made things a little clearer for me somehow. I hope it will do the same for you too.'

Kate found that she couldn't think of anything to say so she just nodded.

'Call me when you're on the train and I'll meet you in that pub we went to before. I think we'll both be in need of a drink by then,' Magnus said.

She hugged him before he left and then walked slowly towards her dad's room. She was walking so slowly that she came to a full stop outside the door to his room. She found that she had no idea what she wanted to say to him.

Come on girl, she said to herself, get in there and wing it like you always do.

She followed her own advice, opened the door and went in.

Magnus was waiting for her when she finally arrived at the pub. He'd got a seat in a corner away from the rest of the other customers and there was a large glass of red on the table waiting for her. She sat down and took a gulp before she said anything.

Magnus gave her a smile and touched her hand.

'How did it go?'

Kate looked at him and then burst into tears. It took her totally by surprise but afterwards she realised that she'd been bottling up a lot of different emotions over the past few days. It all had to come out sometime. She couldn't talk for a while. Eventually she pulled herself together.

'It went well. As well as it could have, I suppose. He told me that he'd been a selfish and uncaring man all his life and that's what I'd always believed anyway. But when he told me everything, I could see that it wasn't quite true. I'm not saying that he wasn't a bastard but I kind of understood why he did what he did. He was warped but, you're right, he wasn't a monster.'

Magnus gave her hand a squeeze as she began to regain her composure.

'You know, I always believed that it was all his fault that mum just gave up, that she gave into her illness. I thought it was all because of him and what had happened to the bank. But it wasn't. He joked that even that couldn't get her attention. The man she truly loved had died and she just didn't want to go on living without him. Dad tried but he couldn't make her want to live. It must be terrible to be so in love with someone and know that you'll always be second best. God, everything I thought about him and mum was just so wrong.'

Magnus gave her hand another squeeze as he asked, 'And are glad that you talked to him today?'

She nodded without saying anything. She couldn't speak as she knew she'd just cry again. Magnus gave her a hug and she felt better afterwards.

'I'm beginning to realise that, if there is any blame for what happened to us, then it might be shared between the two of them,' Kate said. 'We just got caught in the crossfire, that's all.' Wanting to change the subject for a moment she asked, 'How did your call with Nobomi go?'

Magnus smiled, 'Great, she always manages to cheer me up. I'm flying home tomorrow and I must say that I can't wait.'

Home. Kate wondered where that was for her now. Certainly not the sterile flat that she slept in.

'What time is your flight?' Kate asked.

'It leaves at three thirty,' Magnus replied.

'That's good, I don't need to be in work until mid-day so we'll be able to spend the morning together. What do you want to do?'

'Well, I'd like to go and say goodbye to dad and after that perhaps we could get lunch together somewhere.'

'Okay you're on,' Kate said.

Chapter Eleven

The following day Kate said goodbye to her brother at the tube station. He was catching the train to Heathrow Airport and home while she was going back to Letchworth and work. She knew that she was really going to miss him and she was glad that she'd only have a week or so to wait until he returned.

As the train rattled away from London she thought about her father. He'd looked even smaller and frailer than he had before, a million miles away from the powerful and overbearing man that she'd known for all of her life. She realised that, when you're a child, you look up at your parents as though they were some kind of god. She'd still been thinking something like that until quite recently. When you grow up, you realise that they were just people like everyone else, struggling through life as best they could. She felt as if she was finally growing up.

He'd accepted that he was dying and, if the truth be known, he was probably the most cheerful out of the three of them. He was being moved to the hospice in Hatfield later that day so she'd be able to go and see him straight after work.

She thought that it was strange how she felt about him now. She'd imagined that she'd want to have nothing to do with him when he went and that she'd even be glad about the fact that he was dead. How wrong she'd been. When he died, she realised that she'd be an orphan, a lonely homeless orphan. She knew that she was being a little melodramatic but that was genuinely how she felt.

She was glad when the train pulled into Letchworth. Mac was going to pick her up at the station and that was something to be glad about too. It had started raining heavily again. Work was what she needed now, especially as Mac had said that he'd found something interesting in the case file. She wondered what it could be.

'You're looking a little better,' Mac commented as they drove off.

'Am I?' Kate asked.

'Yes, you were all on edge the last time I saw you. You're not now. How was your dad?'

'He's as well as could be expected, I suppose,' Kate replied. 'We talked, for probably the first time in our lives we really talked. It's sad that it takes something like death to make that happen.'

'Just be glad that it happened at all. There are lots of people who never get the chance to make their peace with the people they love.'

'You're right, of course, and I am glad. They're moving him to a hospice near where I live later today. I can pop in and see him this evening after work which is good. So, what was it you found in the case file then? I take it that it has something to do with where we're going?' Kate asked.

'Well, I found a couple of things that were interesting,' Mac said, 'but where we're going right now has more to do with what Martin's found. He's found Anne Foster. She's now called Anne Partington and she's living in Cambridge in an area called King's Hedges. I've been in contact with her and she's waiting for us now.'

Mac crossed over the motorway and headed towards Royston. The rain had eased off slightly but the black clouds they were driving towards promised that there was still more to come.

'So, what did you find in the files then?' Kate asked.

'Two things really and they sort of confirm a theory that I've had since we visited the church. The first was mentioned in a statement from one of the regular church-goers, a Mrs. Helen Mountfitch. She thought that she'd seen Ruth Avaloe on a street near the church at around eleven thirty on a Saturday evening a few weeks before she was murdered. It was dark and she only saw her from behind so she couldn't be totally sure it was Ruth. She said that she'd asked Ruth about this on the Sunday afterwards but she denied that it had been her.'

'So, she only saw her from behind? An identification like that wouldn't exactly stand up in court, would it?' Kate said.

'No, you're right it wouldn't but it's still interesting. Anyway, the other thing was tucked away in the back of the forensics report. Ruth had traces of tree bark under her nails, oak and sycamore mostly. However, the traces weren't new and forensics reckoned that she'd cleaned and cut her nails since the traces were lodged so it couldn't have anything directly to do with the murder. The nearest place that you'd find trees like those would obviously be in the park.'

'So, perhaps she went to the park during the day then,' Kate said.

'And hugged trees? No, I think that I might have a better explanation for it than that but let's wait and see if Anne Partington can shed more light on the case first,' Mac said.

Anne lived in quite an upmarket part of the city judging from the cars that Mac could see in the driveways. He pulled up outside a pair of houses that stood out from the rest. These were rendered white while the rest of the houses were plain brick. They were obviously much older than the other houses and Mac guessed that they might have been built at a time when Kings Hedges was mostly fields.

The door opened almost as soon as Mac rang the bell. Anne was taller than he'd expected, she had blonde hair in a designer cut and an apprehensive look on her face. Nonetheless, Mac thought that she was quite attractive. He showed her his warrant card and she held the door open for them.

She led them into a living room that could have just been done over by one of those decorating programmes that Mac often saw on the TV when flicking channels during the day. Everything was eclectic, spotless and in its place. She gestured towards a 1950's style sofa that looked familiar to him. His aunt had had one just like it in her parlour when he'd been a child.

'So, you're looking into Ruth's case again,' Anne said. 'I guessed you might but I was hoping…well, if I'm being honest, I was hoping that you wouldn't be. I was just about getting used to living without Ruth when, before you know it, five years have gone by and it all starts up again.'

'What do you mean by 'getting used to living without Ruth'?' Mac asked.

She had a long-sleeved top on and Mac couldn't help noticing that she was nervously pulling the end of her sleeves over her clenched hands.

'Well, she'd been a part of my life for just about as long as I could remember and then she was just gone. It was just so sudden and there was no time to…'

Anne stopped speaking and could only shrug her shoulders. Mac could see that she was near to tears so he gave her a little time before he asked his next question.

'Can you tell me why you left Stevenage so suddenly?'

'I just couldn't stand it anymore, day after day seeing all the places where we used to go. I know it was really stupid but, one day near the church, I had this strange feeling. I mean, I knew that she was dead, but I somehow convinced myself that she was going to walk around the corner any minute just like she always used to when we were young. I stood there for hours, hoping beyond hope, but of course she didn't. The day after that I went to the Stevenage train station and caught the first train out. I didn't much care where it took me. I ended up in Cambridge so I walked around for a bit and got a job at a hairdresser's and then I got a flat. I went back to Stevenage to collect my stuff but, apart from that, I've never been back, never wanted to.'

'You're married now, I take it?' Mac asked.

Mac saw her smile for the first time.

'Yes, I met Mike at that first job. I really needed someone at the time. He was just starting out as a hairdresser too and we hit it off. We've got our own business now and we're doing really well.'

'I'm glad for you. I've only got a few more questions. Tell me, as far as you know, did Ruth ever go anywhere outside the church in the year or so before she died?'

Anne thought for a while and shook her head.

'No. After her mum died, she went right into her shell. She was only seventeen when it happened and after that it was like she was in prison. Whether that was all down to her or that bastard of a father she had, I don't know. I suspect it was probably a bit of both.'

'Did she ever mention leaving the church or saying that she'd like to go outside anywhere?'

'No and God knows that both me and Tracey tried to get her to go out with us lots of times but she never would. I think that she was too scared of what her father might say and perhaps Tracey was right in that Ruth had become something of an agoraphobic too.'

'Did she ever tell you if she liked someone, perhaps someone at the church?' Mac asked.

'Well, she liked lots of people...oh, do you mean did she fancy anyone?' Anne asked. 'No, not as far as I know. She never said anything to me anyway.'

'Did anyone at the church fancy her?'

Anne hesitated for quite a while before saying, 'No, I don't think so.'

Mac immediately felt that she was hiding something. He'd take it slowly though.

'Anne, I know you've spoken to the police several times around the time of the murder so I won't go over everything again. In the five years since Ruth's murder have you had any new thoughts or remembered something that you might not have told the police at the time?'

She started to shake her head but then she stopped.

'I told the police everything I knew at the time…well, almost everything.'

Mac said nothing and gave her some time.

'I'm afraid that I lied to you just now,' she said glancing quickly up at Mac. 'There was someone at the church who fancied her, who loved her, who thought that she was a very special person.'

She stopped speaking as she wiped away a tear.

'Yes,' Mac prompted.

'It was me. I loved her,' Anne said. 'I wanted to be with her forever, for us to be a couple, an item. I realised after she died that I'd loved her all my life but she could never see me in that way. I ached for her to kiss me, to touch me and so I kept hanging around hoping that we might be more than friends but it never happened.'

'That's a very personal confession. Do you mind me asking why you're telling us this now?' Mac asked gently.

'I've never told anyone, not anyone. I suppose I just want someone to know, to know that Ruth was loved before she died.'

Neither of them said anything as they walked back to the car. Mac handed Kate the keys. He was more than happy for her to drive. He needed to think.

'Back to Letchworth?' Kate asked.

Mac nodded.

'That was a bit intense,' Kate said as they drove off.

'Yes, it was and it's more than a shame that Anne couldn't tell Ruth about how she really felt. I think Ruth might have been very lonely and, you never know, she might even have been alive today if she and Anne had ended up as a couple.'

89

'But how does that work? I mean, how is it possible for her to be so in love with a woman and then marry a man?' Kate asked.

'Well, they describe lots of things these days as being in a spectrum and sexual preference is definitely one of them,' Mac said. 'For instance, I've never understood what gay men find attractive in other men just as I suppose they wonder why other men find women so attractive. But it's not a binary choice, is it? Some people find both men and women attractive and it can be even more complicated than that.'

'What do you mean?' Kate asked.

'Fancy a coffee?' Mac asked.

'Sure.'

'Okay, I know a place. There's a story that I want to tell you.'

The 'place' was Mac's home. While Amanda would have taken Terry for his walk Mac wanted to check in and make sure that he was alright. He was bouncing with joy as Mac opened the door.

Mac realised that he was a little hungry and made some sandwiches too. When he brought the tray in, he noticed that Kate had sat on the settee and Terry was sitting beside her having his head scratched. He looked up as Mac walked in but he didn't make any attempt to move. This made him smile.

He sat down in the armchair and began his story.

'There's a good friend of mine who is now something very high up in the National Crime Agency. She joined my team as a sergeant some twenty-five years or so ago when she was somewhat younger than you are now. She was brilliant at her job. She was also single, very good looking and someone who really enjoyed life. Because of that she was very popular and she went out with quite a few different men. Then one day she came to see me. She told me that she was now in a long-term relationship with someone, another woman as it turned out. I was quite surprised to say the least, not that I had any problem with it, but because she was probably the last woman who I thought might end up in a same-sex relationship.

It wasn't all that long ago, I suppose, but unfortunately things were quite different then. She felt that she had to keep her relationship something of a secret but she said that she wanted me to know, just in case anything happened to her while she was on the job. I was really curious and I asked her why. Why did she fall for a woman and why that particular woman? She told me that she'd never thought of herself as being gay and she still didn't in a way. She said it just happened that the person she'd fallen deeply in love with turned out to be a woman.'

Kate was silent for a while.

'I think I see where you're going. Anne loved Ruth because of the person she was and she probably loves her husband for the same reason.'

'Yes, something like that,' Mac said. 'The only thing I've really learnt about people is you can never fit them into neat boxes. Life's usually a lot messier than that.'

This had opened up a whole new line of thought for Kate. There was something that she'd been considering for a while and now was the time to do something about it. She decided to change the subject.

'It doesn't really help us with the case though, does it?'

'Well, you never know. All information is useful and, in my opinion, you can never know too much about a victim,' Mac replied.

'So, come on then, what's your theory?'

'It's just a thought at the moment so can we just keep it to ourselves until we get some real evidence to back it up? I think you'll see the reason why I'm saying this soon enough.'

'Yes, of course,' Kate replied.

'Okay then. The original investigation has proved useful as it eliminated most of the possibilities so, whatever the truth is, it has to be something that they didn't consider at the time,' Mac said. 'My main reason for reading the case files is detail was not only for what was in there but to try to identify what wasn't. I've also tried to think about Ruth's murder as a standalone event and that's helped quite a bit too. I also have to say that I've made quite a few assumptions and, as I said, it's just a theory at the moment. So, if you find any flaws in it, please let me know.'

Kate assured him that she would.

'So, from what we know of Ruth she spent all her time in the church. So much so that at least one of her close friends was convinced that she was agoraphobic. Not only that but her father was a very controlling man and, after her mother died, she was even more under his direct influence. She was a virtual prisoner and didn't even have a key to her own front door. However, I think she that she might not have been quite as agoraphobic as Tracey thought and that she might have found her own way of getting in and out of the church unnoticed.'

'The window catch! Do you think that was her doing?' Kate asked.

Mac smiled at Kate's quick thinking.

'I think it's at least a possibility. Perhaps it became a bit loose and then Ruth found that she could not only get out that way but get back in again even though the window appeared to be locked. She wasn't even on the same floor as her father, which seemed to be Ruth's choice up to a point, so perhaps it was something that she'd planned. It might also be no coincidence that the window led onto a small alleyway outside that wasn't overlooked by anyone and that's presumably why it was so handy for the burglars too. I think that she might have been meeting someone when she went out. You see, I've seen something like the tree bark under her

92

fingernails before, a long time ago when I was just starting out as a detective.'

'Really? Was it another murder?' Kate asked.

'Well, we thought so at first,' Mac replied. 'A woman was found in a park near Birmingham city centre one night at the foot of a tree. She was dead and she had an abrasion on her forehead. She had no panties on and had obviously been having sex when she died. We figured that it was probably a rape and murder case and went ahead on that premise. However, that theory was soon blown out of the water by the medical experts. During the autopsy they found that she'd had a massive aneurysm in her brain and that it had suddenly ruptured. It caused extensive internal bleeding in her skull and they reckoned that she must have dropped like a stone and died a few seconds afterwards. One of the old sergeants who worked at the station told us what the bark under her fingernails meant. He told us that she was probably having a 'knee trembler' at the time.'

'A knee trembler? What's that?' Kate asked with a puzzled expression.

'Well, many years ago outdoor sex was very popular. This was because most young people were still living with their parents. Most people were still fairly poor and hotel rooms were expensive and so they used to go to parks and other outdoor places at night and have sex there. They used to do it standing up and that's why it was called a knee trembler.'

'Really? I've obviously led a sheltered life,' Kate said.

'In this case, the woman was bent over and was gripping the tree with both hands while the man took her from behind. That's how come she had the tree bark under her nails.'

'And you think that this was what Ruth was getting up to?'

'I think it's at least a possibility.'

Kate gave it some thought.

'I suppose if, underneath it all, she really hated her father then having sex behind his back would certainly be one way of getting some revenge. Do you think that it might have been someone from the church?'

'I think that's most likely, after all who else did she ever meet? However, we can't be sure if it was the man that she was seeing who killed her, or if she somehow ran into the serial killer on her way to meet him in the park. If she was meeting someone regularly then the killer might have known this, anything's possible. At least it explains why she might have been in the park that night and does away with the need for a kidnapping to have taken place. I never thought that was likely to have happened anyway.'

Mac had to shut the door on a broken-hearted whine from Terry. Although he knew it would only be a while before he would be back, it didn't make him feel any better.

As they walked back to the car Kate said, 'Well, I really hope that your theory's right, Mac. It gives us a way into the case, one that we didn't have before. However, there's another reason why I'm hoping that you're right.'

'What's that?' Mac asked.

'It would be nice to think that Ruth had some fun before she died.'

Chapter Twelve

Mac and Kate arrived back at the police station early and waited for Andy and Tommy to return. The team's room was empty and Mac wondered how Dan and the rest of the team were getting on with the car theft cases. He felt that something must be happening if they were all away at the same time. Kate wandered over to the window and stared out at the rain that was still falling on the car park at the back of the building.

A few moments later she saw a car pull up and Toni Woodgate jump out. She ran quickly towards the shelter of the doorway. Kate knew what she needed to do.

'I'll be back in a minute,' she said to Mac.

Mac smiled. He'd seen Toni too and he had an idea what Kate was up to. He hoped that the story he'd told her might have helped her a little.

She ran towards the corridor and got there just in time to more or less collide with a very damp Toni who was on her way back to her office.

'Oh, I'm so sorry,' Kate said.

'Oh, that's alright. It was probably my fault, I wasn't really paying attention,' Toni said with a smile.

Kate found that she liked Toni's smile a lot.

'It's Kate, isn't it?' Toni asked.

'Yes, Kate Grimsson. I'm working with Dan Carter's team.'

'Yes, you're working with Andy Reid on a case on the moment, aren't you? The Match of the Day Murders. I used to work with Andy and I'm afraid that I asked him about you.'

This gave Kate some courage. She went for it.

'I'm sorry but I haven't got much time. Could we meet up for a drink sometime, sometime soon? I'd like to talk to you about something,' Kate asked.

Toni gave her a look that Kate couldn't quite decipher.

'Yes, sure. How about tomorrow? We could meet at six thirty at the hotel if you like? It's very quiet around then.'

'Great, let's do that. Tomorrow at six thirty then,' Kate said.

Toni started to walk away but she stopped and turned.

'Just turn right after you walk through the main door. I'll be there somewhere,' she said.

She then gave Kate another smile and Kate felt her heart speed up. She wondered what she'd done as she walked back. She'd started something, she knew that much, but she just wished she had some idea of where it was all going to end.

Mac could guess that it had gone well by the little smile that Kate had on her face as she walked in. He pretended not to notice as he continued reading the posters that were pinned to the notice board. Kate went back to staring out of the window at the rain and trying to understand why she felt so excited all of a sudden.

She was shaken out of her thoughts by the sight of Andy and Tommy getting out of their car and, like Toni, they were making a dash through the rain towards the station door.

'They're coming,' she said as she turned towards Mac.

They both turned to face the door.

'I'm sure that someone told me that it was supposed to be summer right now,' Andy complained as he walked in.

He and Tommy took their rain sodden jackets off and hung them up. Water dripped from them onto the floor creating a small puddle.

'We got caught in the rain at the last place we visited,' Tommy explained. 'We couldn't park that close so we just had to brave it.'

'Any luck?' Mac asked.

Andy shrugged.

'Not really but it's early days yet. How about you?'

'Well, we've had some thoughts but we've got nothing concrete as yet,' Mac replied.

'Anyone want a coffee?' Tommy asked.

They all did. Kate volunteered to help and she followed Tommy out of the room.

'How was Kate today?' Andy quickly asked while he had Mac to himself.

'She was good actually,' Mac replied. 'She's had a long talk with her father and I think that's really helped. He's being moved to a hospice near where she lives so she'll be able to see him as often as possible.'

'I know that she talks to you so let me know if there's anything we can do to help,' Andy said.

Tommy and Kate returned with the coffees.

'Okay, so let's start then,' Andy said. 'This is where we've got to on the Alexander case. We interviewed Chloe's mum and dad first. It wasn't the easiest interview that I've ever done. Even after five years, I'm afraid that our visit upset them both deeply. We also managed to interview most of the friends who were with her in Baldock on the night that she disappeared. Some of them even remembered me from the first investigation five years ago. Unfortunately, we've not turned up anything new as yet but there was one thing that I was reminded of. Chloe met a couple of her friends at another pub in Baldock before meeting up with the birthday party and Jackie Hughes was there.'

'Jackie Hughes the footballer?' Kate asked.

'Yes, I'm only mentioning it because he was on the news recently,' Andy said.

'Yes, he's just gone back to Peterborough as an assistant manager, hasn't he?' Mac said. 'I take it that you questioned him at the time?'

'Well, I didn't but my boss did. He'd apparently been on a bit of a bender and went home around ten according

97

to the landlord of the pub. He was picked up by his wife and she said that she drove him straight home.'

'That wouldn't have been too long after his knee went in that international match,' Kate said. 'I take it that's why he was on a bender then?'

'Yes, I remember that tackle,' Andy said with a wince. 'I still think that the full back should have gotten jail rather than a red card and it was supposed to have been a friendly too. Anyway, as I didn't talk to him the first time around, I thought that speaking to him might help me to get a better picture of Chloe's movements that night. So, I rang him to see if we could arrange an interview but he doesn't appear to be living with his wife anymore. She told us that they'd split up a few years ago so we've arranged to see her tomorrow and she's going to give us his new address and contact details. So, we've got Jackie Hughes and umpteen more of Chloe's friends and acquaintances to go through yet. How did you get on Mac?'

Mac told him about the sports centre and the interviews with Ruth's father and friends. He also told him about the case review and his theory.

'A knee trembler?' Andy said in wonder. 'My God, now there's a phrase that I haven't heard in a while. It's all dogging nowadays, isn't it? Anyway, that's certainly something we didn't consider when we were looking into it five years ago. What do you want to do next?'

'I think it's going to be back to the church for us. If Ruth was seeing a man then it would have most likely been someone attending the services there. Unfortunately, it looks as if they've got quite a big congregation so we might be some time doing that,' Mac replied.

'Yes, it looks as if we've all got a lot to do then but, as I said, it's early days and we can only keep digging,' Andy said.

As it was still raining Mac dropped Kate outside the train station before heading for home. As he was about

98

to pull away something that Andy said came back to him. While he was deep in thought a queue of cars was building up behind him and a chorus of irate car horns finally brought him back to the here and now. He didn't go home though, he drove straight back to the police station instead.

Dan and Adil were back. They were drinking coffee and chatting to Andy.

'Mac!' Dan exclaimed. 'How's it going?'

'Not too bad. Tell me is Martin around?'

Martin Selby was the team's computer specialist and Mac needed him right away.

'He's working with the Bedfordshire team on a case of revenge porn. He'll be another couple of days, I'd guess,' Dan replied.

Mac phoned him. He quickly outlined what he needed and Martin promised that he'd send him any results first thing tomorrow morning.

That done, Mac was curious to know how Dan was getting on with his case.

'So, have you caught the BMW thieves yet?' Mac asked.

By the way Dan smiled Mac knew that they had.

'Well, that didn't take long. How did you do it then?' Mac asked.

'It was quite simple in the end,' Dan said. 'We caught the three of them by simply putting an advert up in a few dodgy online car sites offering cash for a BMW in good condition. We implied that no questions would be asked. Adil met with them and they obviously believed that he was shady enough to do a deal with him.'

'De Niro would have been proud of me,' Adil said as he tried to keep a serious expression.

Dan laughed and continued.

'So, they brought him a car to have a look at and everything. They'd changed the number plates but not the VIN number on the engine. We've got it all on video, it's quite funny really, especially the part when me, Chris and six uniforms turn up and nick them all. I'll show it to you when I get a chance.'

'Not exactly criminal masterminds, were they?' Mac observed.

'No, it was all a bit too easy I suppose,' Dan replied. 'Not that I'm moaning, a win is a win after all. Anyway, once we've finished interviewing the Three Stooges and we've tidied up the paperwork, it looks like we'll be free to give you a hand, if you need it. From what Andy was saying it looks like you've still got a lot of interviews to do.'

'Probably a whole church load by the look of it so yes, some help would be really appreciated,' Mac replied.

As Tim was still away in Newcastle Mac went straight home after he'd finished chatting to Dan and the others. Terry was glad to see him even though he'd only left him just over an hour or so before. At least his friend Tim would be back tomorrow evening and he'd enjoy catching up with him and hearing about all his tremendously daring exploits in the sale room. He had a look at what was on TV and, seeing nothing that tempted him, he spent the rest of the evening going through the case file once more, just in case.

He took Terry out for a little walk before going to bed. It had stopped raining and he could even see some stars twinkling in between the dark scudding clouds. He knew there was more rain forecast for tomorrow though.

While Terry was inspecting the base of a telephone pole, Mac's thoughts turned to the upcoming service of remembrance for Nora. Bridget hadn't told him much about what she'd arranged apart from the fact that it would be a small family affair. He found that he wasn't looking forward to it. He'd gone a whole year without his beloved wife and he still felt as if he was hanging on by his fingernails at times. He decided to talk it through with Tim tomorrow evening when he got back from his trip. His friend had also lost his wife and Mac felt that he was the only person he could talk to honestly about it.

His phone went off. By coincidence it was a message from Tim.

'Sorry Mac but I'll now be back in a couple of days. No luck at this sale but there's one in Berwick that looks interesting see you Sunday Tim.'

Mac felt a bit disappointed but thanked God that he had the case to work on. He made his mind up there and then that he'd definitely go with Tim on his next trip.

If he was honest, he missed his friend.

Chapter Thirteen

For the first time in what seemed like ages Kate felt fairly calm. For once she'd had a good night's sleep and she was now on her way into work. Even the overcrowded train didn't annoy her as much as usual.

She'd visited her father the evening before at the hospice but he'd been very tired after the move and had slept for most of her visit. Nonetheless, she still felt that he somehow knew that she was there. At one point his eyelids fluttered and his hand reached out and she grasped it. He then went straight back to sleep. The hospice itself was very nice and she found to her surprise that most of the people looking after her father seemed to be fairly upbeat and cheerful.

Quite a trick, she thought, considering that they were dealing with death on a daily basis.

She'd also had a really long talk with her brother afterwards via Skype and that had helped too. He said that he'd be flying in on Tuesday with Nobomi. He wanted his father to meet her. He'd booked a room for the two of them at a hotel quite close to the hospice. As she watched the familiar scenery speed by, she felt amazed at how her feelings about her father had changed in the past few days.

They'd changed for the better too, she thought. The hatred and anger had gone. It was only once she had gotten those feelings out of her system that she was able to realise the tremendous damage that it had been doing to her.

She suddenly remembered that she was meeting Toni later that evening and felt a flutter of excitement but she had no real idea why. She still wasn't clear in her own mind what she expected from Toni so she decided that she should take it slow and perhaps just talk about being friends. She'd then be able to see where it went from there. If she was being honest, she was still confused about how she felt but the story that Mac had told her the day before kept coming back into her mind.

Did she really like Toni in that way?

She had absolutely no idea. Part of her was excited by the thought of meeting Toni again but another part of her was far more cautious. All of this was new territory for her. The only thing she knew for sure is that she needed to see Toni for some reason and she needed to find out why.

She was surprised to see Mac waiting outside the station for her. He waved to her and she could see that he was already sitting in the front passenger seat. She climbed into the driver's seat.

'I take it that something's happened?' she asked as she started the car up.

'Yes, I think that you might be able to say that. It might be a wild goose chase but, on the other hand, it might just save us from having to interview everyone at the church,' Mac replied.

'Where are we going?'

'Just follow the satnav,' Mac replied.

Kate looked at the satnav. They were going to an address in Shephall, Stevenage.

'What's in Shephall then?' she asked.

'Hopefully, someone who might be able to tell us why men were going into Fairfields Park at night around the time of Ruth Avaloe's murder.'

Mac told her what Martin had discovered. The man they were going to see now ran a small newsagent's shop and Mac hoped that he would have at least some of the answers.

Kate's face showed her surprise.

'Well, you hear about it but I've never actually come across it before for real. I always thought that it was a bit of an urban myth, if I'm being honest.'

'We'll hopefully find out shortly whether you're right or not about that,' Mac said.

'So, how did Martin identify him then?' she asked.

'Well, he took the website down not long after the murder but you can never really delete anything from the web or so Martin tells me. He was able to get the site URL and some idea of what the website was about from the links on other sites that are still out there. From this he could figure out what the domain name was. The site is still active Martin says. Our man has probably forgotten all about it and is still paying out every year for it on his credit card. Martin told me that everyone has to provide some personal information when they buy a domain name. He also said that there's a way you can keep your personal information private but, thankfully, our man didn't seem to know about that and so his details are available to anyone who wants to look. Once Martin had a name the rest was easy. People just don't realise what a minefield the internet can be if you don't know what you're doing.'

They drove through a large housing estate, parts of which looked quite well off while others were clearly more run-down. The newsagent's shop was in one of the more run-down areas. It was small and, just from looking at the adverts that took up most of the window space, it seemed to offer just about everything; alcohol, sweets, groceries, dry cleaning, energy tokens, parcel pick-ups and deliveries, lottery tickets and, presumably, newspapers.

Mac pushed open the door and a bell rang. He looked up as he walked in the door. It was an actual bell and not some electronic gizmo. For some reason this made Mac smile. Behind the counter a tall unshaven man in his fifties was serving a customer. She was looking at an array of lottery scratch cards and couldn't seem to make up her mind which one she should buy. This was clearly annoying the man. Mac waited until the customer was on her way out before showing the man his warrant card.

'You're Mr. Boles,' Mac stated.

On seeing his warrant card Mr. Boles looked worried and Mac wondered if he'd been doing something that he shouldn't.

'Can we go somewhere?' Mac suggested.

'Maggie!' the man shouted out and a large shapeless woman in her fifties slouched out in her pyjamas and slippers. She had a word puzzle book in her hand and she never looked up from it as she took her place behind the counter. The man took them into a shabby living room that was dusty and obviously not much used. Mac and Kate sat down on a sofa that squeaked when they sat on it. The man sat on an armchair opposite. It too squeaked when he sat down.

'So, how can I help the police?' Mr. Boles said with some nervousness.

He could not be described as good looking. His nose was broken, his mouth was somewhat crooked and his hair was long, unkempt and quite grey. His nervous habit was to keep putting a strand behind his right ear, a strand which kept falling back out again.

'Mr. Boles, we're looking for some information, information that I know you can provide,' Mac said.

'What information?' he asked anxiously as he pushed his hair back behind his ear again.

'You're Mr. Horny, aren't you?'

The name got an immediate reaction. Mr. Boles stood up, went to the door and looked down the hall. He then shut the door, came back and sat down again.

'How in God's name did you find that out?' he asked in a low voice.

'We have our ways,' Mac replied. 'There was a murder in the park around the time that you were writing your little blog. Oh, what was it called now? Yes, 'A Dogger's Diary', wasn't it?'

'I thought I'd deleted all that. I wasn't doing anything illegal, was I?' he asked.

It wasn't that warm in the room but Mac could see that he was starting to sweat.

'You were but that's for another day. I want you to tell me exactly what you used to get up to in the park at night five years ago. Now, I must warn you that I know most of the story already so, if you leave anything out, then you'll find yourself in an interview room down at the station. Do I make myself clear?' Mac said.

Mr. Boles nodded.

'Well, it all started off quite slowly, I suppose. We'd heard about 'dogging' in some of the newspapers so me and a friend of mine thought we'd give it a go. Once the weather had started to turn a little warmer, around May I think it was, we used to hang around the park at night. I wrote about it in the blog. I bigged it up quite a bit, of course, especially the number of women who I said turned up which was zero at the start. However, it seemed to work. Within a few weeks we started to get more people in the park and quite a few of them were women too. Then the word spread and it became quite a thing. Most of the women were getting on a bit, widowed or divorced I'd guess, and all they wanted was a quick shag but it was fun all the same. There was a sort of mad excitement about having sex out in the open like that with a stranger, like being a caveman or something I suppose.'

He stopped for a moment and smiled as he remembered some of the highlights. Mac shoved a tablet in front of him. It had a photo of Ruth Avaloe on it.

'What about her? Did you see her in the park during one of your dogging sessions?'

He looked quickly at the photo.

'She's the girl who was murdered. I remember her picture being in the newspapers.' He looked again. 'I honestly don't know. There used to be some younger girls who turned up from time to time, God knows why, but they never seemed to fancy me somehow. I always ended up with the older ones, not that I'm moaning though. It was a shame that it all ended so quickly. After she was found dead the dogging died too,' he said mournfully as he handed the tablet back to Mac.

'Who else used to go there?'

'I don't know anyone else's name, honestly,' Mr. Boles replied. 'That's the way we kept it, strictly no names.'

'You just said that you and your friend 'gave it a go'. I want his name at least,' Mac said.

Mr. Boles hesitated.

'Okay then, it's the station for you,' Mac said as he stood up.

He then gave the newsagent his sternest look and it appeared to have worked.

'It's Rob, Rob Jameson,' Mr. Boles said quickly. 'He owns the betting shop just down the road. The one on the corner.'

Mac was thoughtful for a while. Then he smiled.

'Is there anything else that you can add?' Mac asked. 'Please think carefully as we won't be impressed if we have to drive back here to ask any more questions.'

'No honestly, that's it,' he replied trying to look honest.

He didn't succeed.

'Do you think he was lying when he said that he didn't know Ruth?' Kate asked as they walked back to the car.

'I was watching him closely when I showed him the photo and he didn't really react. But he's feeling guilty about something that was clear enough.'

'What do you think it was?'

'I've got an idea but let's wait until we've finished with his friend,' Mac replied.

The betting shop was quiet, in fact there was no-one in the shop apart from a glum looking man in his early forties who was sitting behind the counter studying some documents.

'Mr. Jameson?' Mac asked.

The man looked up and smiled but the smile soon disappeared when he saw Mac's warrant card.

'So, what have I done now?' he asked as he went back to being glum.

Mac could see that the documents he'd been looking at were bank statements. Even from the little he could make out it looked as if the business wasn't doing too well.

'Nothing as far as we know,' Mac replied. 'We've just spoken to your friend Mr. Boles and he gave us your name.'

'Nick?' he said uncomfortably. 'Remind me to thank him.'

'We're interested in what you used to get up to in Fairfields Park five years or so ago. I want you to tell me everything,' Mac said. 'And I mean everything.'

'This is about the murder, isn't it? I was wondering if you lot would open it all up again. Well, I dare say that Nick has told you all about the dogging then?'

Mac nodded and the bookie's face fell.

'It was all just a bit of a joke at first, something we cooked up in the pub after a few drinks. I'd just gotten divorced and I felt that some quick, uncomplicated sex was just what I needed. It wasn't until a few weeks after Nick had started his blog that it took off. Dogging was in the news at the time and we even got a mention in one of the tabloids. When it got going, we had sex there most weekend nights. There always seemed to be more men than women so you used to have to queue up sometimes.'

'Queue up? You mean that some of the women had sex with more than one man?' Mac asked.

'Oh yes, some of them just couldn't seem to get enough. Not everyone wanted sex though, some of the men were quite happy to just watch and jack themselves off.'

'Did you ever see this girl in the park?' Mac asked as he handed him the tablet.

The bookie only glanced at the photo and returned the tablet.

'I know who she is but no, I never saw her in the park,' he said.

'You're sure?' Mac asked looking at the bookie closely as he replied.

'Yes, I'm sure,' he said somewhat testily.

Mac moved away to the far end of the room and made a call. He talked softly so Kate couldn't quite pick up what he said. He came back and stood in the middle of the room looking straight at the bookie.

After a short but uncomfortable while the bookie said, 'Well, if you've got no more questions...'

Mac didn't reply or even move a muscle.

'So, what are we waiting for exactly?' the bookie asked obviously getting somewhat rattled.

'Have you got your keys handy?' Mac asked.

'Yes, they're here,' he said holding up a bunch of keys, 'but what's that got to do with anything?'

Mac looked at his watch.

'In about three minutes two uniformed policemen are going to come through that door. They're going to cuff you, drag you out to a police car and then drive you to Letchworth Police Station. I just thought that you might want us to lock up for you that's all.'

In fact, as soon as Mac had finished speaking two burly looking uniforms burst in.

'Mr. Maguire?' the older one asked.

Mac showed them his warrant card.

'How can we help, sir?'

'Can you please arrest this man and put him in an interview room at Letchworth Police Station. We'll meet you there.'

'No problem sir.'

109

The bookie looked on with something like horror. He glanced towards a door behind him but this was immediately picked up by the younger policeman. He quickly jumped over the counter and made sure that the bookie was going nowhere. They cuffed him and escorted him out. Mac picked up his keys and locked up after him. He even made sure that the 'Open' sign was turned around to show that the bookies shop was now closed.

As they drove back to Letchworth Kate asked, 'You think that he met Ruth in the park, don't you?'

'Perhaps, anyway I'm as sure as I can be that he's just lied to us and, if I'm honest, I was more or less expecting it. This wasn't the first time that he's told lies to the police.'

'How do you know that?'

'He made a statement at the time of the murder,' Mac replied. 'I only came across it last night. His name stuck in my head as it's the same as the Irish whiskey. While Jan didn't mention the men in the park to the police, her friend Sue did. That's because she recognised one of them and identified him as Robert Jameson. She knew him because he ran the local betting shop on the road where she lived. Five years ago, he signed a statement saying that he'd only been using the park as a shortcut to get to a friend's house. He's now admitted to us that he lied. So, we've got him for perjury and perverting the course of justice at the very least. However, I'd still like to know exactly what it is he's trying to keep from us.'

'Wow! Reading the case file thoroughly really does work,' Kate said.

Mac smiled.

'Only sometimes but this time I got lucky. If his name was Smith or Jones then I'm not so sure that I'd have remembered his statement out of the hundreds that are in the file.'

Kate gave him a look that showed that she didn't quite believe him.

'Anyway, now that we've got some leverage let's see what he's got to say. I'm hoping that he might be able to tell us something useful, something new,' Mac said with some enthusiasm.

Chapter Fourteen

The bookie squirmed in his chair as Mac and Kate entered the room. Mac had suggested that Kate should lead the questioning as technically she was the ranking officer. They'd also agreed what questions they needed answers to but, before they did that, they'd show him the stick. There wouldn't be a carrot.

Kate turned on the recorder and named herself and Mac before reading Mr. Jameson his rights. She then asked him to state his name and address.

'For the record we've told you that you have the right to free legal advice but you've turned this down. However, before we go any further, I'd like you to confirm this for the record,' Kate said.

'I can do without a lawyer for now love,' he replied. 'I want to know what I'm up against and if I can cut myself a deal first. I can always ask for a lawyer later if I want one, I take it?'

'Yes, that's correct.'

'Okay then, love. Just tell me what I'm doing here then.'

He sat back and smiled. Mac thought he looked far too confident. He knew that he was going to be in for something of a shock.

Kate said nothing and just passed him two sheets of paper. It was his statement. He read them both and Mac could see that the thin veneer of his confidence was already starting to peel away.

'I didn't think that you kept these things for that long. Anyway, so what?' he said shrugging his shoulders. 'I told a few fibs to the police that's all.'

Again, Kate said nothing for a while and just looked at him.

'Did you kill Ruth Avaloe?' she eventually asked.

He'd been slouched back in the chair but this question made him sit up straight.

'What? Did I kill that girl? Bloody hell no!' he replied in a strangled voice.

He obviously hadn't been expecting that question and it was also patently obvious that he now knew that things were a lot more serious that he'd thought.

'You were in the park the night that Ruth Avaloe was murdered, is that correct?' Kate said.

'Well yes, but…'

'You'd also had sex with Ruth before the night she was murdered, hadn't you?' Kate stated with absolute certainty.

Kate had absolutely no idea if this might have been true or not. However, they'd both felt that there was an outside chance that the real reason the bookie was lying was because he might have known Ruth too well.

'That bloody Nick. I'll kill him!' he said with anger before returning back to his slouched position. 'Yes, yes I'd had her twice before.'

'So, you were there that night, you'd had sex with the girl who was murdered and you lied to us about it,' Kate said. 'That makes you a suspect, in fact, as suspects are pretty thin on the ground at the moment, that makes you our main suspect.'

She let this sink in. Eventually it did.

'Christ!' was all he could say.

'Tell us about Ruth and I want everything you know,' Kate said. 'If you miss a single thing out then we'll know that you're guilty.'

He licked his lips. His confidence was shredded now and he looked more like a whipped dog.

Mac glanced over at Kate. She was good.

'Well, she started turning up most weekends, around June I think it was, and she stood out. I mean she was young and quite good looking and she was gagging for it. I first noticed her when I saw her watching some people

113

having sex from behind a tree. I could tell that she was turned on. She had her knickers in her hand and she was, you know…masturbating or whatever it is they call it when women do it. I came towards her but she ran off when she saw me. I saw her next a couple of weeks later being shagged up against a tree. That's how she liked it, from behind while she held on to a tree. When the bloke came and finished, I quickly slipped myself in. She didn't seem to mind, she just said, 'Harder, harder.' She was a truly great fuck.'

He stopped and smiled as he remembered. His smile made Kate feel slightly nauseous.

'I came across her the next week and, when she saw me, she just turned around and pulled up her skirt. I took her from behind as before but this time she asked me to strangle her too. I lightly put my hands around her neck but she told me to squeeze harder, so I did. It certainly seemed to turn her on. It was honestly the best sex I'd ever had. The next few times I saw her she was with the same bloke, a tall fair-haired guy in his thirties but I didn't see her at all on the night she died. I honestly didn't even know she was in the park.'

Kate ended the interview and she and Mac left the room.

In the hallway outside she asked, 'What do you think?'

'I think that he might just be telling us the truth at last,' Mac replied.

'Yes, I agree. However, I think we should hold him pending charges and a hearing.'

'That's exactly what I would have suggested. We can pass on the file and let someone else prepare the charges. In the meantime, Mr. Jameson can enjoy some police food while he waits for his bail hearing.'

'Whatever they give him for perjuring himself they should add on a few years for being a total slimeball. Oh yes, and an extra six months too for calling me 'love',' Kate said with feeling.

Mac laughed out loud.

'By the way, we now know exactly what it was that Mr. Boles was hiding from us. I suggest that we bring him in and charge him too.'

Kate smiled and said, 'Well, I'm sure that Mr. Jameson would love the company. Come on then, let's give him the good news.'

They went back into the interview room. After they had seated themselves Kate turned the recorder on and then stated the time and the names of those in the room.

'Mr. Jameson, I can tell you that, while you are still a suspect in the murder of Ruth Avaloe, we will not be charging you with murder at this time. However, we will be preparing charges around the fact that you lied to the police when they took your statement at the time of the murder and for withholding information. What you've just told us we consider as being crucial evidence, evidence that would have helped the original invest-igation greatly. In the meantime, we'll be holding you in custody pending a bail hearing.'

Mr. Jameson's face turned white and he seemed unable to speak.

'Interview ended,' Kate said as she turned off the recorder. As she got up to leave, she said, 'If I were you, I'd get a lawyer and quick.'

Mac followed Kate down the hallway towards the team's room. The hallway was where Kate had first met Toni and she felt a frisson of excitement at the memory.

The room was empty. Mac sat down and looked at his watch, it was only twelve thirty.

'Fancy a coffee, Mac?' Kate asked.

'Yes, please,' he replied.

He was deep in thought when Kate returned.

'So, what do you think?' she asked as she handed him a cup.

'Thanks. Well, it changes our whole perception of Ruth Avaloe and the case, doesn't it?'

115

'Yes, but it's still a bit of a shock to think that someone like Ruth could have been into dogging. I mean on the surface she appears to have been so holier than thou.'

'I've seen lots of cases like this before,' Mac said. 'With some people what you see on the surface is totally different to what they're actually thinking and feeling. Sometimes you can figure out what their motivations might have been and sometimes not. People think in very strange ways. In Ruth's case it seems as if your idea of revenge on her father might have played a part but there's something else too, isn't there? She'd never had a boyfriend, she'd never had sex, she might not have even seen any porn. She must have had sexual feelings which no doubt she kept bottled up. She must have yearned for release from the cage she was living in and she finally found it in that faulty window catch. No doubt she made it even more faulty on purpose and that meant that she could come and go as she pleased after nine o'clock. I'd guess that she might have left it until later to make sure that her father would definitely be asleep. Then she'd let herself out and walk the streets. I'd bet that she felt free for the first time since her mother died.'

'So, that woman was probably right when she said that she'd spotted Ruth out at night,' Kate said.

'Yes, Mrs. Mountfitch, and it would be no wonder that Ruth might have ended up in the park. After all, it's only a short walk from the church and it would be nice on a warm summer's evening. Perhaps she saw people going in there when it was dark and wondered what was going on. Anyway, it looks as if she found out. I wonder what she must have felt like the first time she watched some-one having sex? All those feelings she'd been bottling up must have come out at once. At some point she must have decided to try it, after all it was easy, just turn up and pull your skirt up when a man came near. My guess

116

is that she enjoyed it and that it became something of an addiction for her.'

'What about the strangling during sex?' Kate said.

'Well, God knows how she came across that but she obviously liked that too and that's what might have killed her. I honestly think that there's a chance that the whole thing might have just been some sort of accident.'

'Really?' Kate looked puzzled.

'Okay, let's imagine that Saturday night,' Mac said. 'Ruth turns up probably looking for the same man that she's been seen with quite a few times before. She finds him. Instead of having sex against a tree perhaps Ruth has a better idea. Even if she didn't watch TV people would have been talking about the murders in the church. Perhaps thinking about them, and the way the girls were strangled, turned her on. So, she leads him onto the five-a-side pitch and gets down on her knees in the goalmouth and pulls up her skirt. She's wearing a scarf and she tells the man to pull on it while they're having sex, to strangle her. So, he's behind her with an end of the scarf in each hand pumping away at her. Perhaps she says, 'Harder, harder,' as she did to the bookie and so he pulls harder on the scarf. When you strangle someone with your fingers you get some feedback and you can more or less tell what effect you're having. With a scarf you don't get that, do you?'

Kate thought for a moment.

'So, you think that he might just have pulled a bit too hard and killed her?'

'Well, I can't be totally certain, but I think that it's a real possibility. It would also explain why the MO for Ruth's murder was so different and why she was found the way she was. The man must have panicked and left her just where she fell. He must have heard about the other murders too and was quick thinking enough to take the scarf with him. However, what it doesn't

117

explain is why the man's DNA appeared on the other two girls.'

'So, perhaps Tommy was right and the other samples might have become contaminated somehow?'

'Well, that as good a theory as I've heard so far,' Mac replied.

'So, what do we do now?' Kate asked.

'I'd suggest that we ring Andy and, once we've explained what we've found, we'll let him decide what the next steps should be.'

Mac had a short conversation with Andy.

'He says that he's in Peterborough and about to interview Jackie Hughes. He should be back here in around an hour and a half. Fancy some lunch?' Mac asked.

Kate did. They ended up in the Magnets where they both ordered coffees and burgers.

'You know, I used to be mad on him when I was playing football for the London Bees,' Kate said as she stirred her coffee.

'Who? Oh, Jackie Hughes you mean,' Mac replied.

'Yes, I used to have a poster of him on my wall believe it or not.'

'Well, I dare say that you weren't the only one. He was the player that they all said would win us the Euros and then the World Cup and, as usual, it all went pear-shaped. He gets injured and we lose yet again on penalties.'

'It wasn't just an injury though was it? I mean, if a lad had done that to someone outside a pub on a Saturday night, then he'd be looking at prison for GBH or something,' Kate said with feeling.

'Well, I know all the England fans felt aggrieved but it must have been so much worse for Jackie. He was only twenty-nine when it happened. Anyway, have we got any suggestions for Andy on what the next move in the case should be?' Mac asked.

The burgers arrived and Kate gave this some serious thought while she ate. When she'd finished, she pushed the plate away and stared out of the window at the busy street outside. Mac didn't disturb her thoughts.

'See all those people out there,' Kate said gesturing towards the window.

Mac looked out and nodded.

'They're just ordinary people and probably most of them are quite nice too. If one of them had accidently killed someone then I'd guess that they'd be feeling guilty about it, perhaps very guilty. I'd guess that it might even be like a permanent black cloud over their life.'

Mac had a feeling where she was going and wanted to nudge her along the path.

'So, why didn't he give himself in then if he was feeling so guilty?'

'It's possible that he might have if it had just been the one murder. Well, manslaughter in this case. However, just about everyone was saying that the three murders were definitely carried out by the same person. Perhaps he was afraid that he might have gotten charged for two murders that he knew he hadn't committed.'

Mac prompted her again.

'So, what do you think we should do?'

'I mean, it would be up to Andy, but we could hold a press conference perhaps and speak directly to Ruth's killer,' Kate said. 'We could say that we think it might have been an accident and that it wasn't linked to the other murders and see what happens. We could also say that we're close to identifying who did it but we're giving them a chance to hand themselves in first. I mean, what do we really have to lose? If he doesn't hand himself in then we're not really that much worse off, are we?'

Mac smiled. He'd had a similar thought but he was glad that Kate had come out with it first.

'Well, that sounds like a plan to me. I'd be happy to back you up when you tell Andy.'

'You want me to tell Andy?' she asked.

'Of course. Well it is your idea, isn't it?'

'Okay,' she said with a smile.

He awoke in the night with a start and looked over at the clock. It was only three thirty.

Of course it was, he thought with some bitterness.

Lately he'd been having problems sleeping and he'd also started having the dreams again. Nightmares would be a better description. He'd been wondering if the fifth anniversary of it all would have any effect on him. It was a long time ago he kept telling himself. However, right at that moment it seemed more like yesterday.

The dream was still fresh in his mind as he sat up and rubbed his face with his hands. He felt a click and a sharp pain in his knee and rubbed that too while knowing that it would do no good. The details of the dream were draining away from his mind but he knew what it had been about, what it had always been about. There was a football field, there was a feeling of terrible anger and there was a young girl lying dead on the grass. He could never remember how but he knew he'd desperately tried to stop it happening. He tried and he failed.

He always failed. Guilt as sharp as his pain pierced his heart.

Chapter Fifteen

Andy and Tommy were getting out of their car just as Mac and Kate arrived at the station.

'So, how did it go with Jackie Hughes?' Mac asked once they'd all settled themselves down in the team's room.

'It went okay but we didn't learn anything that we didn't already know,' Andy replied. 'His wife confirmed that she picked him up at the pub in Letchworth around ten that might and then put him to bed as he was very much the worse for wear. As for Jackie he couldn't tell us anything at all. That Saturday he'd been drinking since two and he said that he couldn't remember anything after about five o'clock or so. The next thing he remembered was waking up a day or so later with a hangover from hell.'

'So, he couldn't tell you anything at all about Chloe Alexander then?' Kate asked.

'No, he said that he didn't remember seeing her at the pub and I was also reminded that he's possibly got the best alibi he could ever have for Ana Tomas's murder,' Andy said.

'What's that?' Mac asked.

'He was actually on Match of the Day that Saturday evening and he gave a live interview,' Tommy said. 'I remember watching that episode as I was wondering if he might become one the pundits on the programme. He was a great footballer but unfortunately rubbish on TV.'

'Yes, that's some alibi being on a live TV show in front of about four million witnesses,' Mac said.

'Now, what about you two? Do I detect a slight air of smugness in the room?' Andy asked with a smile.

'You do,' Mac said returning the smile. 'I'll let Kate take you through it.'

Kate told them the whole story.

122

'So, you really think that Ruth Avaloe was into dogging?' Andy asked in amazement.

'It would appear so,' Mac confirmed.

'From what we knew about her I'd never have thought that was possible. So, how did we miss it the first time around?' Andy asked.

'Well, I dare say that anyone who was dogging in the park that night wouldn't have wanted the world to know what they'd been getting up to. So, as soon as news of the murder got out, the website was quickly taken offline and everyone involved kept their heads down. Tell me did you have anyone like Martin in the team at the time?' Mac asked.

'A computer specialist? No, we didn't. I don't suppose anyone thought that there was a need for one,' Andy replied.

'Well, that's probably why then. I had a question in my head about what might have been going on in the park but I wasn't sure exactly what it was. We only found that out through Martin being able to piece together elements of the dogging website from links in other sites that are still around. From that he was able to find the domain name. Luckily for us, the blogger wasn't very knowledgeable about the web and left his personal information open for all to see. That gave us our starting point.'

'Well done, Martin!' Andy said. 'I must buy him a pint the next time I see him. So, you both think that we should do a press conference in the hope that whoever killed Ruth might be willing to give himself up?'

'We do,' Kate said.

'What do you think, Tommy?' Andy asked.

'I think they might have a point. However badly he might have felt about Ruth's death, I doubt that he would have given himself up if he thought that he might have gotten done for three murders, two of which he knew were nothing to do with him. So, if we can make

123

it clear that we're just looking at him for Ruth's death then, who knows? If there was an article in the national papers then he could have driven miles to get to Fairfields Park and so he could be from anywhere. We might have a real job on our hands finding him otherwise,' Tommy said.

Andy gave it some thought.

'Okay, I think we're all in agreement then. I'll give Dan a ring and see what he thinks,' Andy said.

He went into Dan's office and made his call. Mac, Kate and Tommy sat there in silence while they waited for Andy to reappear. It took him longer than Mac would have thought. He began to wonder if Dan might not be buying into the idea but the smile on Andy's face when he returned reassured him.

'Sorry but I've just been talking to someone from the Press Office. Oh, by the way Dan was all for the idea, it was discussing the details for the press conference that took so much time. It's going to be held at ten past six this evening and we'll be doing it from the station at Stevenage. Apparently, they have a good room there for doing press conferences and the like. The Press Officer will be letting all the main TV channels and newspapers know that we'll be making a major announcement about the Match of the Day Murders and she said that there should be a full house.'

'Ten past six,' Mac said, 'a nice time for the evening news bulletins. Get the main headlines out of the way and then link straight through to us. Who's doing it?'

'Well, it looks like I am,' Andy said with more than a little trepidation. 'Dan said that, as it's our case and we know all the details, then it would be best.'

Good old Dan, Mac thought. No-one would have batted an eye if he'd have decided to take it on himself.

'Have you done many press conferences like this?' Mac asked.

'Well, I've done a few but they were nowhere near as big as this one looks like it's going to be.'

Mac could see he was a little nervous about it.

'What are you going to say?'

'Well, the Press Officer said I should keep it short and she suggested that we say up front that we won't be answering any questions. As for exactly what I'm going to say we've got,' Andy looked at his watch, 'exactly three hours and twenty five minutes to put something together.'

They all got straight to work.

Mac knew from experience that trying to write a short statement that both made sense and covered all the facts was usually quite difficult. He always found it easier when he could just talk off the top of his head or answer questions. They were still discussing the finer points of the text some two and a half hours later as Tommy drove them all over to Stevenage.

All that was except Kate.

She'd asked Andy if he needed her as she was meeting someone that evening. He was fine with that and said that they'd all probably be heading home after the conference anyway.

They were met at Stevenage police station by the Press Officer, an interesting looking woman in her mid-thirties with blonde hair who was quite fashionably dressed.

'Hi, my name's Zehra Yildiz-Scott. Have you got your script for the conference?' she asked as she gestured at them to follow her down a corridor.

Andy gave her a sheet of paper that had more scribbling outs than actual words on it. He quickly introduced Mac and Tommy as they walked.

'Okay, let's get this tidied up first,' she said with a reassuring smile.

She opened the door and led them into a small office. She sat down at a computer and her hands started flying across the keyboard. Mac hadn't come across that many people who could key in with all ten fingers. No more than three minutes later she handed Andy a sheet of paper with his little speech clearly visible on it.

'I've made a few corrections, I hope that's okay,' she said.

'More than a few,' Andy said with a grateful smile, 'and all the better for it too. Thanks.'

She looked at her watch.

'Okay, we've still got fifteen minutes to go so we've got lots of time yet. I'll go through what'll happen. At nine minutes past six I'll walk out and remind everyone of the ground rules. I'll tell them that there will just be a short statement and that there will be no questions accepted under any circumstances. When I turn and give you the nod then you walk out and sit down. Are all of you going to be on stage?' she asked.

'If it's okay, I'll just watch,' Mac said.

In truth this was to be a big moment for Andy and he didn't want there to be any sort of distraction. He knew it was more than likely that some of the press might recognise him.

'Are you okay, Tommy?' Andy asked.

'Sure, so long as I don't have to actually do anything,' Tommy replied with half a smile.

'Okay, there'll be three chairs then so Andy, when I give you the nod, you take the middle one and Tommy you take the one farthest away,' Zehra suggested. 'I'll take the other one. Now don't worry if they get a bit rowdy, just sit still and I'll quiet them down.'

Andy nodded.

Zehra continued, 'Okay, so once you're seated, look at the script and remind yourself of what you're going to say. There might be a slight delay while we wait until we're live with all the major TV stations but, once they're ready, I'll stand up and introduce you and Tommy. I'll tell them that you're going to give a short statement and

I'll remind them once again that there will be no questions. I'll then say 'I'll hand over now to DI Reid' and that will be your cue.'

Andy gave her a nervous nod.

'Look, don't worry. It'll be over before you know it. If you want some advice just really take your time, speak slowly and leave gaps between the sentences. It will help you to avoid any mistakes and it looks good on TV, makes you look more serious,' Zehra said with another reassuring smile. 'Once you've finished your statement just say 'thank you', get up and walk off. They'll be firing all sorts of questions at you, even though I'll have told them that they shouldn't, but just ignore them.'

Zehra checked her watch again.

'Okay, it's showtime.'

They followed her down a corridor and Zehra showed Mac the door that would take him into the conference room. He sneaked in and stood at the back of a very crowded room. No-one noticed him as everyone's eyes were glued to the well-lit stage at the other end of the room.

At precisely nine minutes past six Zehra appeared and a number of camera flashes went off.

'As I've already said this is a short statement only by DI Andy Reid concerning one of the so-called Match of the Day Murders. You'll hopefully understand why it's just a statement when you hear it and why there will be absolutely no questions afterwards.'

She looked sternly around the room as she said this. Mac had to admit that she looked like she knew what she was doing. She turned and nodded and Andy and Tommy walked onto the stage. Again, the camera flashes went off but they both managed to sit down without knocking anything over. They waited in silence for something like a minute although it seemed much longer to Mac. Zehra must have gotten a sign from someone because she started talking.

'I'd like to introduce you to Detective Inspector Andy Reid and Detective Constable Tommy Nugent both from our Major Crime Unit. They're part of the team that has been re-investigating the murders of Chloe Alexander, Ana Tomas and Ruth Avaloe.'

Zehra then paused here and looked out at the crowd. Mentioning the girls' names quietened the assembled pressmen down a little and reminded them that the reason they were all there was because three terrible crimes had been committed.

'I'll hand over now to DI Reid.'

Andy looked straight at the cameras and paused for a second.

'We're not here this evening to talk to the press or to the TV news programmes. We're here to talk directly to the person who caused the death of Ruth Avaloe. We're hoping that you can help us to ensure that he gets the following message.

We now have some new evidence and we know what you were doing in the park that night. We know that you didn't mean for Ruth's death to happen. We also know that you weren't involved in the murders of Chloe Alexander and Ana Tomas. If you want to tell us about it then please ring the number that you'll now see at the bottom of the screen. We'll be waiting to hear your story and we'll promise to listen to what you've got to say. I can also promise that you will be treated fairly and with respect at all times. The number is on the screen now and it will remain there for a while. It will also be on the news websites and in the newspapers. We're waiting for your call. Thank you.'

Andy got up and walked off the stage. A barrage of camera flashes and a volley of shouted questions followed him as he went. Mac met up with him in the corridor.

Andy gave Mac a faint smile.

'So, how did it go?' he asked.

Mac's smile was much wider.

'Really well, you were good. Taking it slow, as Zehra here suggested, gave you some gravitas. I believed every word you said.'

'Let's hope the killer does too,' Andy said as he turned to Zehra. 'Thanks, you really made the whole thing so much easier.'

'That's what I'm here for,' she replied. 'You were good Andy, honestly.'

As they drove out of the car park, they were greeted by another barrage of camera flashes and more questions.

'You've got to give it to them,' Tommy said, 'they never give up do they?'

'They certainly don't,' Mac replied. 'So, what now?'

'We wait, I suppose. He might ring tonight, tomorrow or never, who knows?' Andy said. 'One of our trained negotiators will be taking the call and they'll try and get our man to give himself up or, at the very least, try and get some information out of him. If he rings up at all that is. They'll call me straightaway on my mobile if there's any sort of a result.'

'Fancy a drink?' Mac asked.

'Absolutely,' Andy and Tommy said in almost perfect unison.

A half an hour later they were cocooned in the Magnets. Andy was at the bar getting a round in.

'Where's Tim then?' Tommy asked. 'I thought that he'd be in here tonight.'

'Oh, he's still up North on a furniture buying trip. He was due back today but he won't be coming back until Sunday now, some sale in Berwick-on-Tweed,' Mac replied.

'Oh well, it's just as well that Andy and me were thirsty then.'

'Yes, yes it was,' Mac said.

Andy handed Mac a pint and gave Tommy a coffee.

Tommy saw Mac looking at his drink.

'Bridget's working late this evening. I'm going to pick her up in a while.'

They just sat there in silence for a while looking at their drinks.

'I hate this bit,' Mac eventually said.

'What? The waiting?' Andy asked.

Mac nodded.

'Yes, me too,' Andy said. 'I've rang the wife and told her that I won't be back for a while. After we've had a drink, I thought that I might as well go back to the office for a while, paperwork and that.'

More like waiting by the phone for it to ring, Mac thought.

'I'll go back with you for a bit if you like,' Tommy said. 'I've got some paperwork to do as well.'

'If it's okay, I'll come back as well and watch the both of you as you do your paperwork,' Mac said.

Andy and Tommy burst out in laughter.

'Okay, we'll all go back and wait by the phone then. If I'm honest, I don't think that any paperwork will actually get done,' Andy said.

They were all on their second drink when Kate came through the door. She looked around the room and spotted Mac waving his crutch.

'I was hoping I'd find you here. How did it go?' Kate asked.

'Really well,' Mac replied. 'Andy was great. We're just going to have one more drink and then we're going back to the office.'

'Okay, that sounds good,' Kate said. 'I do have some paperwork to do.'

She was puzzled when this set off a gale of laughter until Mac explained.

'So, how did your meeting go?' Mac asked while Andy was at the bar helping Tommy with the drinks.

'Great, yes great. It went really well,' Kate said.

She looked as if she was trying to convince herself. Mac knew that something had gone wrong and wondered what it could have been. As curious as he was, he knew that he'd just have to wait until she told him of her own accord.

Just after eight o'clock they all walked back to the station. The station was quiet and that suited their mood. They made themselves comfortable and Andy took his mobile out and placed it on the table. They all looked at it solemnly.

'So, we just wait. I take it that you've been through lots of cases like this, Mac,' Andy said.

'Yes, quite a few and waiting was always the hardest part. I've never been able to do anything productive when a case is on a knifepoint like this. We always ended up just like this, hanging around the office just hoping that something would happen.'

The door opened and Dan walked in.

'I thought that you might be here. I saw you on the news tonight Andy. Bloody good conference, I thought. Well done.'

'Thanks,' Andy replied. 'I take it that you've got some paperwork to do.'

'Well yes, I thought...'

Dan was stopped in his tracks by four very sceptical stares.

'Oh, okay. If I'm honest, I'll just be staring at the phone along with the rest of you.'

Dan sat down and made himself comfortable. They drank coffee and chatted about football and station gossip and anything else they could think of. In between each conversation there was a long moment of silence as they all just sat and stared at the phone, willing it to ring.

Then it did. It sounded as loud as a police siren in the quietness of the room. Andy looked at the team and then picked up the phone. He listened.

'What? Of yes of course, I was nearly forgetting. Nighty-night Charlotte, nighty-night David, sleep tight. Yes, I'll see you later love.' He put the phone back on the table. 'That was the kids, they wanted me to say goodnight before they went to bed,' he explained.

'Coffee anyone?' Dan asked.

They all nodded. Tommy went with Dan to give him a hand. Kate had wandered over to the window. She was replaying her meeting with Toni in her mind.

It had started out well enough. She'd managed to get there on time and Toni was waiting for her just where she said she would be. Kate had noticed that she was wearing a beautiful black dress, a designer Kate thought, and it accentuated her slim figure. She had make-up on and Kate had to admit that she looked beautiful. In fact, her heart skipped several beats as she realised that she looked more than beautiful. Kate figured that she must be going out somewhere later on. It never occurred to her that all the effort that Toni had taken might have been just for her.

It would have helped if Kate had any sort of clear idea as to why she'd asked Toni to meet her because, after a few minutes of small talk, that was exactly the question Toni had asked.

'Well, I just thought that we should get to know each other better that's all. I mean we're both women and we both work at the station and I don't know that many people there as yet...' Kate was struggling and she knew it, 'so I thought it might be nice for us to be friends,' she hurriedly finished.

'Friends?' Toni asked.

'Yes, that's right. I want us to be friends,' Kate said trying to make it sound like she meant it.

'You've not been working long at the station, have you Kate?' Toni asked.

'No, not that long I suppose.'

'Has anyone told you about me?'

'Told me what?'

'Kate, I'm gay,' Toni said.

'What?' Kate said.

She hadn't been expecting this but then why did her heart start beating so fast?

'I'm gay. Kate. I don't go bandying it around but it's no secret. I'm sorry Kate but I can't do 'friends' with you. If it was anyone else...'

'Why?'

It was all Kate could think of to ask. She'd never felt so confused in her life.

'Why? Oh God, why?' Toni said with some emotion. 'Because with you I'm afraid that I'd always want more and that us just being friends would never be enough. I'm sorry, Kate.'

Toni got up to go but she stopped herself.

'Kate, I know that you're going through a tough time at the moment but I've tried this 'friends' thing once before. It ended up breaking my heart,' she said as she gently touched the back of Kate's hand. 'I'm truly sorry.'

And she was gone.

Kate had sat there in a stupor for quite some time wondering what had happened. Toni's words had been both a massive shock and sort of expected but how could that be? Kate had no idea how she should feel and yet she had still held up her hand and gently kissed the spot that Toni had touched.

She was heading for the train station when she had a thought. She rang the hospice and they told her that her father was asleep and would likely to be so for quite some time as they'd just given him some medication. She was almost glad that she wouldn't have to see him right at that moment. She'd stood on the street outside the hotel for a while not knowing what to do next. Then she remembered one of Mac's favourite sayings.

'If in doubt, go to the pub.'

So, she did. She was more than relieved to see that Mac, Andy and Tommy were already there. She didn't want to be alone with her thoughts right at that moment.

'I thought that you might have gone to see your father,' Mac said breaking into her thoughts.

'Oh, I was planning on doing just that but I rang the hospice and they said that he was asleep. They'd given him something for the pain and they said that he'd be out for some hours. I'll have a look in on him on my way home.'

'So, it's not like a hospital then? The visiting hours, I mean,' Mac asked.

'No, you can go in at any time you like.'

'Just remember that if you need to talk...'

'Thanks Mac but I just need to do some thinking first,' Kate said.

Mac was happy to leave it at that. The coffees arrived and they all gathered around the phone once again.

Tommy was about to say something when the phone went off again. They all looked at each other.

Andy picked it up.

Chapter Sixteen

They all watched Andy intently as he listened to whoever was talking at the other end. They tried to decipher some meaning from his replies but couldn't make much out of the few times he said 'yes' and the final 'thanks'.

'It's our man, he's giving himself up,' Andy said with a huge smile. 'The negotiator's been able to confirm some details with him about Ruth's death that only the killer would know and he's also managed to get his name and address. It looks like it's him alright.'

'Well done, you lot!' Dan said. 'Where's he turning himself in? I take it that it won't be Stevenage with all the press hanging around?'

'No, the negotiator knew that if he was going to give himself up then it couldn't be Stevenage or even here in case the press got wind of it. So, as he lives in Walsworth, he's going to meet us at Hitchin police station. We need to get over there as quickly as possible,' Andy said.

'Best of luck Andy,' Dan said. 'Call me when you can.'

'I will,' Andy replied.

'Yes, good luck Andy,' Kate said. 'I'm going to see my dad in a bit, if that's okay?'

'Yes, yes of course it is, Kate,' Andy replied. 'So, Mac, Tommy are you ready?'

They were. They took another car just in case there were any press hanging around but they didn't see anyone outside the station. Tommy drove them to Hitchin on a route that took them down Wilbury Hill. It was a long straight road and Andy kept an eye out of the back window just in case. Thankfully it didn't look as if they were being followed. Ten minutes later they pulled up outside a large three storied building in Hitchin that was completely hidden behind rows of Victorian terraced houses.

A uniformed officer was waiting for them. He told them that the suspect had arrived and that he was being held in an interview room. He led them to it.

The man seated inside was tall and fair haired just as the bookie had described him. He wasn't particularly handsome or ugly just ordinary. He wore jeans and a black T shirt and he jumped to his feet when they opened the door. Andy and Mac sat opposite him while Tommy took a seat in the corner. The man sat back down and looked at them nervously. Andy turned the recorder on then introduced himself, Mac and Tommy and stated the time. He asked the man to state his name and address.

'My name…,' he said and stopped. He composed himself a little and continued. 'My name is Peter Caldhouse.'

He then gave them an address in Walsworth. It was just a few minutes drive from where they were sitting.

Andy read him his rights and then continued, 'Before we go on, I believe that you're not legally represented by anyone at the moment. Is that correct?'

'Yes, that's right. I just didn't know…I didn't know,' he said with a hopeless shrug of the shoulders.

'I must inform you that there's a likelihood that we'll be charging you with a very serious offence and, in these circumstances, free legal advice is available should you request it. Do you understand?' Andy said.

'Legal advice?' he asked. 'Do you mean a solicitor?'

'Yes. I'd like you to take a few seconds and think about whether you would like us to arrange for a duty solicitor to attend.'

He looked at Andy and Mac as though the he might find the answer in their faces. Mac noticed that Andy gave the suspect an almost imperceptible nod.

'Yes, yes I think that I would like some legal advice,' he eventually said.

'If you wait here then a duty solicitor should be along shortly. If you need anything just ask the constable who will be looking after you,' Andy said.

Andy stated that he was suspending the interview and then turned off the recorder. Mac and Tommy followed him out.

'Okay, so we wait,' Andy said.

'Well, we've waited five years so another hour or so won't kill us,' Mac said cheerfully. 'I'm sure that I've been here before and I'm also sure that they've got a canteen somewhere on the premises.'

The thought of a sausage and egg sandwich seemed quite attractive right at that moment.

'Okay, let's ask, shall we?' Andy said.

They made it just in time as the hot food was just about to finish. Mac smiled as he looked at his sandwich. For some reason police canteen sandwiches were always the best in Mac's opinion. There was silence for a while as they all tucked in. After all it's a well-known fact that waiting can make you hungry.

'Now that hit the spot,' Mac said as he wiped his mouth with a serviette.

'I didn't realise I was that hungry,' Andy said.

'How long do you think it will take?' Tommy asked.

'Well, I dare say that the duty solicitor should be here by now but, as for how long they'll be in conference, who knows? It's up to them, isn't it?' Andy replied. 'What time are you picking Bridget up?'

'Oh, not for another couple of hours yet I should think,' Tommy replied. 'She said she'd ring me when she's ready.'

'Well, I'm glad that he's got a solicitor,' Mac said. 'At least he won't be able to retract any statement he makes saying that he was under duress or whatever.'

'Yes, I always prefer it when they ask for a legal advice too,' Andy said. 'If I'm honest, I think that it helps us sometimes too in making sure that we don't overstep the mark.'

Mac thought that Andy had grown very wise indeed.

It took nearly an hour before they got the message that Mr. Caldhouse and his solicitor were ready to see them. Back in the interview room Andy introduced everyone again for the tape recorder.

'I'd like to say for the record that Mr. Caldhouse has presented himself today at the police station without any duress and of his own accord. He had also asked for legal representation and a duty solicitor has been appointed...'

Andy stopped and nodded at the solicitor. She nodded back. She was in her late thirties with short hair nicely cut into shape, severe black rimmed glasses and a black dress upon which a large turquoise coloured pendant gave a splash of colour. She could hardly be described as slim but somehow it suited her.

Mac thought that she looked as if she knew what she was doing.

'Mrs. Abby Dawkins of Churchley, Old and Dawkins,' she said.

'Do you have any objections to us asking Mr. Caldhouse some questions at this time?' Andy asked.

'No but, if I do, don't worry, I'll soon let you know,' Mrs. Dawkins replied.

Mac guessed that she would too. This only added to the attractions of the interview for Mac.

'Mr. Caldhouse, as I've stated, you've come of your own volition to make a statement but, before we get to that, we'd like to ask you a few questions. Is that okay?'

Mr. Caldhouse looked at Mrs. Dawkins and then nodded.

'For the record, Mr. Caldhouse has just nodded. It would be helpful if you could speak out loud next time,' Andy said.

He nodded again.

Mac now held his breath. The first question was the really important one.

'Mr. Caldhouse did you murder Ruth Avaloe in Fairfields Park?'

'No,' he replied, 'I've never murdered anyone, never.'

Mac wondered if the solicitor had somehow changed her client's mind and that a confession might not in the offing after all. He glanced at Andy but his expression hadn't changed.

'Okay, let me rephrase that question. Mr. Caldhouse, did you contribute to Ruth Avaloe's death?'

Again, he exchanged glances with his solicitor.

'Yes, yes I did.'

Three inaudible sighs of relief were made.

'We know a lot of the story, however, we'd like you to tell us everything you know about Ruth Avaloe and the events leading up to her death,' Andy said. 'Take your time and try not to leave anything out.'

He took a sip from a glass of water and started talking.

'I heard about the park from someone I met at work. He said that he'd been there one Saturday night and that he'd managed to get his end away. I mean that he had sex with someone. I just thought that he was having me on but one Saturday night I went along to see for myself. I was single, alone and I thought, well why not?'

He stopped for a moment so Andy asked him a question.

'What do you work at Peter? Sorry, is it okay if I call you Peter?'

'Yes sure, it's my name after all. I'm a sparky, an electrician. I mostly work on large projects like furnaces, big refrigeration units and we do a lot of work for the oil industry too. I work in Stevenage but I'm away quite a lot of the time too.'

'So, you were in the park...' Andy prompted.

'Well, I was surprised to find out that my friend hadn't been joking. I had sex that first night so I went along the next weekend too and that's when I met Ruth. I didn't know her name at the time, not until I saw it in the papers. She hardly spoke, just a few words every now and again. She was waiting by a tree and, when she saw me, she waved at me to come over. I thought she was beautiful. I was surprised that she wanted me but she did. I went over and she turned around and pulled up her skirt. I took her from behind and then she told me to put my hands around her throat and press. I didn't want to hurt her but she said to do it harder, so I did. She must have liked it because she was waiting for me the next weekend and we did it again. I tried to talk to her, I wanted to get to know her, but she never said very much.'

He stopped and took another sip of water. Mac could see that his hand was shaking.

'I was away for ten days or so and I was really looking forward to seeing her when I got back so, that Saturday evening, I went straight to the park from the airport.'

'Where were you for those ten days?' Andy asked.

'In Aberdeen, there was a failure in a module that was due to go on an oil rig and I had to go and sort it out.'

'I take it that your employer can confirm this?' Andy asked.

'I'd guess so. We were working around the clock sixteen, eighteen hours a day. In all that time I thought about Ruth a lot. So, as I said, when I got back that Saturday evening I went straight to the park. She was there that night and I was so happy to see her. I'd decided that, after we'd made love, I was going to ask her what her name was and see if we could meet properly, get to know each other like. Instead of holding on to a tree she led me into the football pitches. She got down on her knees and told me to take the scarf she was wearing and pull on it as we made love. I thought that it was a bit strange but, right at that moment, I'd have done anything she asked. So, I took the scarf and put myself inside her. It felt exposed doing it there right next to the car park but I suppose that was part of the thrill.'

He took another sip of water. His shaking was worse now.

'So, we were doing it and, like always, she said she wanted it harder so I stroked harder and I suppose I pulled on the scarf harder too. She started making these sounds but right then my brains were in my balls and I just thought that she was enjoying it.'

Another sip and this time his hands were shaking so much that he slopped some water onto the table.

'Then she collapsed, she just went. I was so confused at the time that I just couldn't think straight. I pulled the scarf off and felt at the neck for a pulse. There wasn't one, she was dead. I stood up and looked around but there was no-one there. I pulled my trousers up and ran. It wasn't until I got to the car that I realised that I'd taken her scarf with me. I sat in the car, I was shaking and still very confused. It took me a while to realise what had happened. I'd killed her, I'd strangled her to death. I didn't mean for it to happen. You have to believe me.'

He looked up at Andy and Mac. He could see that they did.

'That wasn't the worst though,' he continued. 'It was an accident but I did kill her. As I sat in the car, I realised that, if I'd acted quickly enough then I might have saved her. I've been trained in first aid and how to resuscitate someone but, when I found that she was dead, it all went out of my head and I ran. God forgive me, I just ran. I just left her and ran...'

He broke down at this point and started sobbing uncontrollably.

Andy paused the interview and then left him with his solicitor until he'd calmed down. He told the policeman in the hallway to get a cup of tea for the suspect.

They waited at the end of the corridor.

'Bit of a sad story that, isn't it?' Andy said.

'It is that,' Mac replied. 'You know it strikes me that both Ruth and Peter in there were obviously lonely and they also obviously found each other attractive. If they'd have met under different circumstances perhaps it might have ended up better for them both.'

Mac thought that poor Ruth had possibly missed out on love twice; first with Annie Foster and then with Peter Caldhouse.

'If what he says is true about being in Aberdeen then that rules him out for the murder of Ana Tomas, doesn't it?' Tommy pointed out.

'Yes, it does,' Andy replied.

Mrs. Dawkins came out and walked towards them.

'He should be okay in a few minutes if you want to carry on,' she said as she turned to go away.

She turned back.

'Oh, and thanks,' she said.

'Thanks for what?' Andy replied.

'For being a bit human for once,' she said.

'Well, we do try.'

'Not often enough in my experience,' she said pointedly.

An hour later and the interview was over. Peter Caldhouse's statement was printed off and signed.

'What do you think he'll get?' Tommy asked as they drove back up Wilbury Hill towards Letchworth.

'Probably less than you'd think,' Andy replied. 'If the judge accepts that it was basically an accident, and that his fear of being charged for all three murders was justified, then three or four years perhaps.'

'He's already done five,' Mac said.

'Yes, I'd guess that, for Mr. Caldhouse, the waiting since Ruth's death has been worse than any prison time,' Andy said.

They were all silent until they got back to the station.

'Are you going to see Ruth's father before the news breaks?' Mac asked.

'Yes, I suppose I should.'

Andy looked at his watch. It was eleven o'clock.

142

'It's a bit late now though. I suppose I'll have to go first thing tomorrow. The wife will love that,' he said with a sigh.

'I'll go if you like,' Mac said.

'No, it's okay. I wouldn't want to impose Mac.'

'You're not imposing. I'll probably be up around six and it would give me something to do as Tim's still away. It might be better anyway as he's met me before, so the news wouldn't be coming from a total stranger.'

'In that case, okay. Thanks Mac, I really appreciate it. I'd better be getting back, the wife will be wondering what's happened to me,' Andy said. 'I'll see you both back here on Monday then.'

'What about you, Tommy?' Mac asked as Andy walked away. 'Is Bridget's shopping trip to London still on?'

'Oh, absolutely,' Tommy replied with a big smile. 'She's been looking forward to it, especially after all the hours she's had to put in at work lately. We've booked a nice hotel for tomorrow night and we're going to a show and then dinner afterwards too.'

Mac could see that Tommy was looking forward to it as well. At that moment Tommy's phone went off. It was Bridget.

'I've got to go, see you Mac,' Tommy said.

'Have a good time in London. I'll see you on Monday,' Mac said.

So, Bridget, Tommy and Tim would all be away for the weekend. As he drove home Saturday and Sunday suddenly seemed like a vast desert that he'd have to trek through to get to Monday and work.

Oh well, I've got the Reverend Avaloe to visit and I can always work the rest of Saturday, he thought. God knows I've done it often enough before.

That thought cheered him up again.

Chapter Seventeen

Mac hadn't been sleeping well lately and, as he'd predicted, he was up early the next morning. He'd filled the bird feeders, had breakfast, drank two cups of coffee, fed Terry and took him for a short walk and it was still only six forty. Amanda was coming to pick up Terry around nine as she was taking her dog out for a day in the country and asked Mac if Terry might come along as well.

Of course, Mac couldn't refuse as he knew his dog would love it but he still had the feeling that it might be something of a lonely Saturday with everyone being away. He thanked God for still being able to work.

He decided that he might as well make his way into Stevenage. If the Reverend went to bed early then Mac reckoned that he probably got up early too. The sooner he saw him the better. He just wanted to get it out of the way. He drove by Amanda's house and popped the spare house keys and a note in her letterbox.

When he got to the church the main doors were open so Mac walked in. He could hear sounds coming from a side room so he opened the door and looked in. The Reverend Avaloe was taking plastic chairs from a high stack and placing them in a circle. He didn't look any more cheerful than the last time that Mac had seen him. He moved another chair before he noticed that someone was standing by the door.

'Oh, Mister Maguire!' he said. 'You surprised me. I wasn't expecting anyone just yet.'

'Can we talk?'

'Yes, yes of course. Just let me finish here, it won't take a moment. It's for our Saturday School.'

'Do you have Sunday School as well?' Mac asked out of curiosity.

'Oh yes, of course,' the Reverend said as he placed the last chair.

Poor kids, Mac thought.

'Perhaps we should go to the church office,' the Reverend suggested.

Mac followed him down the hall to an office containing a desk and three chairs. It was cramped as several large cardboard boxes took up a good third of the available space. One of the boxes was open and Mac could see that it was full of leaflets featuring a very cute little baby with the headline underneath 'Protect her – Join us on the Pro-Life march today'.

Mac sighed.

'So, how can I help you?' the Reverend asked.

'It's more the other way around today. I'm here to tell you that we've caught the man who killed your daughter,' Mac said. 'I wanted to tell you first because it will be in all the papers before too long.'

'Really? I'm surprised at the police being so efficient for a change. Did you find out how he managed to kidnap poor Ruth?'

'He didn't kidnap Ruth and, as far as we know, her death was as much an accident as anything else.'

As kindly as he could Mac told him what they'd discovered.

'Dogging?' the Reverend said in total disbelief. 'Dogging? Are you really telling me that Ruth was letting herself out through that window and having sex with strangers in the park?'

'I'm afraid that's what it looks like,' Mac replied.

'You say that it will be in all the papers? Everything?'

The Reverend looked appalled at the prospect.

'I'm afraid so. There'll be a court case too in due course and it will all come out there as well,' Mac replied with some sympathy.

'A court case too? Oh God, what will people think?' the Reverend said his face turning even more ashen than usual.

'I'm sure that most people won't think any less of Ruth once they hear all the facts,' Mac said trying to comfort him.

'Ruth? Who cares about her? She's dead to me, dead as sin. She's no daughter of mine. Why, she was little more than a whore, opening her legs to any man who'd have her. I wish she'd never been born!' the Reverend said angrily. 'No, it's my work I fear for, spreading the word of the Lord. How can I explain to my God-fearing flock that I brought a harlot into the world? What will people think of me?'

Mac had now had quite enough.

'I'll be going then,' he said as he started walking away.

'My only comfort is that she's now in hell and suffering the eternal tortures of the flesh...'

Mac left the Reverend's complaining voice behind. For some reason he felt as if he needed a shower. His heart was heavy as he headed off for the police station.

Kate sat on the train watching the scenery go by. As it was a Saturday, she'd easily gotten a seat. She felt calm and not unhappy and this was a strange feeling for her. She'd had another long talk with her father the evening before and she realised that she'd forgiven him, really forgiven him. She found it strange that forgiving someone else could help you as much as the other person.

It was raining again when she got off at Letchworth so she pulled her umbrella out of her bag. She couldn't remember when she'd needed to use it so much. She'd woken up early that morning and wondered what to do with the day. She'd gone to the hospice first thing and had sat with her father for a while until he'd fallen asleep. She then decided she might as well go and do some work.

She reminded herself that Magnus would be flying in on Tuesday and that she'd need to take a few hours off to pick him up at the airport. This somehow made her feel a little better about going into work on a weekend.

So, she wasn't a sad case with nothing else to do after all, she was just making up her hours.

She was surprised to see the door to the team's room open and the light on. She pushed on the door and saw Mac looking thoughtfully out of the window.

'And here was me thinking that I'd have the place all to myself,' Kate said.

Mac turned and smiled.

'Me too. How's your father?'

'He's...well, he's as good as he can be, I suppose. It's strange but he seems like he's ready to go. I always thought he'd fight death tooth and nail.'

'Perhaps he's made his peace. With you and your brother I mean,' Mac said.

'Yes, perhaps,' she said with a sad smile. 'So, I take it that you've been to see Ruth's father? How did that go?'

'Not well, I'm afraid.'

'I take it that he got a bit upset then?' Kate asked.

'He was upset alright. He was worried about what people would think of him and his 'mission to spread the word of the Lord'. He called his daughter a whore and wished that she'd never been born.'

Kate shook her head.

'That's not exactly a very Christian attitude, is it?'

'No, it's not. He wished her in hell, do you know that?' Mac said with some anger.

'You feel sorry for Ruth Avaloe, don't you Mac?' Kate said.

'I do, she was trapped and desperate and desperate people do strange things. Anyway, enough of that, how long are you planning to work for today?'

She shrugged.

'The whole day, I suppose. I'll need to take some time off on Tuesday to pick my brother up from the airport. What about you?'

'I'm here for the whole day too but I haven't got your excuse unfortunately. If I'm being honest, I'm just a sad person who's got nothing better to do.'

Kate almost admitted to being a sad case herself but she said nothing. If she admitted it to Mac then she'd have to admit it to herself.

'Any idea of what we should do?' she asked instead.

'Yes, I was thinking about that when you came in. As Andy and Tommy are looking at the Alexander murder, I thought that we could start digging into the Ana Tomas case.'

'That makes sense,' Kate replied. 'Do you want a coffee before we get going?'

Mac did. She was just about to open the door when Andy burst in.

'Thank God! I was hoping that you'd be here. I called you but your phone was off. I didn't know if you were away for the weekend or something.'

Mac pulled his phone out, looked at it and sheepishly turned it on.

'What's happened?' Mac asked.

'They're calling a press conference to announce that we've caught the killer of Ruth Avaloe and they want me to do it. If I'm honest, I hadn't thought past catching him but I suppose it's got to be done. The wife's not exactly thrilled about it though, she had plans for today.'

'When's the conference due to take place?' Mac asked.

'We've got just under an hour and a half. It'll be in Stevenage again,' Andy replied. 'Zehra called me an hour ago, she's arranging it all now. She said they particularly wanted me to do it for some reason. God knows why, perhaps they all wanted Saturday off or something.'

'Well, personally I'm not surprised that they asked you. I thought that you did an excellent job at the last one,' Mac said.

'Well, this one's going to be a bit different. There'll be questions too,' Andy said.

Mac could see that he was somewhat nervous at the prospect.

'Don't worry, we'll be with you.'

They got down and composed a basic statement that covered all the facts as they knew them. Just over an hour later and they were once again on the motorway heading towards Stevenage.

'Will you come on with me, Mac? I could do with your experience when I'm up there,' Andy asked.

'Yes, of course,' Mac replied.

Kate sighed with relief. If Mac was going up then she wouldn't need to.

'You too Kate, if you don't mind. There's safety in numbers,' Andy said.

'Okay,' Kate replied as a number of large butterflies in her stomach started flapping their wings. 'I won't have to do anything though, will I?'

'Well, they'll be asking questions and, as you and Mac know the case better than I do, then you might need to chip in,' Andy said.

Great, Kate thought, and suddenly wished that she'd gone shopping instead.

As before, Zehra was waiting for them and, as before, she took the statement and quickly tidied it up on her computer.

'Okay, are you all ready?' she asked as she checked her watch. 'It'll be the same as the last time except there'll be a question and answer session at the end. Are you okay with that?' Zehra asked.

'Yes, I think so,' Andy replied somewhat uncertainly.

Zehra gave him a reassuring smile.

'As before just take your time and speak slowly. If it was me and I really got stuck for an answer, I might pass the question on to DCS Maguire here,' she said giving Mac a mischievous smile. 'Someone told me that he's done this quite a few times before.'

Andy gave Mac a huge smile.

149

'Now, that's an absolutely excellent idea,' he said. 'After all, having done the case review, you probably know the case better than anyone.'

'Okay then.' Zehra said. 'When I give you the nod, come on stage. Remember that we might have to wait for a minute or so for those TV stations who are taking it live so just take your seat and wait until I introduce you.'

They followed Zehra and waited in the hallway while she addressed the press and TV cameras. She turned and smiled and they trooped onto the stage. Andy sat in the middle as before, Mac in the nearest seat and Kate took the seat furthest away. There were lots of camera flashes as they made their way onto the stage and sat down. There seemed to be a lot of people in the room but, with all the lights in his face, Mac couldn't really see very much. As instructed, they waited but, thankfully, they didn't have to wait long.

'Thank you all for coming today. I'd like to introduce DI Andy Reid, DS Kate Grimsson and Mac Maguire who's acting as a consultant on the case. DI Reid will read a short statement after which there will be fifteen minutes or so when you can ask any questions you have. I'd now like to hand you over to DI Reid.'

Andy read the statement quite well, Mac thought.

Again, he'd taken Zehra's advice and took his time. When he announced that they'd arrested the man who'd killed Ruth Avaloe, Mac could hear the hubbub in the room increase in volume and a volley of camera flashes went off. When Andy had finished Zehra took charge again.

'Okay, raise your hand if you've got a question,' she said. 'Oh, that's all of you then. Okay, Tom Heaton...'

'I thought that the DNA evidence indicated that who-ever killed Ruth Avaloe was involved in the other murders too. Is that now not the case?' the reporter asked.

Let's start with an easy one, Andy thought.

'I can't comment on that just yet but we'll be reviewing the evidence with the forensics lab as soon as we possibly can.'

Tom continued, 'There've been more than a few cases recently where some forensics labs have been shown to have some very flawed procedures. Do you think that this might be a case of that?'

'As I said we'll be reviewing this with the lab,' Andy said as non-committedly as he could.

Zehra quickly picked out another reporter.

'DI Reid, I'd like to ask about the dogging aspect of this case...'

Andy turned and gave Mac an exasperated look. Mac could only shrug his shoulders in response. From his experience he knew that if a case had even a scintilla of sex involved then the press would usually ferret it out pretty quickly.

Mac thought that Andy really handled the rest of the questions well even though an abnormally large number of them seemed to be about dogging. He would have bet that, for some newspapers at least, that's all tomorrow's headlines were going to be all about. He thought about the Reverend Avaloe but, for some reason, he didn't feel all that sorry for him.

Mac found that he was able to sit back and relax for most of the Q&A. However, it turned out that there was one question he had to answer before the session ended. Zehra had picked out Bob Taunton for what was to be the last question. Mac's ears pricked up when he heard the name. Bob was an old hand and Mac knew him fairly well.

'I'd like to ask DCS Maguire a question, if that's alright?' Bob asked.

Mac nodded.

'It's nice to see you again Bob. I'm afraid that it's just plain 'Mr. Maguire' these days though,' he said.

'DI Reid has described some of the circumstances around the case but I'm interested in your role in all this. Is it a coincidence that it was you that helped to break the case? I remember that you used to be pretty good at that before you retired,' Bob asked.

Mac smiled as he answered, 'As DI Reid stated, I work for the team as a consultant these days on a case by case basis and, I'll be honest, it does somewhat soften the blow of being retired. As for my role, it's whatever the team wants it to be and I'm quite happy to take a back seat and take orders for a change. As for it being me that broke the case, well, that couldn't be further from the truth. Don't forget that I had the help of DS Grimsson here, and that was invaluable, however, the person who made the real breakthrough was our computer specialist Martin Selby. He was able to find enough information on the internet to more or less create the content of a website that had been deleted some five years ago and that was no mean feat. Without that we would never have made the progress that we did. I know that resources are tight in most police forces but I think this shows that computer specialists such as Martin can make a really valuable contribution to Major Crime teams.'

After that Zehra started wrapping up the session while Andy, Mac and Kate left the stage.

'Well, that didn't go too badly,' Andy said with obvious relief.

'It went very well indeed, good job Andy,' Mac said.

'Yes, I thought so too,' Kate said. 'I'm glad no-one asked me a question though.'

'Don't worry Kate,' Andy said, 'I've got a feeling that your time will come.'

Kate grimaced and hoped that it wouldn't be any time soon.

'So, what are you two going to do now?' Andy asked as they drove back to the station.

'I was thinking that we could carry on with the Ana Tomas case for a while, if that's okay,' Mac asked.

'Yes, it's more than okay actually but don't forget it's Saturday. You should really take some time off to relax over the weekend, especially you Mac.'

'Don't worry I will. It'll be just a few hours to get a head start, that's all,' Mac replied.

Back at the station Andy rang his wife who was more than ready to go shopping.

'I'd best get going. However, she did tell me that she let the kids watch me live on the news. She turned the sound down though as she didn't want them asking what 'dogging' was. Anyway, they both think that I'm some sort of TV star now,' he said with a laugh. 'See you both on Monday.'

'Fancy a coffee Mac?' Kate asked after Andy had gone.

He did. When she returned, they sipped their coffee in silence for a while. Kate was the first to speak.

'I had a thought last night when I was sitting with dad. It was about Ruth Avaloe and why she went dogging.'

'Go on.'

'Well, I guess that revenge against her father played a big part and she obviously liked the sex but I was also wondering if she was actually trying to get pregnant. There seemed to be so little in her life and I had the thought that she might have wanted something that she could really love, something that would love her back too. After all, she spent a lot of her time in the crèche so it might not have been surprising if she wanted to have a child of her own.'

'That's a really interesting thought. I wonder how her father would have taken it though?' Mac asked.

'Well, no better than he took your news today I'd bet but I doubt that he'd have made her get rid of the baby,' Kate said.

'Why do you say that?'

'I remember that he had a load of leaflets and some posters too in the church foyer that were very anti-abortion so I'd guess that he's a pro-lifer.'

Mac smiled thinking of the boxes of leaflets he'd seen.

'That's well observed and I guess that you might very well be right. It's just a shame that she liked that particular type of sex. I've seen more than a few cases involving strangulation during sex or masturbation that have ended up with someone dying. People just don't realise how dangerous it can be.'

'You never hear that much about it though, do you?'

'I'd guess that a lot of it is hushed up,' Mac said. 'What's the point of making something like that public anyway? I know of one case where the family said publicly that it was suicide rather than admit that it was a sex game that had gone wrong.'

'Anyway, thankfully we've got another case to look at. I don't know that much about Ana Tomas,' Kate said. 'Do you want me to go through the case file first?'

'I've already spent quite a bit of time doing that,' Mac replied. 'Fancy a drive instead? I'll tell you all about the case on the way there.'

'That sounds good to me,' Kate said. 'Where are we going?'

'To Welwyn. I'd like to see where her body was found.'

Outside the rain had stopped although Mac could see plenty of black clouds in the distance and he wondered when this miserable summer would end.

He went through the basic facts as Kate drove them down the motorway towards Welwyn. This didn't take long as there were so few of them. After coming off the motorway they soon passed by signs for the Hertfordshire Police Headquarters building on their right.

'I've never actually visited the headquarters before. What exactly do they do in there?' Kate asked.

Mac shrugged. He didn't know either.

The sports centre was just a few hundred yards further on. Mac told Kate where to park. There was just the one disabled bay free so they were obviously fairly busy. This was confirmed by the number of mostly young people dressed in tight fitting training gear walking to and fro. They all looked very fit and Mac felt decidedly pear-shaped next to them.

'I had a look at the sports centre on Google Earth and, if she was killed elsewhere, then this is how the invest- igators thought the killer might have gotten Ana to the stadium,' Mac said pointing to the wide walkway in front of them.

Mac had to dodge a few people running towards him as they made their way towards the stadium. It was only a short walk of around a hundred yards or so before they passed in between two buildings and found them- selves in the wide-open space of the stadium itself. A number of people were taking advantage of the break in the wet weather and were running around the athletics track. The football pitch in the centre was empty.

'Well, that walkway's more than wide enough to drive a vehicle down,' Kate said as she turned and looked back down the way they'd walked.

'Yes, and, if the killer backed a car down the walkway and had Ana in the boot, then it's only a short walk across the track to get to the football pitch. It would take a few minutes at most,' Mac said.

He waited for a gap in the stream of runners and then scurried across the track onto the football field. He took out his tablet and once again found some photos of the crime scene. He looked carefully at them and pointed towards the goal on his right.

'It's that one I think,' Mac said as he handed the tablet to Kate.

'Yes, you're right,' Kate said as they walked towards the goalmouth. 'I take it that there wasn't any forensic evidence to indicate that someone had carried a body across here?'

'Unfortunately, not. It had actually been very warm and dry that August so the ground was bone hard. As well as that the pitch was apparently well used and was scuffed up so that wouldn't have helped much either. It's a pity that the weather wasn't the same as it's been recently. They'd have had no trouble getting footprints in that case,' Mac said looking down at the mud caking his shoes.

Kate looked down at hers. They were no better.

'I hope that we've got some paper towels or something in the car. Anyway, why didn't the investigators think that she was murdered right here?' Kate asked.

'Well, there was a difference in the way Ana and Chloe were killed. They were both strangled using the same silk scarf, if the DNA evidence is correct that is, but Chloe had a mark on her back. They thought that she might have been forced to her knees and then the killer put his knee in her back to get more purchase while he strangled her. So, while it's still possible that she was killed elsewhere, it's more likely that she was killed where she was found. Ana didn't have any mark on her back and she was also strangled with much more force than had been the case with Chloe.'

'So, how did they think she was killed then?' Kate asked.

'There's no real evidence but one of the investigators, a certain Andy Reid, thought that she might have been picked up on her way home and killed in a car. If Ana was in the front seat and her killer sat in the back seat it would be easy to loop a scarf around her neck and then you'd be able to pull really hard by placing your feet on the back of the seat and using your body weight to apply the force. You wouldn't even need to be all that physically strong either.'

'That makes sense, I suppose.'

156

'The only problem is that her parents and friends say that there's no way that she'd have gotten into a car with someone she didn't know,' Mac said.

'So, it must have been someone she knew then,' Kate said. 'Did she have a boyfriend?'

'Yes, but he was on duty in the Lister hospital from eight that night. He's a nurse and he was working the night shift in the Maternity Unit. Apparently, it was really busy and if he'd have gone missing for even five minutes his boss said that they'd have noticed.'

'Okay, a friend then?' Kate persisted.

'Ana only had a small circle of friends and the investigators checked everyone thoroughly as they did her workmates. Again, they found nothing.'

'I take it that they cross-checked all the suspects from Chloe's murder too?'

'Yes, and most of them had good alibis for the time that Ana was killed,' Mac replied. 'Some had very good alibis indeed.'

Mac looked about him. He'd seen enough. He'd also noticed that the black clouds overhead had gotten somewhat closer.

'Come on, let's have a look at the route that Ana would have taken to walk home.'

They found some tissues in the boot of the car and managed to remove the worst of the mud from their shoes. They then drove out of the sports centre and onto the main road. A couple of hundred yards or so further on they turned right. Mac asked Kate to drive slowly. The road had semi-detached houses on both sides for a few hundred yards and then these turned into rows of terraced houses. They turned left and pulled up outside the house that Ana had lived in.

'It's not exactly a long walk, is it?' Kate said.

'No, it's not. There are houses all along the route so you'd have thought that if Ana had been taken violently then someone might have heard something.'

Mac gave it some thought.

'No-one saw her but, then again it was late, and I suppose that, if they weren't in bed, then they were probably watching Match of the Day anyway. According to everyone she knew she wasn't the trusting kind so, that being the case, then how was it done?'

'Well, people usually trust a uniform, don't they?' Kate suggested.

'Yes, the investigators thought of that too,' Mac said. 'They checked the locations of all the police cars and ambulances that were on duty at the time but again they drew a blank. Anyway, most of the emergency services operate in teams of at least two. The only people on duty who were working by themselves that night were three paramedic units. Two of those were busy treating the wounded at a major accident on the motorway near Letchworth while the other was helping a woman to give birth. Even so, killing Ana and placing her body on the football field might only have taken a matter of ten minutes or less so it's something that we'll need to bear in mind,' Mac said.

'Especially as the Headquarters of the Hertfordshire Police is just over the road from here as well,' Kate pointed out.

Mac was thoughtful for a while before finally looking at his watch. He was surprised to find that it was nearly three o'clock.

'Fancy something to eat?' Mac asked.

'Now you mention it, I'm starving,' Kate said.

As they drove back to Letchworth they decided to finish for the day and go to the Magnets for something to eat and a drink. They'd only just made it into the shelter of the pub when the clouds opened yet again and they watched the crowds of shoppers outside scurrying for shelter. Kate volunteered to go to the bar. Mac looked out as the rain fell like stair rods on the other side of the window.

He was still thinking about Ana Tomas though.

'Here you go Mac,' Kate said as she handed him a cold pint of his favourite lager.

He smiled at the sight of it then raised it to the photo of George Bernard Shaw on the wall and took a gulp.

'So, what have you got planned for the rest of the day?' Mac asked.

'Nothing much really. When we've finished here, I'll go and spend some time with my dad and then I'll go home. I'll probably be tired and ready for bed by then anyway. What about you?' Kate asked.

'I'll just go home, I suppose. Thankfully, Tim will be back tomorrow and early enough to go for a drink, I hope.'

'You've missed him, haven't you?' Kate asked with a smile.

'Yes, I have, although please don't tell him that as I'll never hear the end of it,' Mac said. 'Anyway, until the wanderer returns, I'll carry on digging into the case file. It's beginning to bug me now.'

'Me too,' Kate said. 'There's just so little to go on, isn't there?'

They were saved from talking about the case by the half-time football results coming up on the big TV screen. This started them on a topic of conversation that kept them going until they were ready to leave. Mac phoned for Eileen the taxi driver to pick him up and, as it was still pouring down, he offered Kate a lift to the station. She gratefully accepted.

Terry was overjoyed to see him and jumped up and down for a full five minutes. He read a short note that Amanda had left. Even with the rain they'd all had a lovely day out and she'd even put the time that she'd delivered Terry home. He'd been by himself for all of forty minutes.

Mac smiled. It was nice to be welcomed home anyway.

He made himself a pot of coffee, then turned on his laptop and settled down to work. Terry came over and sat on the sofa beside him and promptly went to sleep. Mac guessed that his big day out had worn him out. He soon lost himself in the case and the hours went by. He was nearly ready to go to bed himself when he came across something that he found interesting. Of course, it might have nothing to do with Ana's murder, yet he kept wondering about it.

Now he knew what he was going to do with at least some of his Sunday.

Chapter Eighteen

It was only nine o'clock and Mac was already on his way back to Welwyn. He glanced over at his passenger who was taking great interest in everything on the other side of the window. The rain had once again stopped and the sun had come out. It was now cheerfully glinting off the sheets of water on the motorway's surface and off large pools on the side of the road. Mac had to scrabble around to find his sunglasses. Although it was supposed to be summer, it was the first time that he'd needed to use them for a while.

He turned left before the Police Headquarters and pulled into Stanborough Park. Mac noticed that this park had a boating lake too but Terry wasn't concerned about that. He was just happy to be allowed out into the freedom of its green spaces. They followed a walkway around the lake and Mac laughed at Terry's reaction to some ducks that waddled across their path towards the water. He obviously didn't know what to make of them and was torn between whether he should be aggressive or friendly. The ducks didn't take any notice at all and were in the water before Terry had quite made up his mind. Mac took him as far as he could and then sat down in a secluded spot and let Terry off the leash for a few minutes.

Mac watched him sniff excitedly around every tree and plant. He remembered Amanda once saying that dogs could see with their noses and he idly wondered what that might be like.

At nine thirty they returned to the car and Mac drove out onto the main road past the Police Headquarters and then past the sports centre before pulling into the car park in front of the hotel that Ana had worked in. Next door to the hotel there was one of a chain of pubs that specialised in steaks and grills. Mac had tried them before and had been surprised to find that they weren't bad. He went over and had a look at their menu.

They also did breakfast!

He'd only had a couple of slices of toast for breakfast and he found that his little walk had made him hungry again. Unfortunately, they also had a notice saying that they didn't allow dogs in the pub under any circumstances unless they were guide dogs.

Mac sighed and looked down. Terry definitely wouldn't pass for one of those.

If it had been overcast and raining then he might have felt better about leaving Terry in the car but, as the sun was shining, he didn't think it would be a good idea so he made his way towards the hotel instead.

An attractive woman in her late twenties smiled at him from behind the receptionist's desk. She was smartly dressed in a dark blue skirt and light blue blouse that had the hotel's name and logo on.

'How can I help you, sir?' she asked.

Her smiled dropped when she saw Terry.

'Oh, I'm sorry sir but we don't allow...'

She stopped talking and looked at Mac's warrant card.

'I'm sorry about bringing my dog along but I had no-one to leave him with,' Mac explained. 'I'd just like to ask a few questions if that's possible. Is the manager around?'

'Yes, yes of course. As for the manager you're looking at her. Is this about Ana?' she asked as the smile totally left her face.

'Did you know her?'

'Yes, I did. I was her line manager at the time.'

Mac looked at her and wondered if she could have been old enough.

'Can we talk somewhere?' Mac asked.

'Yes, of course. I'm just filling in for someone who's off sick. I'll be getting relieved in around half an hour if that's okay?'

Mac assured her that it was.

'I'll wait in the car until you're ready then.'

'You might as well wait in the pub if you like, we can talk there,' she said. 'Don't worry about your dog, just tell them that Kezzie said that it was okay.'

And indeed, it was. While he was waiting Mac whiled away his time tucking into a Full English with an extra sausage on the side. The sausage was for Terry who not only gulped that one down but one of Mac's as well. The walk had obviously made him hungry too. Mac was sitting feeling pleasantly full and sipping at his coffee when Kezzie finally arrived.

'Kezzie? That's short for Keziah, isn't it?' Mac asked.

'Yes, it is,' she replied with a wide smile. 'Not many people have heard of my name before.'

'It's an old Victorian kind of name, isn't it?'

'Yes, I was named after my grandmother who was named after her grandmother and so the name goes back quite a way.'

'I remembered your name from Ana's case file, Keziah Mingoe. Your surname's unusual too,' Mac said.

'Yes, my family are originally from Barbados, except that it's Kezzie Mingoe-Smith now that I'm married. So, a little less unusual now perhaps.'

'You were the receptionists' Team Leader at the time, is that right?'

'Yes, I'd only been promoted a couple of months before…well, before Ana died.'

'Do you mind me asking how old you were at the time?' Mac asked.

'I was twenty-five. They don't mind promoting people when they're young in the hotel business, so long as you know what you're doing that is. They also aren't all that bothered about qualifications which was just as well as I only got a single GCSE in English at school,' she said with a quick shrug of her shoulders. 'That's why I chose hospitality as a career and I think that might have been true for Ana too.'

'Tell me about Ana.'

'She started work at the hotel straight from school when she was sixteen. She started off in housekeeping and spent two years doing that. She was very good at her job too. She hardly ever had a day off and she was very polite with everyone, even at those times when it might have been hardest.'

'What do you mean by that?' Mac asked.

Kezzie sighed audibly.

'Well, people aren't always as polite to the house-keeping staff as they might be. To be honest, some people seem to look down on them a bit. Anyway, with Ana being a young woman and a Filipino too, this made her a target for certain types of people, mostly men, to have a go at her. They'd even ask her for sex and wave money at her. After all, if she's a Filipino then she must be a prostitute. When she politely refused then the racial slurs would start. However, she bore it all with a smile and she never let it bother her too much. Silly men, she used to say, just silly men.'

Mac detected a tear forming in one of Kezzie's eyes.

'She was fun to be with and I liked her a lot. As soon as she was eighteen, she applied for a receptionist's job. You see its company policy that you have to be over eighteen to work on the desk. I have to admit that it was the easiest interview I've ever done and it was great having her as part of the team. She was someone who I could rely on and, as she only lived down the road, she'd sometimes come in as cover when I was really desperate.'

'Did you ever meet her boyfriend or any of her other friends?' Mac asked.

'Yes, she brought Gerry around here once to introduce him to me. I thought he was very nice and quite like Ana in lots of ways,' Kezzie replied.

'That's Gerardo Andrada?' Mac asked.

164

Kezzie nodded.

'In what ways were he and Ana alike?' Mac continued.

'He was quiet and unassuming just as she was. They were good together.'

'What about friends?'

'She sometimes used to go into the pub for a drink and meet one or two of her friends there. The only one I really remember was Angel, Ana's best friend. I met her quite a few times,' Kezzie replied.

'And what was Angel like?'

'Well, she was certainly different to Ana. She was a little more outgoing perhaps. She loved parties or any sort of social occasion or so Ana said. I believe that they'd known each other since they were children.'

'Did Ana or any of her friends ever talk about the sports centre at all?' Mac asked.

Kezzie shook her head.

'No, not that I ever remember. Ana really wasn't into exercising, she always said that we get enough exercise at work and that's true enough. We're always on our feet.'

'Thanks. What you've told me makes her a little more real to me now. I'd also like to ask you about something that happened just a week or so before Ana died,' Mac said.

Kezzie thought for a moment.

'Oh, do you mean the robbery? That was big news for a while, well until Ana was found that is. What do you want to know?' she asked.

'Whatever you can tell me,' Mac replied.

'Well, an old couple were staying with us for the weekend, a Mr. and Mrs. Gilmour. They'd never stayed with us before and they brought just the one piece of luggage with them and a carrier bag. I didn't know it at the time but the carrier bag contained fifteen thousand pounds in twenty pound banknotes. It was never clear to me, even afterwards, what the money was for as they

165

changed their story several times. First, they said they were going to the races, except there weren't any on, and then they said the money was for an antiques auction except they couldn't say which one. Anyway, it was definitely their money as the police said that they'd withdrawn it from their bank account just the day before. They came down for dinner here in the pub and when they returned to their room the money had gone.'

'Were you on duty at the time?' Mac asked.

'No, Ana was. She called the police first and then the hotel manager and then me,' Kezzie said.

'Who was the manager at the time?'

'That was Dalvinder, Dalvinder Singh. He was manager from the time the hotel first opened. I took over from him a couple of years ago.'

'And where is Mr. Singh now?' Mac asked.

'Oh, he went back home,' Kezzie replied. 'Although he'd lived in Hertfordshire for nearly ten years, he couldn't wait to get back. All his family were still there and I think that he was a bit homesick towards the end.'

'And where was home?'

'Oh, Bradford. He comes from Bradford.'

Mac smiled. He'd been expecting her to say the Punjab or somewhere else in India.

'So, what happened then?'

'Well, the police came and even a couple of those people in white suits…'

'Forensics,' Mac prompted.

'Yes, that's right. They even fingerprinted some of the staff including Ana. Anyway, they found out soon enough who it was. He'd left his fingerprints and DNA all over the place they said later.'

'And who was it?'

'One of our bar staff, more of a glorified glass collector really,' Kezzie said. 'The Gilmours were silly enough to leave their key card on the table while they ate and he borrowed it for a few minutes, long enough to get into their room and make off with the money. They'd only hid it under the mattress, hadn't they? Anyway, his name was Glenn Gove.'

Mac thought it was a strange name and sounded more like a place in Scotland than anything else.

'Well, Glenn was a nasty piece of work,' Kezzie continued. 'I've come across his type before, always on the lookout for an opportunity to rip people off or do them down. He was a racist too.'

'How did that manifest itself?'

'He mostly collected glasses and plates but when Ana or myself were in here he'd never come near our table,' Kezzie replied. 'It was the same when he was serving at the bar. He was always magically busy when we wanted a drink. I noticed it was the same with other black people.'

'Why didn't the hotel sack him?' Mac asked.

'The pub's run separately from the hotel so it was up to the landlord really. I had a word with him but he was so short-handed that I think he was willing to put up with him. Of course, he never asked any of his black or Asian customers if they were willing to put up with Glenn. Anyway, the police caught up with him a couple of weeks later in London. He'd managed to gamble away most of the money by then and only had five hundred left of the fifteen thousand he'd stolen. It wasn't Glenn who killed Ana though, if that's what you're thinking. He was apparently caught on CCTV in some casino in London losing more of the Gilmour's money at the time that Ana was taken.'

Mac thought about this. He remembered from the case file that the investigators had ruled out Mr. Gove as a suspect and, after that, it seemed as though they hadn't looked at anything to do with the theft at all. However, he wasn't going to dismiss it quite so quickly.

'In the five years since, have you, or any of the other staff, had any thoughts about who might have killed Ana? Have there been rumours of any sort?' Mac asked.

Kezzie gave it some thought and then slowly shook her head.

'I'm sorry but no. There was lots of talk in the weeks afterwards but no-one had a clue really. Since then just about all the staff have moved on. Out of all the people who were working here at the time there's just me left.'

'We're still trying to figure out how Ana was taken. One theory is that she was intercepted by someone on her way home who manged to get her into a car. How likely do you think that might have been?' Mac asked.

'Incredibly unlikely unless she was taken by force. Ana was quite small and she was well aware of how vulnerable she might be. She was always very careful, especially around men. After all, she knew what they could be like from the hotel. She always carried a can of pepper spray in her bag and I don't think that she'd have hesitated to use it,' Kezzie said.

Mac thanked her and gave her a card in case she thought of anything else. Mac suddenly realised what was on the card.

'Oh, I know it says that I'm a private detective there but...'

Kezzie smiled, 'Don't worry Mr. Maguire, I know you're working with the police. I saw you on TV doing the press conference.'

On the way back Mac pulled into the park again in the hope that he and Terry might walk off some of their breakfast. He was sitting down watching Terry sniff some bushes when his phone went off. It was a message from Tim.

'Started early so I'll be in the Magnets around 3. Got some bargains too, see you Tim.'

Mac smiled and looked at his watch. It was nearly twelve. He'd stay a little while longer and make sure that Terry had a good run out before he left him for a few hours. He was sure that Tim would be ready for his bed by seven or so after such a long drive home so Terry wouldn't be left too long by himself.

Mac watched the black clouds gradually coming closer but he hung on as long as he could. Just over an hour later and they were forced to make for the car as the heavens opened up again.

Oh well, Mac thought, he'd had a good breakfast, a few sunny hours in the park and he'd soon be in his favourite pub listening to all his best friend's latest adventures.

Things could definitely be worse.

Chapter Nineteen

Kate had managed to spend a few hours with her father before he'd once again fallen asleep. He was sleeping a lot now and she knew that it wouldn't be long before he would go to sleep and never wake up again. She had been surprised that her father seemed ready to go and she was even more surprised to discover that she was more or less ready to let him. For the first time in her life she could think about her father without feeling angry or resentful. It felt quite strange.

It was nearly twelve o'clock on a Sunday and she had no idea what to do with herself. Almost without thinking her feet had led her to the train station and she boarded a train for Letchworth.

She no longer had the excuse of making up her hours for Tuesday when her brother was to arrive but she just didn't know what else to do with herself. The sun was shining as the train sped down the tracks and everywhere looked bright and clean after being washed by the rain. The rain held off while she walked to the station. Before going to the team's room, she went upstairs and had a peek into the room where Toni's team worked.

It was empty and she felt disappointed even though she knew that she was being stupid. She was sure that Toni had better things to do on a Sunday than hang around the police station. She stood leaning against the door jamb as she gazed into the empty room.

What was it with her and Toni anyhow? Did she really feel something for her or was it just some sort of mental tic due to all the stress that she'd been undergoing?

She wished she knew.

She went down to the team's room and that was empty too. She started up her computer and started looking at the Ana Tomas case file. She got interested in the boyfriend and even more so when a Google search turned up some very interesting photos. She made a few phone calls and smiled. She might have something. She'd been working for a couple of hours now and she felt a bit stiff. She stood up and stretched her arms. She heard a car door slam and went over to the window.

It was Toni!

She was with a man, someone Kate hadn't seen before, and they were heading for the door. Kate moved to the side of the window so she couldn't be seen. Her eyes never left Toni's face.

She's grown even more beautiful, Kate thought.

The man said something that made Toni smile and Kate felt her heart speeding up. They disappeared inside and Kate didn't know what to do next. Should she go and bump into Toni again by accident? She hesitated thinking that doing that a second time might seem a bit lame. Then she had a thought that stopped her in her tracks. What if Toni was seeing this man? After all he was young and very good looking. Kate could only glumly think that Toni might be on some sort of a date.

By the time she'd gone through all the 'what if's', Toni and her companion were back in the car park. He got into a car and drove off. But before he did this Toni had given him a big smile followed by a hug and a kiss on the cheek.

Kate stood there as still as a statue as the car drove off and Toni walked away out of sight.

She'd kissed him! Perhaps Toni wasn't as gay as she'd said she was and maybe she'd decided that a man was what she really wanted after all. Kate had them as good as married in her mind before she reminded herself that it was just a hug and a kiss on the cheek and probably meant nothing. Then the picture of them kissing went through her head again and the whole mad carousel of thoughts sped around her head again.

It took her a good while to realise that she was jealous! She'd never been jealous of anyone in her life

171

before, at least not in a romantic way, and she'd often wondered at the mad behaviour it had caused in others.

She got herself a coffee and tried to settle down again to read the case file. She was okay for a while until once again she thought of them kissing. It made her feel uneasy and somewhat desperate. She finally closed the computer down and gave up. It was now past three o'clock and she decided that she might as well go back home. Home? She once again realised that she didn't have one. Her flat definitely wasn't home, it was just somewhere she stored her clothes and slept occasionally. When she could sleep that is.

The rain was coming down again and that made her feel even sadder. She decided that she might as well go and have a quick drink before she caught her train. She remembered Mac saying that Tim wouldn't be back until the evening so she should be safe enough. Right then she just wanted to be alone.

They say that misery loves company, she thought. It certainly wasn't true in her case.

She didn't want to intrude on Mac and Tim too much anyway. They might come to the conclusion that she was desperate and friendless and she didn't want them thinking about her in that way. Even if it was true.

She walked towards the pub door and was surprised to see someone waving at her from the other side of the window. It was Mac and Tim. They were telling her to come inside. She stood still for a moment wondering if she should just walk away. Then she realised that would be just plain rude so she sighed again and went inside.

Tim was standing up as she walked over.

'Ah Kate, it's so good of you to show up, Mac and me are in great want of a referee just now. A large red?' he asked giving her a big smile.

'Yes, thanks,' she said as she returned the smile.

'Have you been working today?' Mac asked.

'Just a few hours,' she said.

'Yes, me too,' Mac admitted.

'I honestly didn't think that you'd be here until this evening.'

'That's what I thought too but Tim set off at six this morning and that's why we're here early. He'll be tired in a few hours I'll bet but it sounds like he got some real bargains. So, all the travelling was well worth it he said. I dare say that you'll hear all about it soon enough.'

Mac looked over at Kate and he could see that she was uneasy.

'Look, don't feel that you're intruding or inflicting yourself on us in some way,' Mac said in a quiet voice. 'We're happy to see you and we both know what it's like, the interminable waiting and the not knowing what to do with yourself in the meantime. So just relax for a while and enjoy Tim's tall tales of his adventures up North.'

'Thanks Mac,' Kate said. 'You're right, I don't know what to with myself half the time. I just feel so alone. To be honest I can't wait until Tuesday when Magnus flies in.'

'Well, you've only got tomorrow to go and hopefully we'll have enough to do to keep us both busy and our minds off things for a while.'

A glass of wine appeared in front of her.

'Oh, thanks Tim,' Kate said. 'Mac said that you've been up North looking for some bargains.'

That was all the prompting Tim needed.

'Just wait until I tell you…'

And he did. Kate was more than happy to relax and let Tim's words wash over her. She had to admit that the way he told it was really funny too. As Mac had predicted by seven o'clock Tim was nodding off so he sent him home and then ordered a taxi.

'Are you going to the train station?' Mac asked.

'Yes, I'll have another look in on dad and then go home. I'm feeling a bit tired myself now if I'm honest which is good. I haven't been sleeping that well lately.'

'I'll drop you around if you like.'

'No, you're okay, it's only around the corner,' Kate protested.

'It's started raining again,' Mac pointed out, 'and it's really no bother.'

Kate looked out of the window. The rain was coming down so hard that it was bouncing off the pavement.

'Okay then. Oh, what about poor Tim! Does he have far to go?'

'He'll be okay. He only lives a hundred yards or so down the hill, he has a little flat over his shop. He'll be asleep and dreaming of more bargains by now I dare say.'

'I'd never heard of a Viardot table before. The way he described it made it sound wonderful.'

'You should go in and have a look in his shop someday. He has loads of interesting stuff...' Mac said.

He was interrupted by the sound of his phone going off. He looked outside and could see that a taxi was waiting across the road for them. Mac scurried towards it through the heavy rain as quickly as he could.

'My God, where is all this water coming from?' Mac exclaimed as the taxi pulled away. 'They say that sea levels are supposed to be rising and it's not surprising given this weather.'

'Thanks, Mac,' Kate said. 'Even with my umbrella I'd have been soaked by the time I'd have gotten there.'

It had been a strange day Kate thought as she looked out of the train window. It was an August evening outside but the dark clouds made it look gloomy and autumnal. She was thankful now that she'd run into Mac and Tim. They'd cheered her up, especially Tim. Otherwise her whole day would have been as gloomy as it was now outside.

Again, she thought of Toni and how beautiful she'd looked. And that kiss of course.

She sighed audibly. She quickly looked around the train carriage but there was only one person near her and he had his headphones on. She knew that she'd have to do something about it and quickly too, otherwise it would end up driving her crazy.

She decided to see if she could have a word with Mac tomorrow. He might know what to do.

After the Sunday night drama had ended, she sat there in a daze. The news was on next and she wondered afterwards why she'd made no move to turn the TV off. She'd been avoiding anything to do with the news for a while now.

She felt sick as she watched a re-run of the police news conference. They'd caught the man who had killed Ruth Avaloe. The team answering the reporters' questions looked very professional and now she knew that they'd be looking somewhere else for whoever had carried out the first two murders. This made her feel even more nauseous.

It had all seemed like a bad dream at the time and even more so after five years. It belonged to the past so why couldn't they have just left it there? She stood up and went over and picked up a framed photo. He was safe and she supposed that was the important thing but she found that she was still filled with such a fear that her legs literally shook.

Something was coming, she knew that, and it would be nothing good.

Chapter Twenty

Mac had gone to bed early too but he'd woken up in the night in pain and it had taken him a while to get back to sleep. He'd set his alarm for seven but he felt so tired that he'd turned it off and thought about staying in bed. He grudgingly got up and checked his back for pain as he stood up. It was always there but thankfully it wasn't as bad as it had been during the night.

The pain's always worse when it's dark, he said to himself.

A shower helped to wake him up. He took his pills and watched the birds squabbling over the feeders in the garden as he drank his first cup of coffee. Mac remembered once again that the anniversary of his wife's death was just over a week away and he had a seriously sad moment.

He'd had a chat with Bridget on the phone the evening before and she said that everything had been arranged. There would be a small family service only at six thirty next Tuesday evening. He found that he wasn't looking forward to it. He didn't need reminding that Nora was no longer with him.

He had another cup of coffee and some toast and tried to think about the case. He wasn't entirely successful. As soon as he'd finished his coffee, he wrote a note for Amrit and left for the station.

Work is always the best pain killer, he reminded himself.

As early as it was Kate was already there when he arrived.

'Couldn't sleep?' Mac asked.

Kate nodded.

'You too?'

It was Mac's turn to nod.

'So, any ideas as to what we might do next?' he asked.

177

Kate was about to answer when the door opened and Dan and Adil walked in.

'Come to give us a hand?' Mac asked with a smile.

'Well, that was to have been the general idea. I say 'was' because it looks like at least some of the criminal fraternity have finally returned from their holidays,' Dan replied.

'What have you got?'

'Multiple stabbings outside a pub in Hertford town centre just before closing time last night,' Dan said. 'Two men were seriously injured and another one's just hanging on by his fingernails so it might be murder yet.'

'That sounds serious. Do you need any help?' Mac asked.

'We might if we can't identify who's behind it fairly quickly. We were there last night and we've got some ideas from the initial interviews, plus there's plenty of CCTV footage, so it might be fairly straightforward. If not then, don't worry, I'll soon let you and Andy know if I need any help. So, it's back to Hertford for us. Chris is already there and luckily Leigh is back today as well. I only dropped in to pick up something,' Dan said before he disappeared into his office.

As he came out, he was about to make for the door when he stopped and turned.

'I was nearly forgetting, Andy called and he said he won't be in for a while so he asked if you could find yourselves something to do. He and Tommy are with Mrs. Alexander. She's volunteered to do a live appeal on TV and it'll be happening in a couple of hours or so. You never know, they sometimes work,' Dan said with a shrug before he and Adil disappeared.

'Do they?' Kate asked.

'What?' Mac asked.

'Those televised appeals, do they ever work?'

'In my experience very rarely. However, I've found that it can often help the family quite a lot. It makes them feel as if they're doing something positive and, as Dan said, you never know. What were you about to suggest when Dan came in?'

'Oh, only that we might go and see Ana's boyfriend. I checked up on him and he's still working at the Lister hospital as a senior nurse and I also found out that he's now married. Guess who to?' Kate asked.

Mac could only think of one name.

'Angel Santos?'

'That's right. It might be nothing but when someone falls in love with their best friend's boyfriend…'

'It can lead to trouble,' Mac said as he gave this some thought.

'Well, he's still working at the hospital and he'll be on shift right about now,' Kate said.

Mac smiled.

'Good work! Okay, let's do just that.'

As they drove towards Stevenage Mac turned towards Kate.

'I had an idea too. I was looking at the book about the murders and I thought we should go and have a word with the author. She's a local journalist and you never know what she might have picked up while she was doing her research,' Mac suggested.

'It looks as if we've got a plan then,' Kate said.

She was glad that they were keeping themselves busy. She didn't want any time to think. Just one more day to go she told herself.

Gerardo Andrada worked in the Maternity Unit. It was towards the back of the sprawling hospital site and they were luckily able to park right outside. The unit was a long three storied generic hospital building. Inside a couple of harassed looking receptionists were trying to deal with several women who had the most massive bumps. Almost all of the women were accompanied by their white-faced partners whose only job seemed to be to stand there and look both embarrassed and nauseous at the same time. Mac and Kate stood in the queue and waited.

'Oh, it's Gerry you're after then,' the receptionist said when they finally reached the desk. 'If you want to sit down, I'll give his ward a ring.'

Mac was happy to do so. Looking at all the comings and goings reminded Mac of when they had Bridget. He'd almost forgotten that she'd been born in this hospital. Of course, it hadn't happened in this building, it was far too new. He couldn't remember exactly where in the old hospital it had been but, then again, he wasn't too surprised. A lot of his memories of that day were quite hazy.

He remembered driving down the motorway after Nora's waters had broken and having to tell himself to drive safely as he found himself speeding up all the time. Like the expectant couples around him now, he first had to book Nora in and then get her examined. They then took her straight through to the midwife and less than two hours later Bridget was born. His memory of that moment was crystal clear as well as the first time he'd held her.

'You wanted to see me?' a man's voice asked.

Mac looked up to see a dark-skinned young man with jet black hair who was dressed in a regulation hospital blue top and matching trousers. He had a half-smile on his face as if he wasn't quite sure what expression he should be using in such a situation.

Mac stood up and showed him his warrant card.

'Oh, it's okay,' the man said, 'I remember you both from the news conference on the TV.'

'Mr. Andrada, can we talk somewhere?' Mac asked.

'Yes, sure but please just call me Gerry,' he said with a genuine smile.

They followed him down a corridor and then another one. Mac looked at him as they walked. He'd never be described as tall but he moved with a grace and litheness that reminded Mac of a cat. Gerry looked in a couple of rooms before he found one that was empty. He held the door open and they walked into a small consulting room with little more than a desk and a few chairs.

'We've all been following the case on the TV and in the papers,' Gerry said as they all sat down. 'When we heard that you'd caught the man who killed Ruth Avaloe then that gave us some hope even though we now know that he had nothing to do with Ana's death. Yes, we're still hoping even after all this time.'

'We?' Mac asked.

'Yes, Angie and me and Ana's family of course.'

'You still keep in touch with Ana's family?'

'Of course, they're very old friends of my mother. They came over to England together from the Philippines years ago,' Gerry replied. 'Ana and Angie and me all grew up together.'

Mac could see real sadness in his eyes as he looked down towards the floor.

'In the five years since have you had any further thoughts about Ana's murder?'

Gerry shrugged and both policemen could see a tear fall down his cheek.

'No, but I wish I had. These five years have been terrible, especially for Ana's mother. She just wants to know what happened to her daughter and why. We all do.'

'I believe that Angel and you got married. How did that come about?'

Gerry smiled and shrugged.

'I suppose we were just there for each other after Ana...well, after she was taken from us. She was at least as shocked and depressed about it as I was, perhaps more so. We spent a lot of time together consoling each other and I suppose that, over the years, it turned to love. Angie and I got married last year. We both still miss our Ana but I guess life must go on.'

'Just a final question. Did Ana ever say anything to you about a robbery at the hotel where quite a lot of money went missing?' Mac asked.

'Oh yes, she talked about that quite a bit. I think it was the only robbery they'd ever had while she was working there. It was the first time she'd ever been fingerprinted too and I remember that it took a while before she got all the ink off her fingers. She said that the woman who took her fingerprints was funny and made her laugh. She wasn't all that surprised when it turned out to be the barman. He wasn't a nice person from what she told me.'

'By the way what exactly do you do here?'

'Well, while the midwife looks after both mother and baby, I'm concentrating only on the baby,' Gerry replied. 'I'm responsible for analysing all of the data we get from the baby and ensuring that it's not in any distress.'

Not an unimportant job then, Mac thought.

He asked a few more questions and then gave up. Remembering the queue of women in the lobby, Mac figured that Gerry had better things to do with his time. Outside he got quickly into the car as the heavens opened once more.

'So, what do you think?' he asked.

'Well, if he was lying then he's the best liar I've ever come across,' Kate replied.

'Yes, I agree. Anyway, he's given us the address of the school where Angel works. Let's see what she's got to say.'

Angel worked as a classroom assistant at The Holy Mother Catholic Primary School while she was studying to be a teacher. The school was situated only a couple of minutes drive from the sports centre and it served what looked like an old council estate. The school itself consisted of a couple of two quite large two storeyed buildings, one obviously a lot newer than the other.

The outside gates were locked and Mac had to speak into an intercom and show the camera his warrant card before they were let inside. They were told to immediately report to reception. Mac wondered at the security in schools these days, it had certainly been nothing like this when he was taking Bridget to school. However, Mac was all too aware of the very good reasons behind it.

A nice middle-aged lady looked at their cards and then they waited. There were lots of colourful drawings on the walls and again Mac was reminded of Bridget when she was very young and how wonderful both he and Nora thought she was at drawing. He remembered Nora tacking a particular drawing of a bright yellow sunny morning to the fridge.

'If I'm feeling a bit down then all I'll need to do is look at this and it'll cheer me up,' she'd explained.

Mac suddenly felt like crying and he had to stand up and turn away from Kate for a few seconds while he composed himself.

'Is your back playing you up?' Kate asked with some concern.

'Yes, something like that,' he replied as he quickly wiped away the single tear that had made it through.

He was saved by the arrival of a young woman. She had jet black hair cut into a bob and wore a light blue top over a darker blue skirt. She could have been Ana's older sister.

'I've been hoping you'd call,' she said with a sad smile and a totally open face.

At that moment Mac forgot about any theory around Ana's murder that might have involved Gerry and Angel. She led them into an empty classroom and sat down on top of one of the small desks.

'We've already been to see your husband at the hospital. We're just making sure that you've had no new thoughts in the five years since Ana died,' Mac asked.

'Was killed you mean,' Angel said fiercely. 'I'm sorry but this anniversary has been the hardest one by far for us all. They say that time softens everything but that just isn't true. Until they catch whoever did that to Ana, we'll all keep suffering. As regards to any new thoughts then no, I'm sorry to say that I haven't had any. Gerry and I have talked about it endlessly. We've even tried to carry out an investigation of our own but, just like you, we got exactly nowhere. Then I saw your conference on the TV and heard that you'd caught the man who'd murdered Ruth Avaloe and, for a few minutes, I thought that you'd caught him...'

She stopped and, just as Mac had done earlier, she stood up and turned away. Mac gave her a few seconds.

'They say that hope can kill you. Right now, that feels like the truth,' she said bleakly as she turned back to face them. 'However, I'll keep hoping and I'll pray for you every day.'

'Thank you. I'd like to speak with Ana's mother too. Will she be at home? If not, then do you know where I might find her?' Mac asked.

'I'm glad that you want to see her. She thinks that the police have forgotten all about Ana. My mother and Ana's mother own a shop in tow. She'll be there now. I'll phone her and let her know that you're on the way.'

Angel gave them the address. The 'shop' proved to be one of those small places where you can get your shoes repaired and keys cut. Mac also noticed that they did tailoring and clothes alteration too.

Two ladies in their fifties were standing behind the counter waiting for them. They were both quite short, had black hair going grey, wore glasses and had identical expressions on their faces. They both looked scared. They could easily have been mistaken for sisters.

'You're the police?' one of the women asked.

The other woman took hold of her hand as she said this.

Mac showed her his warrant card.

'Is there somewhere we can talk?' Mac asked.

The woman who had spoken gestured at them to follow her. The other woman opened up a flap in the counter to let them through. They followed her into a small back storeroom full of cardboard boxes that smelt of leather and then into a little kitchen. It had a little fold-up table and two chairs. The woman looked at Mac and Kate uncertainly.

'It's okay, I'll stand,' Kate said quickly guessing that the lack of seats might be the problem.

The woman smiled at her and sat down. Mac took the other seat.

'So, you're still looking for him,' she said. 'I'm glad of that at least.'

'We're doing everything we can,' Mac assured her.

'I know but it hasn't been enough so far, has it?' she pointed out.

'We'd also like to speak to your husband if that's possible,' Mac said.

'He's with Ana now. He died six months ago. He wanted to die.'

Mac sighed. There would be no easy way to do this but he had to continue. He asked her the same questions he'd asked of Gerry and Angel and he wasn't surprised when he got the same answers. He kept the interview as short as possible as he could see that Mrs. Tomas was getting quite upset.

'It's like a nightmare that never ends. There are times in my dreams when I see Ana and even speak to her. She's happy where she is now and I sometimes see my husband and he's happy too. The nightmare happens when I wake up and I have to face the fact that I might never see my daughter or my husband ever again.'

Her face crinkled up and tears started streaming from her eyes. Mac quickly ended the session and, on his way out, told Angel's mother that she was needed in the kitchen.

'When someone kills, it's not just about the person who's murdered and the murderer. It sends out a ripple affecting everyone who ever knew them or, in this case, more like a tsunami I'd say. There are more things than just the person who has died that can never be put back together,' Mac said.

He was starting to depress himself and he knew he'd have to snap out of it. He looked at his watch. It was nearly twelve o'clock.

'Fancy something to eat?' Mac asked.

It was as good a way to cheer himself up as any.

Chapter Twenty One

They found a coffee shop that had some sandwiches on display that looked tasty enough. Neither of them said anything until they'd finished eating.

'That wasn't exactly the cheeriest morning I've had,' Kate said gloomily.

'No, it was pretty grim but it had to be done. It was always possible that one of them might have been known something. All we need is something to go on but we're getting nowhere, are we?' Mac said with a frown.

'Well, maybe this journalist might know something,' Kate said trying to cheer Mac up.

'Maybe,' Mac said not looking all that convinced.

He felt his confidence wavering a little. The case had been a dead end for five years now. What made him think that he could crack it when no-one else could?

Five years, a little voice whispered inside his head, that's why.

Mac had learnt to trust that little voice. Kate was surprised to see him smile a little.

'Well, there's always hope,' Mac said. 'Come on, let's see what Mrs. Rebecca Ferrante has to say for herself.'

Mac contacted the paper who informed him that she no longer worked full-time for them but fortunately they did have a phone number. Mrs. Ferrante was in and happy to see them which cheered up Mac even more.

She lived in the Old Town in Stevenage in a row of little old houses each of which had a bright red door. The houses were originally single storeyed but each now had a dormer window peeping out of the tiled roofs.

'Well, it certainly looks like somewhere a writer might live,' Kate said as Mac rang the bell.

A woman in her late fifties opened the door and smiled on seeing them. She had long grey hair that was tied up in a ponytail and a pair of very intelligent eyes peered out at them from behind a large pair of purple rimmed spectacles. Mac noticed that her nails were painted with exactly the same shade of purple as her glasses. She definitely looked her age but Mac guessed that she might be one of those lucky women who just didn't care.

'Mrs. Ferrante?' Mac asked.

'Oh, please call me Becky. Come in, Mr. Maguire, and you too, DS Grimsson.'

She showed them into a little room that was jam-packed with books. A large table was covered in more books and papers and a laptop was open.

'That's partly your fault,' she said with a rueful smile. 'I've had to kick off a very quick rewrite in light of recent events.'

'I'm sorry about that,' Mac said.

'Oh, don't be. I'd like nothing better than seeing the bastard who killed those girls behind bars. Although I should say bastards now, shouldn't I? I'm sorry but, when I was writing the book, I had to interview all the families and you'd have to be made of stone to not let it affect you.'

'Yes, I know. We've just spoken to Ana's mother.'

'How is poor Maria?' Becky asked.

'Not good I'm afraid. I didn't know that she'd recently lost her husband as well.'

'Yes, poor Aurelio more or less gave up when he found out that he was ill. I think he wanted to go. They're all very devout Catholics and I guess that he just wanted to see his daughter again.'

'That's more or less what Mrs. Tomas said too. Anyway, we're here in the hope that you might have some new information that could help us. Is there any chance of that?' Mac asked.

'Not very much, I'm afraid,' Becky replied. 'I've never stopped looking into this case. I'm afraid that I've got a bit stuck, although perhaps obsessed might be a better word. Anyway, even with all the time I've spent on it, I've still gotten exactly nowhere. It's been the most frustrating experience I've ever had and, believe me, I've had some very frustrating experiences in my time.'

Mac thought for a while.

'I'd guess that you'd at least have a pet theory or some sort of gut feeling about the case. I'd also guess that you face the same problem that we do in that the evidence refuses to stack up to support any of our theories. So, let's forget about the evidence for a while. I'm going to put you on the spot and ask you for your best guess of who the killer might be. This will be strictly off the record of course.'

It was Becky's turn to think for a while.

'As it's off the record I'll tell you, otherwise I might get sued for what I'm about to say. For me there are three in all, two possibles and one very possible. All of them are related to the Chloe Alexander case. I never came up with even a single suspect for poor Ana's murder.'

'Go on,' Mac said getting interested.

'Okay the two possibles are called David Sternberg and Aaron Farzan and the very possible is called Will Hecksmith.'

The names didn't ring a bell with Mac but, then again, he'd only skim read the Alexander case file.

'I know that I said it's off the record but would you mind if we record what you're going to say?' Mac asked. 'It's just so we don't miss anything.'

'That's no problem so long as you don't mind me reminding you on the recording that it's definitely off the record.'

'That's okay with me,' Mac said as he nodded towards Kate.

She got her phone out, tapped the screen a few times and then positioned it between Mac and Becky.

'Can you go through each name one by one and tell us why you've got your suspicions?' Mac asked.

'As I said, Mr. Maguire, this is definitely off the record.'

'Agreed, so tell us about Will Hecksmith,' Mac prompted.

'Now, Will's my personal favourite,' Becky replied. 'He was an ex-boyfriend of Chloe's and she was the one that had dumped him. He was a bit of a control freak, you know the type.'

Mac did and all too well. It was this impulse to control someone that often led to a lot of domestic violence and, sometimes, to murder.

Becky continued, 'She'd met Will at a party around three months or so before she died. He was good looking and dressed fashionably. She dated him for just four weeks. By the end of that time he'd already started telling her what clothes she should wear and passing comments on the people she hung around with. According to a friend of Chloe's she was beginning to get a bit scared of him. She said that he was 'starting to get creepy'. So, she dumped him and he didn't take it well. Then again, those types never do. They think they own the world.'

Mac had a feeling that Becky was speaking from experience.

'Nothing happened immediately afterwards but a month or so later she started getting trolled on social media and being called a 'slut' and a 'whore'. Then some little stories were published telling the world that she'd slept with half the college and exactly what she'd done with each of them. That was enough as far as Chloe was concerned so she told her Uncle Ben. He's a sergeant in the Marines and he and Chloe were very close. So, Ben caught hold of Will one night as he was walking home and threatened to pull all his teeth out with pliers if he carried on. I've met Ben and I honestly think that he'd have done it too. Anyway, Will must have believed him because the trolling stopped instantly after that.'

'Did the police know about this at the time?' Mac asked.

'Well, I'd guess that the Alexanders wouldn't want the police to know about what Ben did but they did tell the police about their suspicions. Anyway, Will had an alibi for both Chloe's and Ana's murders. When Chloe died, he was playing an online game with three friends. The police checked his log in and someone was playing under his name for the hours between nine until nearly four in the morning. His three friends swore that he was with them all the time. Not the greatest alibi, I suppose, but he had a much better one for the time of Ana's murder. He'd gotten into a fight at a student gig in Hatfield and ended up cooling his heels in a police cell from around ten o'clock onwards. They let him go without any charges the next morning.'

'Well, as alibis go, that's a pretty good one,' Mac said.

'Yes, it is,' Becky said. 'Now for David Sternberg. He was a college friend of Chloe's and they'd fallen out badly over something. I never did find out exactly what. Anyway, just a couple of days before Chloe died, they had a really big argument, one that was seen by one of Chloe's friends. I say seen because she was looking out of a window at the college so she couldn't hear what was said but she could see that Chloe was quite upset. However, David had an alibi for Chloe's murder. Just like Will, he says that he was at a friend's house playing one of those football games all night. Boys and their toys, I suppose. They weren't playing online so we only have his friend's word for it. It wasn't until around a year ago or so that I heard that this friend of his was the shady sort and that he was up in court for several burglaries. He also asked for several more to be taken into account and one of these happened on the night that Chloe had been killed. However, the burglary did take place around three in the morning and David's friend still insisted that he hadn't lied about being with David until after two. Even so, I still think that there's a fairly good chance that he might still be lying. Unfortunately, David's alibi for Ana's murder was much stronger. He was very drunk and at

191

a family wedding in Glasgow and there's some timed videos to prove it.'

'Okay, so what about Aaron Farzan?' Mac asked.

'I'm really not all that sure about Aaron,' Becky said, 'but there was something in the way he reacted when I questioned him about Chloe. Chloe was in a sort of gang at school that liked to think of themselves as misfits and rebels. There were six of them in all, three girls and three boys. Aaron was one of the boys. He said that they'd drifted apart since they left school and he hadn't seen her for some time. He also had an alibi for the time that Chloe was killed, he was at home with his mother apparently, and he wasn't even in the country when Ana was killed.'

'Where was he then?'

'He was in Iran visiting his father. His mother and father split up some years ago and his father went back home. It seems that he liked it out there because he went there to live a couple of years ago. He's become quite religious from what I've heard.'

'So, what made you suspect him then?' Mac asked.

'Well, it certainly wasn't because of the wealth of evidence against him,' Becky said. 'I don't know, perhaps he seemed a little too upset about someone who'd just been a friend at school, and perhaps he was just a little too nervous generally. Then again, when someone you know gets murdered perhaps you have every right to be upset and nervous. I don't know, you asked me about gut feelings and I must admit that I had one about Aaron but God knows why.'

'Is there anything else that you can tell us?' Mac asked.

'No, I'm sorry but that's it and anyway I've probably just wasted your time as it's all total nonsense,' Becky said.

'Why do you say that?'

'Basically, because there wasn't a trace of any of their DNA at either crime scene so it makes it highly unlikely that it's them, doesn't it?'

Mac could only agree. However, her comment did get him thinking once again about the DNA evidence.

Mac thanked her as Kate picked up her phone and turned the recording off.

'If what I've told you is of any help would there be any chance of an exclusive interview afterwards?' Becky asked as she showed them to the door.

'There's every chance, I'd have thought,' Mac replied.

'Anyway, just do your best and catch whoever did that to those poor girls,' Becky said.

Mac thanked her again and said that they would indeed do their best.

They sat silently in the car for a while. Kate had put the key in the ignition but she made no move to start the car. She was thinking and Mac was happy to let her carry on. It was nearly two minutes before she said anything.

'They all had really good alibis for Ana's murder, didn't they?' she said.

'It looks like it, one was in a police cell, one was in Scotland and the last was thousands of miles away.'

'I wonder if they had anyone who really loved them.'

'What do you mean?' Mac asked.

'Someone who'd kill for them,' Kate said as she turned and gave Mac a sombre look.

It was Mac's turn to think.

'So, you're thinking that there might have been a point in at least one of them having such a good alibi? You think that someone else might have killed Ana to prove that it couldn't have been them. Yes, that might explain the scarf. As the same scarf was used in both murders everyone assumed that there was just a single murderer.'

'Is it likely do you think?' Kate asked looking somewhat doubtful.

'No, I don't, although I remember a Maigret story that featured it as a plotline. In the book a wife kills a girl to prove that it couldn't have been her husband who was being held in jail for five other murders. However, it's certainly not something I've come across too often in real life, outside of the criminal fraternity anyway.' Mac could see Kate's disappointed expression. 'But this case has been so intractable that it's probably going to be something unlikely that's going to break it for us.'

'So, you think there might be something to it?'

'Perhaps, enough anyway that I'm going to suggest that we all concentrate on the Alexander case. If we do find who killed Chloe then, if you're right, that might lead us to Ana's murderer too.'

Kate smiled. She was about to start the car when her phone went off. Mac watched her as she looked at a text. He was half expecting for it to be bad news about her father but it wasn't. When Kate had finished reading there was a smile on her face.

'That was Magnus. He's managed to get an earlier flight so I've got to pick him up at the airport at six o'clock tomorrow morning.'

'Heathrow, I take it?' Mac asked.

'Yes, that's right. What's the traffic like on the motor-way at that time?' Kate asked as they drove off back towards the police station.

'Well, at around five or so in the morning I'd say that it will probably be absolutely dreadful. After that it just gets progressively worse,' Mac replied.

'You think that I should leave a bit early then?'

'As early as you can, I'd say.'

Mac looked at his watch. He was surprised to find that it was nearly four o'clock.

'I take it that you're going straight to see your father after you pick up Magnus?'

'Yes, that's the idea. Magnus is worried that he might go before he gets there. He really wants dad to meet his wife.'

'Well, if I were you, I'd go straight home when we get back to the station and try and get some sleep,' Mac suggested.

'Yes, you're probably right. What are you going to do tomorrow?' Kate asked.

'Well, I'm certainly not going to be running around breaking any doors down that's for sure.'

This made Kate smile.

'No, I thought that I might get stuck into the case file again,' Mac went on. 'There's months of work in those files and I probably haven't read half of it yet. There's also another case that I want to have a look at.'

'What's that?' Kate asked.

'The robbery at the hotel.'

Kate turned and gave him a puzzled look.

'Do you really think that the robbery might have had some bearing on Ana's murder?'

'If I'm honest, I've no idea. All I know is that it's something that the investigators seemed to have dismissed once they confirmed that the thief had a rock-solid alibi.'

'Then why?' Kate asked. 'I'm sorry, I'm just interested in your thinking as I'd have probably dismissed it too.'

'Because it's unusual and unusual things should always be looked at a little more closely,' Mac replied. 'However, if I'm being honest, there's something about it that's just stuck in my head. It's like an itch and the only way I can scratch it is to look into it as closely as I can.'

'Do you always follow your hunches?' Kate asked.

'Yes, more or less. They get annoying if I don't so I've always found it best to follow them up and get them out of my system.'

'Do you solve many cases through doing that?'

Mac gave this some thought.

195

'Well yes, some cases have gotten solved when I've followed through on a hunch but usually it just gives me another piece of the puzzle. When it works that is.'

'That's interesting,' Kate said. 'I'll hopefully be back in on Wednesday and I'll be looking forward to seeing how you get on.'

Kate pulled into the police car park and parked up. They checked the team's room but everyone was out except for a young man with a somewhat extreme hair style who looked nothing like a policeman.

'Martin! You're back,' Mac said with some surprise.

'Have you missed me then?' Martin asked with a smile.

'Of course. How did the revenge porn case go?'

'Really well. The ex-boyfriend tried to get rid of his phone and laptop but, even though they were damaged, we managed to get enough evidence from them to nail him. It was fun actually.'

Mac thought that Martin's idea of fun was strange but he then had to remind himself that he was quite looking forward to doing a case review. He knew that most of his colleagues would think that very strange indeed.

'I need a favour,' Mac said. 'There was a robbery at the hotel where Ana Tomas worked just a week or so before she was killed. Can you get me everything you can on it?'

'Sure, I'm afraid that I can't do it straight away though. I've got something to finish off,' Martin replied.

'That's no problem, I'm in no rush. Thanks, Martin.'

Kate still wanted to have that chat with Mac and this seemed like a good chance.

'Do you mind if I buy you a drink while you're waiting? I'll get myself back home after that. Who knows but it might help me get to sleep?'

Mac gave her a thoughtful look.

'Yes, why not?'

Chapter Twenty Two

Mac looked out of the window into the car park. It wasn't raining but it looked as if another shower wasn't too far off.

'Martin, is there any chance that you could send me that case file by email?'

'Sure Mac, no problem,' Martin replied with a smile. 'Look for it in a couple of hours or so. Enjoy your drink.'

They took their time walking to the pub. It wasn't far but it seemed like it to Mac. His back was beginning to feel quite painful.

'Are you alright, Mac?' Kate asked seeing that he was slowing down a bit.

Mac tried to smile.

'I'll be okay. It's not far now and I'll get a taxi home straight from the pub.'

The sight of the Three Magnets approaching cheered him up. It was just as well as fat, heavy drops of rain started falling on the pavement like miniature explosions. He was luckily only mildly damp by the time he got inside. He saw that his usual table was free and made for it while Kate made for the bar. He sighed with relief as he sat down.

On the other side of the window the rain was falling heavily and the streets had suddenly cleared of people. One of the papers had dubbed it the 'Summer that never was' but the one that caught on was 'A Summer for Ducks'. People had started calling it the 'Duck Summer' and the name had stuck.

Kate returned with the drinks and sat down opposite him. She stared out of the window at the rain falling. She wanted to talk to him about Toni but she didn't know where to start.

Mac gave her some time.

'I remember you saying to me not long ago that I'd never been in love,' Kate said as she glanced up at Mac. 'That really stuck in my head. Then something happened on Sunday, well nothing happened but...'

Kate took a gulp of wine.

'Well, when I was in the station Sunday Toni dropped by. She must have had to pick something up, I suppose. Well, she was with someone, a man, quite a good-looking man I suppose and, well, she kissed him before they left. It was just a kiss, I suppose, but...'

'You felt jealous of him, didn't you?' Mac said.

'Yes, I guess I did,' Kate admitted. 'I've never felt that before. I mean I've never met him but, in that moment, I hated him. That's really stupid, isn't it?'

'No, it isn't. You've got it bad, haven't you?' Mac said.

Kate's face and shoulders slumped.

'I'm so confused, I just don't know what to do, Mac. Oh, and I'm sorry for dragging you here and boring you with my personal stuff. I used to have friends you know, where I worked before. Good friends too but, when I left my husband behind, I left them as well for some reason. It seems as if I've cut myself off from everyone, everyone except for my brother that is.'

Mac knew exactly how she was feeling. He'd done exactly the same after Nora had died.

'You have friends here too. Me and Tim at the very least,' Mac said.

Kate's face broke into a warm smile.

'Thanks Mac, that's really good to know. So, as a friend, have you any advice for me? I just don't know what I should do or even if I should do anything at all.'

'I definitely think you should talk to Toni and be totally honest about what you've been going through. You never know but you might be able to work it out between the two of you.'

'I'm not sure how I'd even do that. I arranged to meet her once and I that didn't turn out too well. I'm not sure she'd be up for that again.'

'Why don't you go and knock on her door then? She only lives a few minutes walk from the station,' Mac said.

'Really? I didn't know that. You don't know her address, do you?' Kate said feeling her face redden as she did so.

'No, but I know where she lives. All you need to do is turn left out of the station car park then left again and Toni's about half way down on the left. It's a house that's been turned into two flats and it has a bright blue door. Almost turquoise really. You can't miss it.'

Kate felt her heart rate speed up at the thought of seeing Toni again.

Left, left and the turquoise door on the left, she said to herself.

'Thanks Mac, really thanks,' she said.

They were interrupted by the arrival of a very sodden Tim.

'God, I'm soaked,' he said with some exasperation. 'It's only a hundred yards and I ran as well.'

'With all that junk in your shop couldn't you find an umbrella?' Mac asked. 'Go on sit down and talk to Kate for a minute and I'll get them in.'

They talked about the weather and football for a while and Kate enjoyed it. At around six Kate left them to it and headed home.

'Ah, young Kate's going through a tough time at the moment, isn't she?' Tim said.

'Yes, she is but, with some luck, it might all turn out okay for her in the end.'

Mac hoped against hope that he might be right.

As Kate stared out of the train window she felt as if her emotions were on some sort of roller coaster ride. Up one second with the thought of seeing Toni again and then plunging into the depths as she went through all the ways that things might go wrong. She was quite surprised when she arrived in Hatfield. She was also surprised that she hadn't thought about her dad once on the trip home.

She knew that Mac was right though. She had to see Toni and she had to find out once and for all what was going on.

She put her umbrella up and hailed a taxi to take her to the hospice. She'd spend a couple of hours with her father and then get a takeaway on the way home and go to bed early.

She just hoped that she would get some sleep.

Chapter Twenty Three

Mac had slept well. He too had gone to bed fairly early and woke up just before seven o'clock. He smiled as he realised that he'd had a good night's sleep for once. Uninterrupted nights were tending to get rarer lately. He sat up and checked his pain levels. It wasn't too bad so he stood up and then smiled again. It was bearable and he was more than thankful for it, especially as it had been so painful the evening before.

He went out and filled up the bird feeders while the kettle was boiling. He thought of Kate who would be somewhere on the M25 by now driving her brother and his wife to Hatfield to see her father. He was glad that she'd have the support of her brother during what was going to be a difficult time for her.

He also remembered that Nora's remembrance service was exactly a week away. He was dreading it. He just wanted to get it all over and done with.

He watched as the birds descended on the full feeders while he sipped at his coffee. He always had a sense of Nora being somewhere close by when he did this. Perhaps it was because she had loved the birds so much. He watched as a group of starlings descended on the feeders sending the smaller birds scattering.

He remembered that he'd once called them bullies when they did this. Mac could hear her reply in his mind.

'Ah well, and don't they need feeding just as much as the smaller ones? They're not as greedy as people anyway. They'll only eat what they need and there'll be plenty for the smaller ones when they've finished.'

Mac smiled at this but it was a sad smile.

He filled up his cup again and went to work. He sat down on the sofa and turned on his laptop. Terry managed to walk over to the sofa and climb up beside

Mac without opening his eyes. He went straight back to sleep, if he'd ever been awake that is.

He looked at his emails. There was one from Martin. A fat case file on the hotel robbery. Mac smiled and got to work.

Kate was cursing under her breath at the traffic as she drove back from the airport. She looked in the rear-view mirror and she could see that both Magnus and Nobomi were fast asleep. They'd caught the overnight flight and neither had been able to get any sleep on the plane. She smiled as she looked at her brother. She remembered when he was small and he used to fall asleep on the sofa. Mum would have to pick him up and take him to bed. She felt suddenly tearful at the memory.

Whoa girl! she said to herself. Today was going to be hard enough without adding to it.

It was stop-start for another hour or so until she got past Watford and she could eventually speed up a bit. Twenty minutes later she pulled up outside the hospice.

'We're here,' she said as she turned around to see both Magnus and Nobomi stirring and rubbing their eyes.

'My God, did we sleep all the way here? Sorry, sis,' Magnus said.

'No, don't be sorry, you both obviously needed it. Come on, let's go and see dad.'

As they walked down the corridor towards her father's ward her heart was thumping and she said a little prayer that he'd still be there. He had seemed very frail the night before and as though a puff of wind might have carried him away. He'd only woken up for a few minutes.

'Kate?' You're by yourself again then,' he'd said. He'd then given her a sad look. 'I've been thinking and I'm sorry. You always look so sad. I think that you were a lonely little girl too and perhaps that was my fault. I hope you're not lonely anymore, Kate. It's such a waste of life being by yourself, such a waste.'

He'd then gone straight back to sleep.

His words had been echoing around her head ever since. He was so right, being lonely is a waste of life.

She was surprised to see him sitting up and smiling at them as they walked in.

'At last,' he said, 'I get to meet the wonderful Nobomi.'

Her father could always be utterly charming when he wanted to and he put a good show on for them all. He chatted and smiled and asked lots of questions about South Africa and their life there. She could see that Nobomi had immediately warmed to him. Kate was happy to just sit and listen. There was something of her old father there and she remembered how good he was to talk to some-times. When he was there that is.

Even though he was obviously trying to fight it they could all see that the tiredness was winning. He eventually fell asleep and they quietly left the ward.

'Shall I drop you at your hotel?' Kate asked.

'Oh, yes please. If I'm honest I could do with a few more hours sleep,' Magnus replied. 'They've got a rest-aurant there. Do you want to come and meet us around lunchtime and we'll get something to eat before we come back here?'

Kate did. The thought of a few hours in bed appealed to her too. She hadn't slept well, thinking about Toni had seen to that.

She'd fallen asleep as soon as she put her head on the pillow. It only seemed as if she'd been asleep for five minutes when the alarm woke her up. It took her a few seconds to realise that she hadn't set an alarm. It was her phone.

She looked at the screen. It was the hospice. She felt strangely calm as though she already knew what they were going to tell her.

They told her that her father had passed away in his sleep just a few minutes before. He went peacefully the nurse said.

She sat there stunned for some time. She knew that it was going to happen and yet she was still shocked to her core. For good or bad he'd been a major part of her life and now he was gone. She suddenly thought about Magnus and decided to leave the self-pity for later. She quickly dressed and got in the car. She didn't want to tell him over the phone.

She knocked on his door and he answered it with a smile on his face. The smile disappeared when he saw his sister's expression.

'He's gone, isn't he?' Magnus said.

Kate nodded.

'They rang me half an hour ago. He went peacefully in his sleep they said.'

Magnus stepped forward and hugged Kate as she burst into tears. Kate was once again taken by surprise by the strength of her emotions. She noticed that Magnus was crying too.

Nobomi came out of the bathroom. When Magnus saw her, he turned and took her in his arms. His wife held him and kissed him and said all the right words. Kate's heart was breaking as she realised that she had no-one who could do that for her. She felt utterly desolate.

Kate drove them to the hospice. Her father's bed had a screen around it. He looked as though he was still sleeping and there was almost the hint of a smile on his face.

'I'm glad that I got to see him again before he went,' Magnus said.

'I think he could have gone anytime but he hung on. I think that he was waiting for you,' Kate said.

After standing there in silence for a while Magnus touched his father's hand.

'Goodbye dad,' he said and turned to go.

Kate did the same. She found it difficult to keep the tears at bay.

They stood outside the hospice looking at each other for a few seconds.

'I need a drink,' Magnus said.

'Me too,' Kate replied.

She drove them back to the hotel and parked up. She'd come and get the car later, right now she just wanted to find the bar.

As it was only two in the afternoon the bar was quiet which suited them all.

'So, what happens now?' Magnus said.

'Dad's arranged the funeral himself. The people at the hospice have already phoned the undertakers,' Kate said. 'They've got my number, I daresay they'll let us know if we need to do anything.'

Magnus gave her a strange look.

'He told me about the will, Kate. I'll be getting just about everything.'

'Really?'

'Yes, he's left quite a bit and he said that he wanted me to set up some sort of charitable foundation in Africa with it. He told me about it because he wanted to make sure that I was okay about the idea. Are you okay about it?'

Kate smiled.

'I'm more than okay about it. I don't need or want the money and at least it will be doing some good in the world. I actually think it's a great idea.'

'I've been thinking and I want to call it the Emer and Einar Foundation after mum and dad. What do you think?'

Emer and Einar. As a couple they almost sounded poetical. If only their lives had been like something from a poem too.

'That sounds great,' Kate replied. 'You're going to make it all happen. I know you will. I'm so proud of you.'

'Me too,' Nobomi said with a smile as she squeezed her husband's hand.

For some reason that small sign of affection triggered something in Kate. She'd had enough.

She'd had enough of self-pity, enough of just sitting around and hoping that things would get better, enough of being alone. She thought of her father's words again and she suddenly felt a sense of urgency in her. She was going to do something about it.

'I'm sorry Magnus but I have to be somewhere. I can't explain right now. Can I call you later?' she said as she stood up.

'Are you sure you're okay, sis?' Magnus asked with a concerned expression.

'I honestly don't know but there's something I need to find out and I need to find out right now.'

She got a taxi to the train station and was back at the police station in Letchworth just after three o'clock. She had a look in the local detective's room but Toni wasn't there. She asked one of the detectives and he said that Toni had gone out to do some interviews and then she was planning on going straight home afterwards. She hung around the station for a while until the thought struck her that Toni might have gone home early.

It was lightly drizzling as she walked down the street towards Toni's flat. She had no trouble finding it as the door was indeed a shade of turquoise just as Mac had described it. It had a little covered porch where she could wait and keep dry.

She waited and watched the rain fall.

Chapter Twenty Four

Mac had spent some hours going through the case file as thoroughly as he could. However, it didn't tell him much about the hotel robbery that he didn't already know. He then looked through all the photos taken at the crime scene. In one of them the mattress had been pulled to one side and a white suited figure was taking samples using a swab from around the base of the bed. Presumably that's where the money had been hidden.

Mac's pulse speeded up slightly when he noticed Ana in the background of one of the other pictures. She was talking to another white-suited figure, a woman. He thought for a moment until he remembered something that Ana's boyfriend had said.

He said that 'the woman who took her fingerprints was funny and made her laugh.'

He looked at the photo quite closely. Mac had met quite a few of the forensics team during the past months but not this woman and, for a moment, he wondered who she was. He decided to ask Bob Yeardley, the forensics team leader, when they next met and carried on looking through the photos.

He eventually got up and stretched his arms. He looked out of the window. It was still raining and Mac thought of Kate. He wondered if everything had gone okay with her brother. He decided to ring her later that evening and see how she was.

Kate was looking at the rain falling down too. She was also wondering what on earth she was doing standing outside Toni's flat.

She might be hours yet, Kate thought.

It didn't matter. She knew that she was going to wait however long it took. She had to know. She started preparing what she was going to say to Toni for when she turned up. She was still in the process of doing this when Toni actually turned up. Kate jumped with surprise.

Toni had a puzzled look on her face as she walked up to Kate.

'Kate, I wasn't expecting...I...,' Toni said.

She seemed as surprised and tongue-tied as Kate felt.

'I'm sorry, can I help you with something?' Toni said as she regained her composure.

Kate had rehearsed some lines, lines that were supposed to be considered and intelligent, but at that very moment they all flew out of her head.

'My dad died,' she blurted out.

She bit her tongue. That was not what she had wanted to say. She didn't want Toni's pity but as to what she did want she still wasn't sure. However, Toni's face softened when she said this.

'Come in, you look like you need a drink,' Toni said.

She did.

Toni hung their coats up, put on some soft music and returned from the kitchen with two large glasses of red wine.

'I'm really sorry that your dad died. I lost mine four years ago so I know how you feel,' Toni said.

'Did you?' was all Kate could think to say.

'Yes, it's strange, I was only talking about it to my brother on Sunday. It still seems like it was only yesterday somehow.'

Her brother? Of course, that's who she was with in the car park, Kate thought. Thinking back, she could clearly see the resemblance. Her heart started thumping even faster.

'Do you want to talk about it?' Toni asked.

Kate didn't but there was something she wanted to talk about. Unfortunately, she didn't know how to broach the subject or even what the subject really was. Then she remembered Nobomi and how she'd touched her brother's hand. She looked up at Toni. She found it strange but she suddenly knew exactly what she wanted.

She was beautiful, Kate could see it now. In fact, she was more than beautiful, in that moment she was perfect. Kate looked into her eyes, they were warm and brown, and her body made up her mind for her. She leant forward and planted the most passionate kiss she had in her on Toni's lips. When she pulled back and looked at Toni's face, she had a moment of panic. What if?

The panic subsided as she watched the smile grow on Toni's face. She returned Kate's kiss with every bit as much passion.

Two minutes later a trail of clothes led towards the bedroom.

Kate awoke with a smile. Even before she opened her eyes, she could feel it on her face. That had never happened to her before. She opened her eyes. The steely grey early morning light was creeping in around the edges of the curtains. Her smile widened as she thought of what had happened. Her body still hummed with the pleasures of the evening before, pleasures that were new and entirely wonderful. Her heart was full in a way that she'd have thought impossible only the night before. She moved onto her side so she could look at Toni's face.

In the dim half-light she could just make it out. It was a beautiful face, the most beautiful that she had ever seen. She just lay there looking and she felt totally happy. She could see now that it wasn't a perfect face but that made it even more unique and all the more wonderful in Kate's eyes.

Her lover's face, Kate thought.

She'd always thought that all the songwriters and romantic novelists had been lying when they sang or wrote about love. Of course, that was because she'd never really experienced love before. Now, she thought that all the songs and the books were far too limited and could never come close to describing the soaring feeling that now lifted her heart. It had only been one night but, even if that was all it was going to be, she wouldn't have regretted a second of it. It had opened her eyes and she knew that a door into a new life had also opened.

She lay gazing at Toni's face and at those lips, those luscious lips. She just couldn't resist it. She raised herself on one elbow and planned to just brush Toni's lips with hers so she wouldn't wake her. The touch of a butterfly's wing that was all. As their lips touched, she felt Toni's hand gently hold the back of her head ensuring that the kiss was both deeper and longer than she'd planned.

When Kate pulled away those same lips formed a wide smile as Toni opened her eyes. She turned on her side too so that they could both look into each other's eyes.

'I was awake,' Toni said as she held Kate's hand in hers. 'I could feel you beside me but I was afraid. I was afraid that I was only dreaming and that as soon as I opened my eyes you'd disappear in a puff of smoke.'

Kate looked deeply and unflinchingly into Toni's eyes and could only see love there.

'I'm not going anywhere,' she said.

'Good, I don't want you to,' Toni said, her voice husky with emotion.

It was wonderful just lying quietly in each other's arms and watching the light gradually grow stronger. Showering together was actually fun rather than just something she had to do. However, the best part for Kate was breakfast. She couldn't remember the last time she'd had breakfast at home. Eating on her own had seemed such a lonely way of starting the day so instead she usually went straight into the office and grabbed a coffee there. That first breakfast with Toni, simple as it was consisting of just coffee, toast and yoghurt, was the best meal she'd ever eaten by far. Toni asked if the breakfast was okay and what Kate liked to eat. They chatted and started revealing little things about them-selves to each other.

They both knew that they had only just started their exploration each other. They'd just set foot on a beach while a whole new continent lay before them.

Chapter Twenty Five

They walked together to work that morning. Toni stopped before they reached the station and gave Kate a nervous look.

'Can I ask you a question?' Toni asked.

'Of course, anything.'

'Last night, I mean I'll understand if it was, but...'

Kate had a feeling about what she was going to ask.

'Are you wondering if the only reason I came to you last night was because my dad died?'

'Well, yes. As I said I'll understand if you don't want to see me again but I suppose I was hoping...'

Kate's heart fluttered as she saw fear in her lover's face. She quickly stopped Toni's question by kissing her.

'My dad dying did have something to do with last night. Almost his last words to me were about being alone. He said that it was such a waste of life. He was right, I don't want to be alone anymore, I want to be with you.'

Toni smiled and gave Kate a serious hug.

'Would you like to meet me tonight then?' she asked.

'Just try and stop me. I'll be waiting outside your flat at six o'clock sharp,' Kate replied.

'So, I'll take that as a yes then,' Toni said with a wide smile.

Kate watched as Toni disappeared into her office and stood there feeling like she wanted to run in after her. A minute without her felt like a minute of life lost. She wondered at these feelings and she realised that her life could now be divided into two parts, before and after Toni.

She knew that nothing would ever be the same again.

It was only then that she thought of her brother. He must be wondering what was going on. She rang him and said that she'd meet him at his hotel in an hour or so. She'd tell him everything. She walked into the team's room and Andy, Tommy and Mac were already there and in deep conversation.

'Kate! I wasn't expecting you back this soon,' Andy said.

'It's only a quick visit. I just wanted to let you know that my dad died yesterday. He passed away just a few hours after seeing my brother,' Kate said.

They all expressed their sadness at the news. Mac was looking closely at Kate and, for some reason, he didn't think she was as sad as she might have been. In fact, there was a lightness about her that he'd never seen before.

'Take as much time off as you need,' Andy said.

'I think I'd like to keep working, at least for a while. I'll only be thinking otherwise,' Kate said. 'I'm going to see my brother but I'll be back in a couple of hours. I hope you don't mind waiting, Mac?'

'No problem. We were just talking about what we should do next,' Mac said. 'Go on, go and see your brother. I'll let you know what we're doing when you get back. I've always got the case file to fall back on in the meantime.'

Kate could once again see her reflection in the train window. This time she was smiling. She thought she'd be so desolate after her father had died, and she was in a way, but thinking of Toni somehow made every bad or sad feeling disappear. There was some sort of magic there.

She told Magnus and Nobomi what had happened and about her feelings for Toni. She wasn't entirely sure as to what their reaction might be and so she was more than a little nervous when she finished. She needn't have worried.

'I'm so happy for you sis. You look different today, the sadness has gone,' Magnus said as he gave her a hug. 'If I'm honest, it's a relief that you've found someone. I really wouldn't have liked leaving you here all by yourself when I went back home.'

Nobomi gave Kate a big hug too.

'I've never had a sister before, only brothers, but now I'll have two sisters. You must bring her to meet us.'

Kate had tears in her eyes as Nobomi said this but they were not tears of sadness.

As she travelled back, she felt so light that it was a wonder that her feet still touched the ground. Magnus had decided to try and have the best time he could while he was here. He'd be in England for at least two weeks as he needed to spend some time setting up the foundation with her father's lawyers. Nobomi had never been to Europe before so he wanted to give her a tour of the country starting with London. They decided to meet up again on Saturday. Kate would be glad to get back to work. It would pass the time until she could see Toni again.

When she got back Mac was sitting by himself.

'Where is everyone?' Kate asked.

'Well, I saw Dan for about fifteen seconds earlier on. The stabbing case is still ongoing but I think he's hoping for an arrest before long. He was picking up Martin who'll be helping him with some facial recognition software. As for Andy and Tommy they're both out doing some interviews. Andy's determined to cover everyone they talked to during the original investigation. He's left Will Hecksmith, Aaron Farzan and David Sternberg to us. Unfortunately, as Becky Ferrante said, Mr. Farzan now lives in Iran but his mother still lives here so we can hopefully talk to her.'

'Okay then, want to get on with it?' she asked with a smile.

He looked closely at Kate and wondered.

'So, I take it that Toni was in last night then?' he asked.

Kate's eyes widened and her mouth fell open.

'You should be glad you live now, Mac. A couple of hundred years ago they'd have burnt you at the stake. Anyway yes, you're right Toni was in.'

'I take it that things went okay then?'

Kate's smile widened and Mac could see a dreamy look come into her eyes.

'Things went better than okay Mac, far better.'

'Well, it's after twelve now and I'd guess that you'll want to get off on time this evening, so shall we get going?' Mac said returning Kate's smile.

'Okay, so who are we seeing first?' Kate asked as they walked towards the car park.

'I couldn't get hold of Mrs. Farzan so we'll try her later. I've contacted David and Will but Will said he won't be available until four o'clock or so. He said that he'd meet us at the station. David lives in North London, near Mill Hill, and he said he'd take the afternoon off work and meet us there at around one thirty or so.'

They didn't talk that much as they made their way into London on the motorway. Kate was wrapped up in her thoughts about Toni while Mac was still carrying on a mental case review. With all the information the case files held he was sure that there must be some sort of a clue in there somewhere.

As David lived in North London it meant that they only had a couple of miles of London traffic to negotiate. Kate was glad as it was slow going. They eventually pulled up outside a new development. The flats were obviously quite up-market and wouldn't have come cheap. Mac wondered how David might be able to afford such a flat.

It was just before one thirty when Mac rang the buzzer. A voice asked them who they were. Mac told the voice. The door buzzed and Mac pushed it open.

David's flat was on the third floor but, luckily, there was a lift. A young man was waiting for them at an open doorway as they walked down the hall.

'David?' Mac asked.

215

His voice sounded doubtful as the young man somehow didn't match Mac's mental model of what David might look like. This young man was small and very slim. He was also very obviously of Asian origin.

'David will be here in a minute or two,' the young man said in a light sing-song voice. 'Please come in.'

The flat was light and airy and had furniture that looked both stylish and useful. The young man gestured towards a white sofa.

'And you are?' Mac asked as he gratefully sat down.

'I'm Imran, David's partner. Can I get you something? I do a really good espresso if you're interested.'

Mac and Kate were.

So, David is gay, Mac thought. Well, if there was any sexual motive for Chloe's death that would probably rule him out. Still, he knew Chloe well and Mac hoped that he'd be able to tell them something that they didn't already know. His thoughts were interrupted by the front door opening. A young man entered the room. He was tall and had a mop of unruly black hair that looked as if he'd just got out of bed. He was dressed in an old T shirt, torn jeans and a pair of red Converses. He had a green canvas man-bag over one shoulder that reminded Mac of the bags that workmen used when he was a child for bringing their lunch into work.

'I'm sorry, I was a bit late and I had to run from the station,' the young man breathlessly explained.

Imran emerged from the kitchen with two small cups. He gave these to Mac and Kate and then went over to David who had to bend down slightly so he could kiss him on the cheek.

'Would you like one too, love?' he asked.

'Yes, please,' David replied.

He sat down in the armchair opposite.

'I've been more or less expecting someone to call. I saw the press conferences on TV and Mrs. Alexander too,' David said a sad expression. 'It doesn't seem like five years somehow.'

'How long have you been living in London?' Mac asked.

'Over a year now, ever since I got a job at the BBC. I'm a designer there, you know websites mostly. I'm working on the new radio website at the moment,' David replied. 'That's where I met Imran, he works there too.'

Mac now understood how they could afford such a flat.

Imran came out and handed David a cup. He sat on the arm of the chair and draped his arm around David's shoulder. He obviously felt very protective of him.

'I just wanted to ask you if you'd had any thoughts in the past five years about Chloe, anything at all that you feel might be helpful,' Mac asked.

'I'm sorry I haven't but I wish I did. She was a good friend to me when I really needed it. It's so crappy when someone dies like that. There were things that I wanted to say to her. I never really thanked her or anything.'

'Someone saw you having an argument a couple of days before Chloe was killed. You were asked about it at the time but you said it was nothing. Was it nothing?'

David looked up at Imran before answering.

'I lied. We did have an argument. Chloe was absolutely furious with me, if I'm being honest. It was about me being gay. I just couldn't admit it to anyone at the time, except to Chloe that is. She was so easy to talk to. Anyway, she thought that I was wrong to keep it hidden. She said that I should find some courage and come out. She was right, of course, but I was just too scared at the time. My dad's a builder and he's from Glasgow too and so I figured that he wouldn't want a poof for a son. I thought it would break my mum's heart as well and so I said nothing, even though it was killing me.'

Imran gave David's arm a sympathetic squeeze.

'After Chloe died, I figured that life was too short and so I did as she'd advised and came out.'

'How did it go?' Mac asked.

'Well, mum told me that she more or less already knew and, while it was a bit of a shock for dad, he seemed to get over it fairly quickly. You forget sometimes that your parents do actually love you,' David said.

'Can you tell me anything about Will Hecksmith or Aaron Farzan?' Mac asked.

'I've never met Aaron, although Chloe mentioned him a few times. She'd been good friends with him at school but I only met her when I went to college. As for Will, he must have been one of the biggest tossers I've ever come across. I warned Chloe about him but she had to find out the hard way.' David looked up at Mac. 'You don't really suspect Will though, do you?'

'Unfortunately, we don't suspect anyone at the moment. We're just asking questions about anyone who knew her,' Mac replied.

'Well, I doubt if Will had anything to do with Chloe's death. Yes, he was a toad and small-minded with it but he was basically a coward. He accused me once in public of being a 'shirt-lifter'. Although where he got that phrase from, I'll never know. Anyway, I punched his lights out and he never said another word about me after that.'

'Will said that he was playing an online game with friends the night that Chloe was killed. Do you believe that?'

'If I were you, I wouldn't believe a word he said,' David replied.

He suddenly became thoughtful.

'What is it?' Mac asked.

'It's just something I remembered. Why I don't know.'

'Is it about Will?'

David nodded.

'A couple of weeks after Chloe died, I saw Will and one of his friends in a corridor at the college. They were

218

arguing about something. All I heard was his friend say, 'After what I did, you really owe me'. I don't know what he meant by that but it sort of stuck in my head.'

Mac had an immediate idea of what it might have been about.

'What was the friend's name?' he asked.

'Troy Gartner.'

'I don't suppose you know what Troy is doing these days?' Mac asked.

'I've no idea. I couldn't stand Will or any of his hangers on. They'd be the last people I'd want to keep in touch with,' David replied with certainty.

As they drove back Mac rang the station and asked one of the local detectives if they could dig up an address for Troy Gartner. Mac reckoned that, with a name like that, it shouldn't be too hard. He got a call back just as they were entering Letchworth. It hadn't been hard at all as Troy was already known to the police. He'd been cautioned several times for anti-social offences and he'd also served six months in a young offender's institute for smashing the plate glass window of a chip shop that had refused to serve him.

Mac surmised that Troy might have some anger issues.

Troy still lived in Letchworth on the Jackmans housing estate. He lived in a housing association flat on the second floor but this time there wasn't any lift.

'Will you be alright, Mac?' Kate asked seeing the apprehensive expression on his face.

'Oh, of course,' he lied. 'I'll just have to take it slowly that's all.'

There was no bannister either so he took it one step at a time while leaning against the wall. He took it as carefully as possible, just one slip might put him back in bed for weeks and he'd already had a good dose of that fairly recently. He smiled at Kate when he reached the top of the last flight of stairs. It should be a little easier going back down.

The paint was peeling from the door of Troy's flat and it looked as if someone had tried to kick the door in at some time. There was no doorbell so Mac knocked.

After a while they could hear sounds from behind the door and eventually it opened a tiny crack. A girl's face peeked out at them. Mac suspected that she had no clothes on. He showed her his card.

'I'm looking for Troy. Is he in?'

'I'll go and ask him,' she said as she shut the door again.

A few minutes later the door opened again and the girl emerged dressed in a pink top and ripped jeans. She didn't even look at them as she scurried off down the hallway. They waited some more. Then the door opened and they walked in. There wasn't much in the way of furniture but to Mac's surprise it was tidy enough.

Troy was sitting on a broken-down old sofa lighting up a cigarette. He was dressed in a scruffy T shirt and boxer shorts. He glanced up at them without any fear.

'What have I done now?' he asked wearily.

Mac had a feeling of déjà vu. He remembered that the bookie had said exactly the same thing.

'Nothing. We're not here about you, we want to ask you some questions about Will Hecksmith. Do you still see him?'

'Will? No, not for ages. He went a bit funny, didn't he? Anyway, I don't see any of the old crew these days. Is this about that Chloe Alexander? I saw a bit about her on the telly the other day.'

'Yes, we're looking into her case again,' Mac replied.

'Well, it wasn't Will if that's what you're thinking.'

'Yes, he was playing games with you, wasn't he? All night you said. Was that true?'

'Yes, of course. Why would I lie about that?' Troy said looking offended.

Too offended, Mac thought. Despite his protests he had a feeling that Troy was lying. He had an idea.

'Bartholomew Warboys, also known as 'Bazza' I believe, has told us that Will actually went out for a while that evening. He's signed a statement to that effect too. Any comments?'

Troy thought for a while.

'Is Bazza going to be in trouble? I mean it was a long time ago.'

'I told Bazza that, so long as he told me the truth, there'd be no further action. I'm saying the same to you,' Mac said.

'What about Tunde? What's he said?'

'If you're referring to Tunde Adebayo, we're visiting him next,' Mac replied.

'Yeah, Tunde. He's got all religious these days,' Troy said. 'He was a sneaky little liar when we were a crew but that's what I liked about him. I might as well tell you then, as Bazza's already told you, and I'm pretty sure that Tunde will too. Jesus won't allow him to tell a lie these days.'

Kate gave Mac an excited look.

'Yeah, Will went out that night. He was out for about an hour or so.'

'And you, Bazza and Tunde lied about it?'

Troy shrugged and told them all about that night.

'Do you believe him?' Kate asked as they drove towards Will Hecksmith's house.

'Well, I believe that he believed what he told us. However, it does mean that Will had a motive and we now know that he had the opportunity too. Anyway, let's not wait until four. I've got his address, let's go and see what he's got to say.'

Will lived in a big house in quite an upmarket part of Letchworth. A woman in her late forties opened the door. Mac showed her his warrant card.

'I'm looking for Will Hecksmith. I take it that you're his mother?' Mac asked.

'I don't know what I did to deserve it but yes, I'm his mother,' she said with a weary expression. 'Come in. It's only three o'clock so he'll probably still be asleep.'

She left them in a large, well-furnished room. Mac went over and looked at some photos in frames on a dresser. They all had a boy in them and featured him at various ages as he grew up. The people in the photos looked happy.

He was interrupted by the sound of a woman's voice shrilly shouting something that he couldn't quite make out. Mrs. Hecksmith joined them a moment later. She looked a little upset.

'He'll be down in a minute. I take it that this is about Chloe?' she asked.

'Yes, tell me did you ever meet her?' Mac asked.

'Just the once. I thought she was a lovely girl, good looking and smart too. If I'm honest, I wondered what on earth she was doing with Will. Anyway, it didn't last long, they never do. Will was always a bit selfish I'm afraid to say but Chloe's death really hit him hard. In fact, I don't think he's gotten over it yet.'

She turned around as a sleepy Will entered the room. He was still dressed in a pair of pyjamas and was rubbing his face as he entered the room.

'Would you like anything?' Mrs. Hecksmith asked.

'I'd love a cup of tea,' Will asked hopefully.

'Not you, them,' his mother replied with more than a touch of anger.

'I'm okay, thanks.' Mac replied.

'I'm okay too,' Kate said.

'Okay then, I'll get you some tea then,' she said begrudgingly to her son before she left.

Will sat down and looked nervously at Mac and Kate.

'It's just as well you've come. I forgot to turn the alarm on so you'd have been waiting for me a long time at the station. So, what do you want to know?'

Mac thought that he'd ease his way in and, as he was interested in Will's alibi for the time when Ana was murdered, he decided to start with that.

'The weekend after Chloe died you were arrested for fighting. Tell me what happened,' Mac said.

'Oh that, I was at some student gig and I heard someone talking about Chloe,' Will replied. 'He was a bit drunk, as I was, and he said that she was probably asking for it or something along those lines. I'm not usually the bravest person you'd meet but that night I totally lost it and just jumped on him. He was with four or five friends but I just didn't care. I got a few good punches in too before the bouncers came and dragged me away. The police took me in and they were going to charge me too. Then I told them what he'd said and, when they found out that I knew Chloe, they were okay with me. I was totally pissed so they let me sleep it off in a cell and even gave me some breakfast the next morning. When I got outside, the guy that I'd hit was waiting for me. He'd been waiting for hours to apologise. Yeah, he was okay actually it was just everything else that was shit.'

What Will had said indicated that he felt guilty about something but what? Mac decided to cut to the chase.

'Where did you go when you left Troy, Bazza and Tunde the night that Chloe was killed?' he asked.

Will almost jumped in his chair when Mac said this.

'You know?'

'We know,' Mac replied flatly, 'but tell us anyway.'

'I thought I was so clever those days, terminally stupid was more like it. I wanted to get back at Chloe for dumping me. God, I was such a pratt and she was so right to dump me but all I could think about was getting some revenge. I settled on death by strangling.'

Chapter Twenty Six

Mac looked at Will with an expression that was in equal part amazement and puzzlement.

'Her hamster? You strangled her hamster?'

Will looked embarrassed and more than a little sad.

'Yes, that was me alright. While Chloe was getting strangled to death, I was in her house killing her hamster. Christ, you can't get any lower than that, can you?' he said with a dejected expression.

'Tell me how you did it.'

'Oh, it was easy enough. I got another mate of mine to sit in with Troy, Bazza and Tunde and play the game while I slipped out. It only took me about fifteen minutes or so to walk to Chloe's house. I'd been there a couple of times before with Chloe and she told me that her mum always kept a key under the backdoor mat. So, I let myself in and crept up to her room and strangled her hamster. That bit was easier than I'd thought it would be. I was just holding it and it tried to get away so I tightened my grip. I was wearing a pair of my mum's rubber washing-up gloves so I wouldn't leave any prints and I suppose that I couldn't feel how tightly I was holding it. Anyway, I found that I'd killed it without meaning to. I panicked, put it back in its cage and ran. That was it really.'

'How did you know that Chloe's family would be out that night?' Mac asked.

'One of Chloe's friends said that they were all visiting family up North somewhere. She said that Chloe didn't want to go with them as it was her friend's birthday. So, what happens now?' he asked.

'Nothing unless Mrs. Alexander wants to press charges.'

'I hope she does. I was so stupid, I deserve to be punished,' Will said as he gave them both a bleak look. 'I loved her you know.'

He suddenly started crying and rocking back and forth in his chair.

'Will, listen,' Mac said. 'Listen!'

Will looked up at him.

'It wasn't your fault that Chloe died. She didn't die because you killed her hamster. You were just being young that's all. It looks to me like you've been punished enough. Punishing yourself even more won't bring Chloe back.'

Will nodded and Mac could only hope that his words had somehow sunk in.

His mother entered the room with a cup of tea. She put it down and went over to Will and hugged him.

'I'm sorry Mrs. Hecksmith but we've had to ask some difficult questions.'

'I just wish that I knew what to do with him and why he's so sad all the time,' she said with some desperation as she showed them to the door.

'Ask him after we leave. You might just find out,' Mac said.

Outside they both took a deep breath of air.

'That's a hell of a price for killing someone's hamster, isn't it?' Kate said. 'From what he said it looks like he didn't even mean for it to happen.'

'Yes, it is. Anyway, I think we can safely rule out Will but we'll need to go and check out his story with Mrs. Alexander anyway. Come on, let's go and get a coffee somewhere.'

The 'somewhere' turned out to be the Magnets. It had gone four and so Mac thought that having a chat around what they knew so far might be as beneficial as anything else.

'What time are you meeting Tim at?' Kate asked as she gave Mac a coffee.

'Around six. What time are you meeting Toni?'

'Same time,' Kate replied with a wide smile.

It was strange but even just hearing her name was somehow magical.

'So, are we any further ahead?' Kate asked.

'Definitely, we've ruled out David Sternberg and Will Hecksmith and that's something. I'll try and get hold of Mrs. Farzan tomorrow but I wouldn't hold your breath on that one. All we've got there is Becky Ferrante's gut feeling.'

'I wonder if Andy's doing any better?'

'He's determined to interview everyone that they talked to before so you never know. The best hope we've got is that someone's changed their mind over the last five years.'

Kate's phone rang. She looked at the screen and she looked puzzled. She spoke to whoever was on the other end and only said 'yes' finishing with 'We'll be right there.'

'I thought that might be my brother but it wasn't. It was the station. Someone's walked in and wants to talk to us about Chloe's murder. They tried Andy first and then tried me.'

'Who is it?' Mac asked.

'Alicia Hughes, Jackie Hughes' wife,' Kate replied.

Mrs. Hughes was waiting for them in the reception area when they got there. Kate found an interview room and they all seated themselves. Kate introduced Mac and herself.

'We were told that you had some information about the murder of Chloe Alexander. Is that right?' Mac asked.

'Yes, yes I think I might,' she replied nervously.

Mac looked at her closely. She was young, in her late twenties possibly, blonde and really pretty. She was dressed in a bright and expensive looking light summer dress. Mac thought that it was slightly incongruous considering the weather they'd been having.

'Do you mind if we record this conversation?' Mac asked.

226

She shrugged and he took that for a 'yes'.

Kate started the recorder and Mac introduced himself and Kate again for the record and asked Mrs. Hughes to do the same and also give her address.

'You've told us that you have some information regarding the murder of Chloe Alexander. Can you tell us what it is?' Mac said.

She looked up at the ceiling briefly and was obviously making a final decision on whether she should go ahead. Mac could only wait and hope. She started talking.

'It was just five years ago but it seems like a lifetime away now. It was one of the darkest times of my life for several reasons. Until Jackie had sustained his injury, we'd had a great life, lots of money and travel. Yes, it was great but Jackie's injury ended all that. I mean we still had the money, neither of us really spend that much, and with the insurance we probably had more than enough for a couple of lifetimes. No, it wasn't the money.'

She stopped and coughed nervously.

'I'm sorry, can I have some water please?' she asked.

'Sure,' Kate replied and left to get some.

Mac stopped the recording while she was gone. He and Mrs. Hughes just looked at each other. She definitely didn't strike him as being anything like the stereotype of the footballer's wife he'd often seen on TV. She spoke well and she was clearly an intelligent woman. Kate came back and Mrs. Hughes took a big gulp of water.

'Thanks,' she said.

Mac started the recorder again.

'You were saying that it wasn't the money,' Mac prompted.

'Yes, unfortunately for Jackie he loved the game and why not? After all, football had been his life for as long as he could remember. It was all he knew or wanted to know. I think that injury did more than just shatter his knee, it killed something inside him. Anyway, even though he should have felt lucky that he could still walk,

227

he could only think about his career being over and he took to the bottle in a big way. It really wasn't like Jackie. He'd never been a big drinker when he'd been playing. No, football always came first with him. Anyway, he was out getting drunk the night that Chloe Alexander was...,' she stopped and took another sip of water.

'Yes, we already know that he was in the Red Lion in Baldock. In your statement you said that you picked him up there at ten o'clock. Is that correct?' Mac asked.

'Yes, that's right but I never told you what happened after that,' she said nervously.

'So, what happened?'

'Well, Jackie and I had a bit of a fight when we got back home. I was getting a bit sick of his drinking and his self-pity and I told him so. We had a right shouting match.'

'Was Jackie ever violent?' Mac asked.

'No, never, not even when he was drunk. Anyway, that's what I've kept telling myself these five years. Then I saw that poor Mrs. Alexander on the TV and I knew I had to get it off my chest.'

'What?' Mac asked.

'After we got home that night Jackie went out again in the car. I told him not to go. He was so drunk that I was afraid he'd kill himself, or someone else, but he went anyway. I went to bed and I managed to sleep for a while. I woke up around four and Jackie still hadn't come home so I started to worry. I had a good idea of where he might be so I drove out in our other car and I found him there.'

'Where was he?'

'He was just a hundred yards or so from the school playing fields. He was in the car fast asleep and slumped over the steering wheel. I managed to move him into the passenger seat and then I drove him home. When we got back, I somehow got him awake enough to get him into bed. He slept for almost a day,' she said.

'Why was he at the playing fields?' Mac asked.

'It was where it had all started for him,' Mrs. Hughes replied. 'He didn't go to that particular school but he was in one of the local kid's teams that used the football fields at weekends. I'm afraid that after the injury he used to get drunk, get maudlin and then go there and feel sorry for himself. He did it quite a few times.'

'So, you're telling us that your husband was asleep in a car a hundred yards or so away from where Chloe's body was found?' Mac asked.

She shivered.

'Yes, that still gives me goosebumps thinking that Chloe was lying there on the field while I was trying to get my husband into the passenger seat. After I'd got him to bed, I took all his clothes off to put in the machine. They were covered in dirt, especially the knees of his trousers, so I guess that he'd made it to the football field after all. I checked the pockets as I always do. He always left something there for me to find, usually tissues, but this time he really surprised me.'

She stopped and sipped some more water.

'What was it?' Mac asked.

'It was a pair of women's panties.'

'What did you do with them?'

'I threw them in the bin of course. I thought he'd been with someone although, thinking about it later I couldn't see how. He was so drunk you see. Anyway, it wasn't until much later that I heard that Chloe Alexander's panties were missing and you can guess what I began to think. I just couldn't see Jackie doing anything like that though and so I dismissed any thoughts I had about Chloe's murder. The next Saturday he was doing a live interview on Match of the Day. He was really up for it and he promised to keep out of the pub and so I thought that he'd be okay. I thought that having Gary Lineker interview him might keep him sober for at least one night. It wasn't though and he disappeared on me again.

He eventually called me to come and get him from Welwyn train station. He said that he'd missed the last train home. He never told me what he'd been doing there, I asked him but I honestly think that he couldn't remember.'

'What time did you pick him up?' Mac asked.

'It was after twelve thirty.'

'But how did he get so drunk if he'd been doing a live interview at ten thirty?' Mac asked.

'I only found out later from a friend at the BBC that they did a test run with Jackie and he was awful. They had to do the interview several times and then edit it all together.'

'So, it wasn't live then?'

'Yes, that's right. The way they did it made it look like it was live but it was all done much earlier. Of course, as soon as the interview was over, he went straight to some pub or other.'

Mac was thoughtful for a while.

'So, let me get this straight. You're not only telling us that your husband might have killed Chloe Alexander but that he was also in Welwyn on the night that Ana Tomas was killed. Is that right?'

'Yes, but I still don't think it was him,' she said. 'Jackie's no murderer. I could never believe that.'

'So, if you think it wasn't him then why are you telling us this?'

'Because, if I'm honest, I'm not totally sure. After five years of thinking about it, I'm just not sure,' she said giving Mac a despairing look.

'Is there anything else you can tell us?' Mac asked.

She shrugged and then slowly shook her head.

'Okay, if you can bear with us, we'll need you to make a formal statement. Someone will be along in a few minutes to do that. Is that okay?' Mac asked.

'Yes, it'll be a relief to finally get it all off my chest.'

As soon as they left the interview room Mac tried to get Andy on the phone. He got nothing. He tried Tommy's number and had better luck.

'Where are you?' Mac asked.

'We're just on our way back to the station. Why has something happened?' Tommy asked.

'You could say that. I'll tell you both about it when you get here. Oh, and tell Andy that he can switch his phone back on now.'

Andy and Tommy both had a half puzzled, half expectant expression on their face when they burst into the team's room.

'What is it Mac?' Andy asked.

Mac told him what Alicia Hughes had said.

'Well, we were looking for a new lead and it certainly looks like we've got one now,' Andy said with a smile.

The smile dropped a notch when he saw Mac's expression.

'You don't think it's him, do you?'

'I'm not saying it's impossible but I must admit that I have my doubts,' Mac replied.

'Go on,' Andy said.

'Well usually, when we identify the correct suspect, it explains a lot of things that didn't make sense before. For me this just raises a lot more questions. Jackie and Chloe hadn't met before that night, had they?'

'No, they hadn't. Well, as far as we know.'

'And did Chloe speak to Jackie at all when they were in the pub together earlier in the evening?' Mac asked.

'I'll need to ask Chloe's friends again to make sure but no, not from what I remember.'

'The landlord called Jackie's wife to take him home so I take it that Jackie must have been genuinely drunk if he did that?'

'Yes, I remember that the landlord said that he'd started on the double whiskeys at around eight or so,' Andy said. 'He said that he must have had at least seven or eight in the two hours before he was picked up by his wife.'

'Okay, so his wife was probably right when she said that he was drunk. Tell me, you've spoken to Chloe's family and friends, was she really the type of girl who would go to a football field in the middle of the night with a stranger who was drunk even if he was a famous footballer?'

'I'd guess not. That bit puzzled us all, not only how Chloe got to the football field but what she was doing there in the first place,' Andy replied.

'So anyway, let's assume that Jackie magically sobered up a bit and managed to drive back to Baldock. There he picks up Chloe, without anyone noticing him which is unlikely in itself as he's so well known, and somehow convinces her to go to the football field with him. When he gets her there, perhaps he tries it on and she wasn't having any. So, they fight and Jackie ends up strangling her. So, drunk as he is, he takes her panties off and puts them in his pocket, takes the scarf too and then goes back to the car and falls asleep.'

'Yes, it all sounds a bit unlikely doesn't it?' Andy said.

'Not only that but what did he do with the scarf? Anyway, as unlikely as it all sounds, let's assume that it happened that way. Somehow Jackie hung onto the scarf, perhaps he hid it in the car boot or something. So, then he takes it with him to the Match of the Day studios the next Saturday. It was supposed to be a live interview late that evening so why would he take the scarf with him? Was he really going to talk to Gary Lineker and then go out later that Saturday night and find some random girl and strangle her? And why Ana Tomas? Jackie didn't have a car that night so he'd have had to walk for fifteen minutes or so from the train station to the hotel where Ana worked or take a taxi. If you're intending to kill someone taking a taxi there and back would seem a little unlikely. So, he walks there, waits for Ana and follows her as she walks home. He then either strangles her and then carries her dead body across a main road in his arms or somehow persuades her to come with him to the sports centre. From what I've been told that's something that Ana would never have done.'

'Perhaps Jackie had stayed at that hotel and knew Ana that way?' Andy suggested.

'Well, that's certainly something that we can check out. So anyway, after killing her he then goes back to the station and rings his wife to pick him up. He's also a good enough actor to convince her that he's blind drunk.'

'And, on the other hand, he might have never met Chloe Alexander at all and he just drove to the football field and then went back to his car and fell asleep. Then he might have gotten drunk again after the embarrassment of how badly the interview went, got off the train at Welwyn by mistake and then fell asleep on the bench,' Andy said.

'Well, that seems a bit more likely doesn't it?' Mac asked.

'Yes, it does. Nonetheless, unlikely as it is, we'll have to check it out anyway.'

'There is one way it could have happened though, only slightly more likely perhaps, but still,' Mac said.

'What's that?' Andy asked.

'It was an idea that Kate came up with. If Jackie did kill Chloe in some sort of drunken rage what if someone else killed Ana to give Jackie an alibi? Everyone assumed that because the same scarf was used in both murders that the same person must have been present at both murders but what if they weren't? What if there were two killers? In that case they needn't have known Ana at all. Any girl would have done and she might just have been unlucky that they picked her.'

'As you say unlikely but really interesting. It would certainly explain why Ana was strangled with Chloe's scarf, in fact that would have been the whole point of the exercise.'

Andy gave it some thought.

'Okay, I suggest that, as we've already interviewed him, Tommy and I'll go and speak to Jackie Hughes and follow up on that. We'll have to careful though, if any word of this gets out to the press then they'd have a field day. I'd hate to be the one who ruined his second career as a manager if he's innocent.'

'I can have a word with the manager of the hotel and ask her about Jackie Hughes, if you like,' Mac offered.

'Yes, please do and let me know what she says. I remember you saying that you had Sondra Mason's address, is that right?' Andy asked.

'Yes, I've got it on my phone.'

'Good, can you go and see her too? I know that she was in the pub before Chloe that night so she should know if there were any interactions between her and Jackie Hughes. It would also be interesting to see what Chloe's take on Jackie was. Was she impressed by him or thought he was good looking or whatever?' Andy said.

'We'll also need to speak to Mrs. Alexander tomorrow,' Mac said. 'We'll need her to confirm something that Will Hecksmith told us earlier.'

Mac told Andy and Tommy all about the murder of Chloe's hamster.

'He really killed Chloe's hamster then?' Andy said. 'He sounds as if he must have been a bit unhinged at the time.'

'Weren't we all a little bit unhinged when we were teenagers? Anyway, I think he's paid for his crimes such as they were,' Mac said.

'Okay then, we all know what we're doing tomorrow so let's call it a night then,' Andy said.

Mac looked at his watch. He was surprised to find that it wasn't too far off six o'clock.

'I'll walk you to the corner,' Mac said to Kate.

She nodded but didn't say anything. Mac thought she'd be all excited at seeing Toni again but she looked more nervous than anything else.

'Are you okay?' Mac asked as they neared the corner.

'I'm not sure. I've always found second dates a bit strange. I mean the other person has had some time to think and you know...' she trailed off.

'You think that Toni might have changed her mind?'

Kate shrugged.

'Well, there's only one way to find out, isn't there?' Mac said.

Kate kissed him on the cheek and gave him a brave smile before she said goodbye.

That evening Mac found himself wondering how Kate was getting on. That was until he and Tim saw that the Villa were actually a goal up in a crucial top six game. After that everything else that wasn't football related was forgotten.

Chapter Twenty Seven

Toni had to be up early that morning and so Kate got up with her. She wasn't going to miss having breakfast with Toni for anything. They walked to the station together and kissed before they parted. She stood in the team's room looking out of the window at the rain but this time it didn't make her sad. It was just rain. She smiled as she thought back to yesterday evening and how worried she'd been as she'd walked towards Toni's flat.

She'd had to wait outside again but she didn't mind. She felt as if she needed a little time to calm down anyway. For some reason negative thoughts were swirling around her mind almost convincing her that it would all go wrong. Then, as Toni walked towards her, one look at her face sent all Kate's doubts tumbling away. Her eyes were warm and her smile was radiant and Kate knew that it was all for her. As soon as Toni closed the door, they found themselves in each other's arms and once again a trail of clothes led to the bedroom.

They'd been happy to just lie in each other's arms and talk afterwards. Eventually Toni had asked Kate if she was hungry and she found that she was. Toni disappeared for a while and came back triumphantly with some fish finger sandwiches which they ate in bed accompanied by a glass of red wine. This had made Kate laugh out loud with delight.

Kate had loved fish finger sandwiches when she'd been young and eating them with Toni made her feel like a naughty schoolgirl again.

She'd woken up early anyway and once again found herself staring in rapture at Toni's face. She'd wondered if her feelings for Toni would be the same as they had been the previous night and she found that they weren't. They were even stronger and deeper. She knew that she was getting into something that she would never be able to get out of and she found that she didn't care.

Of course, there were practicalities. She'd need to go back to her flat at some point if only to get some clothes. She found that she didn't want to spend a single night away from Toni even though she'd only known her for a couple of days. She felt as if she'd known her for a lifetime.

Even so she decided that she should go back to her flat that night and give them both a chance to think things through. She mentioned this over breakfast and Toni agreed that it might be a good idea. Kate could see that she was disappointed though and that made her feel sad. However, she didn't know what else to do.

After all they'd only known each other for two days, she reminded herself. Perhaps they should slow things down a bit.

'Couldn't wait to get to work?'

She turned around to see Mac standing there.

'Well, Toni had to be up early so I got up with her.'

Mac looked closely at her. She looked happy enough but there was something in her look.

Was she having doubts? he thought. Oh well, he was sure that it would all work out.

'So, what's first?' Kate asked.

'Well, I've arranged to speak to Mrs. Alexander at eleven so we've got some time. Fancy a coffee?'

'Yes, why not?'

'Okay, the only problem is that it's in Welwyn.'

Mac told her on the way that he'd rang the hotel yesterday evening and he'd arranged to meet the manager before nine thirty as she started work then.

'There's a pub next to the hotel. She said she'd meet us there,' Mac explained.

'So, how come you just didn't ask her while you were on the phone?' Kate asked as they headed towards the motorway.

'I suppose that I could have but I prefer to talk face to face when I can,' Mac replied.

Kate smiled.

'That's so you can see whether they're lying or not,' Kate said with a smile.

'Well, not just that. There are other things you can pick up too besides which they do a very nice coffee there. The breakfast's not bad either,' Mac said with a smile.

'Ah, we get to the real motive at last,' Kate said trying to sound serious and not at all succeeding.

Kate watched Mac as he tucked into his Full English. As this was her second breakfast she'd settled for a Danish pastry and coffee. Mac had only just pushed his plate away when a very smartly dressed woman came towards them and sat beside her and opposite Mac. Kate guessed that she must be the hotel manager but she was much younger than Kate had been expecting.

'Kezzie, I'd like to introduce you to my colleague Detective Sergeant Kate Grimsson.'

She turned and shook Kate's hand.

'So, how can I help you, Mr. Maguire?' she asked.

'Well, I only have two questions really. The first one is, have you had any other thoughts since the last time we spoke?'

Kezzie thought for a while then frowned and shook her head.

'I'm sorry, I wish I had.'

'Okay the second question is, did Jackie Hughes ever stay at the hotel or did Ana ever mention meeting him?'

Kezzie's face screwed up in puzzlement.

'You're talking about Jackie Hughes, *the* Jackie Hughes, the famous footballer?'

'Yes, that's right.'

'No, he's never stayed at the hotel, not ever. I mean we'd have been talking about it for months afterwards if he had. Anyway, we're just a budget hotel and I'd guess

238

that Jackie Hughes would be more used to something a little more upmarket. I'm also pretty sure that, if Ana had ever met him, she'd have told us all about it too. Why are you asking? Is he a suspect?' Kezzie asked.

'No, no he's not,' Mac quickly said. 'We're only asking because he happened to be in one of the pubs that Chloe Alexander visited on the night she died. We have to check everyone out, even if they're famous. However, I'd appreciate it if you could keep this to yourself. It could be quite damaging if the press ever got hold of it,' Mac asked.

'Yes, of course. I can see how it might look. I promise that I'll keep it to myself,' Kezzie said.

'Thanks and don't forget that you've got my card just in case you do remember anything,' Mac said.

As they walked to the car Kate said to Mac, 'We're walking on a bit of a tightrope when it comes to Jackie Hughes, aren't we?'

'It's always been the same when it comes to celebrities. We have to ask the questions but it only takes one person to go to the press and, before you know it, they'll have Jackie hung, drawn and quartered on every front page in the country. However, I trust Kezzie to keep it to herself.'

'So, it's Mrs. Alexander's next?'

'Yes, I'll give her a call just to make sure that it's still on.'

It was still on, in fact Mrs. Alexander seemed to be more than anxious for the interview to go ahead. They pulled up outside a fairly modern detached house, not massive by any means, but Mac reckoned that you could at least swing a cat in it unlike some other new houses he'd been in. Mrs. Alexander was waiting for them at the door.

'Come in, Mr. Maguire. It's so nice to see you again,' she said as she held the door open.

Mac introduced Kate.

'Oh yes, I remember seeing you at Gerry's wedding,' she said with a smile as she led them into the living room.

'So, what do you need to know?' she asked as they sat down.

'On the night that Chloe died is it true that you were away?' Mac asked.

'Yes, it was a little trip up to Northampton to see my mother-in-law. That's where my husband John is from. There was no specific reason for the trip but she was getting on and my husband liked to keep an eye on her. We always stayed overnight at a hotel there and took the chance to catch up over a drink with John's brothers and some old friends of his. He had that Monday off work so it seemed like a good time to do it.'

'Did Chloe normally go with you when you went to see your mother-in-law?'

'Yes, but it was a friend's birthday and she'd promised she'd definitely go. That was before she knew about us going up to Northampton. Even though she'd promised, she nearly changed her mind anyway. If only,' she said as her face crumpled.

Mac caught a glimpse of the despair that Chloe's mother must have been experiencing for the last five years. She quickly regained control.

'Anyway, we were back here late the next morning. We arrived just as the police car did,' she said bleakly. 'John's mum died a month later too. I don't think that it was a coincidence either, Chloe had always been her favourite.'

She stopped speaking and Mac gave her a little time.

'I'm sorry but there's just a few things I need to check,' Mac said.

'Don't be sorry, I'll help in any way I can.'

'Is it true that you used to keep a key under the back mat?'

'Yes, a bit silly I know but Darren, Chloe's younger brother, was always locking himself out. Why?' she asked.

'When you got back that Sunday did you notice that Chloe's hamster had also died?' Mac asked hoping that his question didn't sound too strange.

'Her hamster?' Mrs. Alexander said looking puzzled.

She gave it some thought.

'Oh God yes, I remember now. I couldn't go into her room. It was John who told me that Harry was dead.'

'Harry was the hamster?' Mac asked.

'Yes, at the time we'd bought it for her she'd liked One Direction and she said that it looked a bit like Harry Styles. God, I'd completely forgotten all about that,' she said as her face crumpled again. 'I'm sorry.'

She disappeared into the kitchen and shut the door behind her. They both heard her crying. They could only sit there, look at each other and wait. She came back in a few minutes later, red-eyed and clutching a wad of kitchen towel.

'I'm sorry, I find that it's the little things nowadays that set me off. Anyway, why were you asking about Harry?'

'Do you remember a boy that Chloe went out with called Will Hecksmith?' Mac asked.

'Yes, I remember Will. A bit full of himself, I thought.'

'Well, he told us that, on the night that Chloe died, he broke in using the key you kept under the mat and killed Chloe's hamster.'

She sat there in stunned silence for a while.

'Why on earth would he do that?'

'Chloe had dumped him and he wanted to get some sort of revenge. In the end I think he killed the hamster more by accident than anything else.'

'I always thought that it was some sort of spiritual thing, the hamster dying like that at the same time as Chloe. Wrong again,' she said.

'I think Will did love Chloe in his way. He's been punishing himself for what he did ever since,' Mac said.

'Yes. Her dying has fucked us all up,' she said with a sudden savagery. 'I feel like I've been on autopilot for the last five years. I've been alive but I haven't been living, none of us have. I know that we buried Chloe but we still haven't had any closure. I need to know at least why Chloe died. Was it through hate or lust or just bad luck? I need to know, otherwise it's just as though we hadn't buried her at all.'

'We'll do our best,' Mac said.

She looked at Mac and managed a smile.

'I know you will. You did well to catch the man who killed Ruth Avaloe. God, I was so hopeful after that. Anyway, it must have been of some comfort to her father,' she said.

She had obviously never met the Reverend Pritchard Avaloe, Mac thought.

'We'll keep trying. We won't give up, I promise you that,' Mac said hoping that it would give her some comfort.

As they walked back towards the car Kate said, 'Well, it looks as if Will's story holds up.'

'Yes, it does.'

They sat in the car but Kate didn't start the engine. She looked over at Mac and gave him a doubtful look.

'Are you sure that you should have promised her that? You know, that we'd keep trying. We've probably only got another couple of weeks if we don't come up with something.'

'But that doesn't mean that I have to stop, does it?' Mac replied.

'So, you'd carry on by yourself then if we don't come up with anything?'

'Yes, if I have to. I'm afraid that this case has gotten under my skin. I don't think I could stop thinking about it now even if I wanted to.'

242

'Fair enough,' Kate said knowing just how he felt. 'So where to now?'

'To see Sondra Mason except that she's called Sondra Harrington now. She got married a couple of years ago. She works in a bank on the corner of Leys Avenue. She said to drop by anytime.'

The bank actually looked like it had originally been built as a bank with an ornate Georgian style carved stone lintel over the door and a façade of stone columns running down each side of the building. Inside it looked as if it had been recently decorated in an attempt to make it look modern but Mac thought it didn't quite succeed. It had a high ceiling and more than enough space to swing several cats at once.

Mac smiled. It reminded him of how banks used to look when he was young.

He approached a young woman who was sitting at a desk. She had a name badge pinned to her uniform which said 'Angela' so he knew he was safe in asking for Sondra. She went to the counter and Mac saw another young woman look over at him and nod. She walked out from the behind the counter and held the door open to a small room. This was obviously where they held private meetings with their customers.

Mac looked at Sondra closely as they seated themselves. She was in her mid-twenties, or perhaps a few years older, had long brown hair and wore glasses. She was dressed in a business-like trouser suit that was dark blue. However, she had an open face and a nice smile and Mac liked her instantly.

'Have you been to see Auntie Karen?' she asked.

'Yes, we've just come from there,' Mac said.

Sondra's smile was suddenly replaced with a look of concern.

'Was she okay?'

'Not really, I'm afraid that she got a bit upset at one point.'

'You'd think that after five years had gone by that the edges would have at least worn off a bit, wouldn't you?' Sondra said. 'It hasn't though, not for any of us. I'm sorry, what was it you wanted to ask?'

'I wanted to ask you about your last meeting with Chloe in the Red Lion. I believe that you were already in the pub when Chloe arrived?'

'Yes, I'd been out shopping with some of my friends that afternoon and we'd planned to end up at the pub for a few drinks before going home. I knew that Chloe was going to be in Baldock so I arranged to meet her there before she went to her friend's birthday party.'

'Did you see Chloe interact with anyone there?' Mac asked.

'You mean a man, I take it?' Sondra thought and then shook her head. 'No, she just talked to me and my friends. Then, when we left, she left with us and I walked with her to the pub that she was meeting her friends in. It was on the way for me anyway.'

'Did you see Jackie Hughes in the pub that evening?' Mac asked.

'Oh yes! I nearly forgot all about that. God, I was absolutely mad on him in those days. Oh, he was so gorgeous even though he'd obviously had a few.'

'Did Chloe go anywhere near him?'

'Chloe? No. She didn't like football,' Sondra said. 'I don't think she even knew who he was, if I'm honest. I've got two older brothers who are mad Arsenal fans so I'm afraid that I got sucked into the whole football thing but Chloe wasn't into sports at all.'

'Did you see anyone else talking to Jackie?' Mac asked.

'Well, yes lots really. I mean he was famous, wasn't he?' Sondra replied.

For some reason Mac thought that she seemed a little uncomfortable.

'Did you speak to Jackie Hughes yourself by any chance?' Mac persisted.

244

She looked up to the ceiling before answering.

'Well, I tried to but he was either too drunk or he was blanking me. I even tried to get his autograph but that didn't work out too well either.'

'Tell me.'

She looked quite ashamed and Mac was more than curious as to why.

'Well, before Chloe joined us, I told my friends that I was going to get him to autograph something for me, for a laugh really. As I said I'd been shopping so...' She paused for a moment and looked down at the table top. 'Well, I gave him a pair of panties I'd bought and asked him to sign them for me.'

'What did Jackie do?'

'I don't think he understood what I wanted him to do to be honest. He just gave me a strange look, stuffed the panties in his pocket and disappeared into the gent's toilet.'

Outside Mac stood for a moment thinking and looking at the traffic going by.

'So, now we know where Jackie Hughes got the panties from,' Kate said.

'Yes, it's not him. Then again I never thought it would be.'

Mac looked at his watch. It was nearly one o'clock.

'As we're just a few yards away from the Magnets fancy a bite to eat?' Mac asked.

Kate did.

Kate ordered some food and returned with two coffees.

'I've given Andy a call and told him the news,' Mac said.

'So, how did he take you more or less ruling out his one and only suspect?'

'He was okay. I don't think he thought that Jackie Hughes was ever really in the frame anyway,' Mac replied.

'So, where are we then? Have we made any progress?' Kate asked.

'Of course, we have. We've managed to rule out some suspects and that can only be good. We'll get there eventually, trust me,' Mac said.

If he was honest, he wasn't sure whether he was reassuring Kate or himself.

Chapter Twenty Eight

Having already had a big breakfast Mac settled for a tuna sandwich. Kate had the bagel with avocado.

'I take it that we'll be seeing Mrs. Farzan next?' Kate asked in between taking bites out of her bagel.

'Yes,' Mac replied dreamily.

He was looking out of the window at the people passing by and letting his thoughts wander. Kate said nothing and left him to think. A good five minutes went by before Mac said anything.

'Sorry,' he apologised. 'It used to drive my wife mad sometimes when I did that.'

'Have you thought of anything?' Kate asked.

'No, not really.'

He had thought of something but it was still unformed and shapeless. He needed to think a bit more before he'd say anything.

'Do you think that we should give Mrs. Farzan a call before we turn up on her doorstep?' Kate asked.

'I tried earlier on but she wasn't in.'

Or perhaps she might not want to see us for some reason, Mac thought.

'Why don't we just turn up on her doorstep and see what her reaction is?' he said.

That's just what they did but Mrs. Noor Farzan still wasn't in. Mac rang the bell several times just to make sure.

'Let's sit in the car and wait, shall we?' Mac suggested.

Mac went quiet. He looked over at the house. It was rendered white, as was usual for Letchworth cottages, but it was far from being a cottage. It was a detached house on Pixmore Way, not as big as some in Letchworth perhaps, but big enough. There was a large garage on the side of the house and enough space to park three or four cars in front. There were no cars parked outside so

Mac guessed that either Mrs. Farzan was out or it was in the garage. He guessed that she was out, hardly anyone seemed to use their garages these days to actually park cars in.

He let his thoughts run free again and even he was unsure of where they were leading him. He was still thinking when a large black BMW pulled into the parking space and a woman got out and let herself into the house.

'Let's give her a minute,' Mac said.

They gave her three and then they made their way over to the front door. Mac rang the bell again.

A woman in her fifties answered. She was well-dressed, slim and quite elegant. From her long jet-black hair, her complexion and the oval shape of her face Mac guessed that she, or her family, were not originally from England.

Mac showed her his warrant card and watched her closely. She went pale for a few seconds and then quickly collected herself. Mac was curious again.

'Can we come in?' Mac asked.

'Yes, yes of course,' she said although her body language was saying something quite different.

She led them into a very elegant living room that didn't appear to have been much used.

'Do you live by yourself these days?' Mac asked as he sat down on a comfortable looking sofa.

'Yes, unfortunately I do. Both my husband and son are in Iran at the moment,' she said in a flawless upper-class accent.

'Are you originally from Iran?' Mac asked.

'Yes, my family came over here in 1979. They were fleeing the Islamic Revolution. I was only eleven or twelve at the time so I don't remember all that much about it if I'm honest.'

Mac wondered if this was the reason why she was still in England and living alone.

'I take it that you still can't go back to Iran?'

'That's right, they've made it quite clear to all my family that we wouldn't be welcome there. Anyway, England is my home now. I've been living here almost forty years and I have no wish to go back to Iran. I take it that you're asking these questions because of Chloe Alexander?'

'Yes, I believe that your son Aaron was a friend of hers at one time. Is that correct?' Mac asked.

'Yes, he knew her when they were at school together and I think they were quite close for a time. However, they ended up going to different colleges and they didn't keep in touch. I suppose they both made new friends and forgot about each other.'

'How did Aaron take it when he heard that Chloe had been killed?'

Mac watched her really closely once again. She was going to say something but she hesitated. Mac knew that she was being very careful with what she said.

'He was upset, very upset actually,' she said looking straight at them. She lowered her gaze as she continued, 'Although he hadn't seen her for ages, I think he still thought of her as…well, as a friend.'

Mac felt excited. He knew that he was on the scent of something.

'Where was Aaron on the night that Chloe was killed?'

'He was home, he was with me all evening,' she said nervously.

'Where was he the weekend after that?'

'Oh, when the other girl got killed you mean? He was visiting his father in Iran. I think that he needed to get away for a while.'

Mac felt that she was telling the truth when she said this.

'Can I ask you why you're so interested in Aaron after all this time?' she asked anxiously.

249

'We're not really. As it's the fifth anniversary of Chloe's murder we're just ensuring that the original investigation didn't miss anything. We're talking to everyone who knew her,' Mac replied.

His eye caught something. He stood up and winced. The wince was for real as a sharp pain ran down his left leg. The pain was short lived but it gave him an idea.

'I'm sorry but I suffer with back pain. I can't always sit down for long without needing to get up again.'

Mrs. Farzan gave him a pitying smile.

'Of course,' she said.

'So, had the visit to Iran been arranged for a long time?' Mac asked as he prowled around the room.

'No, not too long. A couple of weeks, I think.'

'Can you tell me why your husband went back to Iran? I take it that you're still married?'

'Yes, we're still married,' she replied. 'He's a professor at the University in Tehran, Urban Planning. I think that's why he wanted to live here when he came to England. He thought that Letchworth and the whole Garden City movement was wonderful.'

Mac had moved to the back of the room where a table was covered with framed photos. He looked at them intently. There was one with Mrs. Farzan, a tall dark-skinned man and a young boy.

'Is this your husband?' Mac asked holding up the framed photo.

'Yes, that's him with Aaron when he was about seven, I think,' she replied.

Mac continued looking at the photos. Then one caught his eye even though it was right at the back. He looked closely at it and smiled. He then held his back and let out a sharp yell.

'Mac, are you okay?' Kate asked clearly concerned.

His face was twisted with pain. Kate went over to him.

'Please don't let her see me like this,' he whispered between gritted teeth. 'Get her out of the room for at least two or three minutes. Tell her that I need a glass of water or something.'

Kate did as she was told. She explained what the problem was to Mrs. Farzan. After four minutes had gone by Kate went back and peeked into the room. Mac was still holding his back. He had his phone in his hand and she saw him quickly put it back in his pocket. He took the water she'd brought and drank it down.

'Let's go,' he said as he started hobbling towards the door.

'I hope you get better soon,' Mrs. Farzan said after she'd shown them to the front door.

Mac hobbled slowly to the car and winced again as he bent down to get in. Kate gave him a concerned look and drove off.

'Shall I take you to the hospital?' she asked as they neared the end of the road.

'Oh, that won't be necessary,' Mac replied brightly.

She glanced over at him. He pained expression had gone and a smile had replaced it.

'Well, you got over that very quickly!' she exclaimed.

'I was never in pain in the first place. Well, I was in pain but I mean that it wasn't anything abnormal.'

'So, what was all that performance about then?'

'I had to get Mrs. Farzan out of the room,' Mac replied. 'I'll tell you why when we get back to the station. I need Martin to check something out for me first.'

Mac and Kate looked on and waited breathlessly while Martin went about his business. It only took him a few minutes to confirm Mac's suspicions.

'I think that we'd better call Andy now,' he said.

Andy and Tommy were back at the station in less than fifteen minutes. Mac showed them what he'd found and told them about his suspicions.

'Wow, I never really thought about that,' Andy said. 'This is going to be difficult, isn't it?'

'Yes,' Mac replied. 'We need a plan.'

251

It took them over an hour before they came up with something that they thought might work. Although it was Tommy who came up with the original idea, it was Andy who put the finishing touches.

'So, what do you think Mac?' Andy asked after he'd gone through it all once again.

'I like it. I think it could work but you'll need to make that phone call first.'

Andy did. They all watched him while he did so. They knew it was on when he gave them the thumbs up sign.

The old familiar excitement coursed through Mac's veins. At last they were on their way!

A little later Kate slipped out into the office next door. It was empty. She picked up the phone and made a call.

Becky Ferrante was getting a bit stuck with the rewrite of the book and wished that she had something else to do. She was quite glad when the phone rang and interrupted her. She was surprised when she realised that it was the red-headed policewoman on the other end. She was even more surprised at what she told her.

'Becky, do you remember asking about an exclusive interview when we last saw you?'

She did and immediately wondered where this was leading.

'Well, I can give you something better than that. After receiving some new evidence, the police will be arresting Jackie Hughes at the Peterborough football ground first thing tomorrow morning. They'll be charging him with the murder of Chloe Alexander and Ana Tomas,' Kate said.

'What? Is this for real?' Becky almost shouted.

'Yes, it's for real,' Kate said with conviction.

'Why are you telling me this?' Becky asked.

Kate knew this was the vital question.

'Because he's famous and rich and he'll get off with it if we're not careful. They're all trying to keep it very quiet here but I don't want it be kept quiet. He's guilty and I want all the world to know.'

'Again, I'll ask why?'

Becky still wasn't convinced. Kate had to improvise.

'Look, I can't tell you but it's something personal, something that happened to me,' Kate said not being exactly sure what the mythical 'something' might be.

'Let me guess then. I'd bet that someone famous once raped you, or tried to, and got away with it. Is that right?'

Kate's silence seemed to confirm this.

'Okay, we don't need to go into detail about that but tell me everything that you can about Jackie Hughes.'

She'd bit!

The story was all over the papers and the news early that evening.

'Well, I suppose we might as well go and arrest Jackie now as it's in all the papers. I wonder how that got out so quickly?' Andy said with a rueful shake of his head.

Andy and Mac turned up at the football ground and had to drive past a baying and ever-growing pack of the press. Several TV cameras had already been set up. Andy was also accompanied by Dan and Adil and several uniforms. It was Adil who was seen manhandling Jackie into a police car. Not long after they got him to the police station, they videoed him taking a DNA sample. This was sent to the forensics lab marked 'Urgent'.

Andy held a press conference that evening. Despite all the questions that were thrown at him he refused to give any details. All he said was that they had some new evidence and that they were only waiting for confirmation from the DNA test results before laying any charges. Everything depended on the DNA tests he stressed more than once.

The whole team met at the station and once again they were waiting for a phone call that would make or break the investigation. Andy was nervously pacing up and down.

'Are you sure that they said that Veronica Allsop herself would be doing the tests?'

'Yes,' Dan said. 'She told me so herself and she should know as she runs the lab these days. She's supposed to be their best DNA profiler too or so I've heard.'

'I don't know, it's such a long shot, isn't it?' Andy said.

'It might be but I still think that it's got a good chance. Let's just wait and see,' Dan said trying to sound calm but not feeling it.

They waited.

Three hours later they finally got the initial results via email. Andy read it anxiously.

'Yes,' he exclaimed as his fist pumped the air. 'She's saying that they've got positive results. Traces of the same DNA were found at both Chloe's and Ana's crime scenes. She's saying that Jackie Hughes is guilty!'

Dan smiled, 'Come on then. What are we waiting for? We've got a lot to get organised before we can make the arrest.'

Chapter Twenty Nine

The lab stood behind a sturdy looking steel barred gate that was situated just off the Broadwater Road in Welwyn. Most of the street was lined with industrial units and Foursight Forensics PLC seemed to have one of the bigger and more modern ones. They'd waited until nine thirty the next morning. They wanted to ensure that everyone who worked there would be on site.

A marked police car pulled up at the gate. Inside were Dan, Andy, Mac and Adil.

'Hello?' a tinny voice asked.

Dan pushed the button on the intercom.

'Hi, it's Detective Superintendant Dan Carter. I've come to pick up a DNA report. It's urgent.'

'Can you show me your warrant card please?' the voice politely asked.

Dan held his card close to the camera. The gate swung open. Dan drove inside and was tailgated in by three large police vans. They all pulled up outside the main entrance. It was a white two-storied building that looked like a warehouse, it also looked quite extensive. They'd learnt that over forty people usually worked there.

Dan walked straight into the reception area. A young woman looked at them in astonishment from behind a counter.

'I didn't think there'd be quite so many of you,' she said with surprise as she looked at the lines of uniformed police getting out of the vans outside.

'Move back and away from your desk, please,' Dan ordered.

She looked at him as though he'd just spoken in a foreign language.

Dan leant over the counter and said, 'Now!'

She did as she was told.

'Where's Mrs. Allsop's office?' Dan asked.

'Up the stairs on the right,' she replied.

'Thanks, someone will now take you outside. You will not be allowed to take any phones or any other personal possessions.'

Dan nodded to one of the uniformed officers who led the young woman outside.

Some of the police went into the downstairs areas. They'd been told exactly what to do. They were to get everyone out immediately and they were to ensure that no-one touched their computers or even their mobile phones. All personal possessions were to stay inside the building. Dan, Andy, Mac and Adil all headed upstairs. Tommy and Kate weren't too far behind and they were followed up by a squad of uniformed policemen. The office was easy to find. It had a sign outside 'Veronica Allsop–Managing Director'. It was mostly glass and they could see that the woman inside was looking at them in some surprise as they all walked into the office. She looked through the glass at the squad of policemen fanning out across the working area outside with something like horror.

Dan showed her his warrant card.

'Move away from your desk please and turn and face the wall,' he said sternly.

'What?' she said.

She looked totally stunned.

Dan was getting slightly annoyed now so he repeated what he'd said but even louder this time. She seemed to finally understand what she had to do.

Mac watched her closely. She was in her mid-forties perhaps but looked older. Everything she wore seemed to be a shade of grey. She had her hair cut short and wore large black rimmed glasses. He guessed that she was the type of woman who usually gave the orders and that was probably part of the reason why she was having problems taking it all in.

'Kate, can you search her?' Dan asked.

256

Kate went over and told Mrs. Allsop to put her hands up against the wall. She frisked her thoroughly and placed a phone on the desk. She then went through a handbag that was on the floor underneath the desk and produced another phone.

'Can I ask what this all about?' Mrs. Allsop asked nervously.

'No, you may not,' Dan replied brusquely. 'Cuff her and take her away.'

Two uniformed officers did just that. She looked back at them as they escorted her off the premises. All Mac could see was disbelief in her face.

Dan's phone went off.

He said, 'That's great,' and then rang off. 'That was Chris and Leigh. They're bringing in Mrs. Farzan too.'

A young man wandered in. He had a vague smile on his face, spiked up hair and he was clutching a backpack. He looked around the office with some interest.

'Ah Martin, you're here. It's all yours now. I just hope that you can come up with something,' Dan said.

'I've got someone coming over in an hour or so from the Met to help me out. Between the two of us we should be able to find what there is to find,' he replied confidently.

'Good, I'll let you get on with it then. Adil, Kate and Tommy can you keep an eye on what's happening here? Make sure that we get the personal details of everyone working on site. At some point we'll have to interview them all. Andy and Mac, come with me and let's see what Mrs. Allsop and Mrs. Farzan can tell us.'

Having met Mrs. Noor Farzan, Mac reckoned that she wouldn't put up too much of a fight. However, he reckoned that Veronica Allsop, once she'd regained her composure, might prove to be a bit more of a challenge.

In that he was right. Noor Farzan caved in after half an hour and her story confirmed all their suspicions. Knowing the full story should make the interview with

Mrs. Allsop a little easier. Dan and Adil went down to the cells to see her.

'She wants a lawyer,' Dan said when he returned. 'Oh well, it's an ill wind and all that. I'm starving, anyone fancy a sandwich?'

Mac did, in fact he was ravenous. Raids always had that effect on him. They were notified that Mrs. Allsop's lawyer had arrived an hour and a half later by which time they'd had a conversation about how they should approach the interview. It was agreed that Dan and Andy would lead. Mac would sit behind them and pass them a note if any ideas came to him.

Veronica Allsop was already in the interview room flanked by a middle-aged man in a black suit. He had a long mournful face and, if he'd been asked, Mac would have guessed that he was an undertaker. When he introduced himself as Edward Himbury, Mrs. Allsop's personal lawyer, Mac was certain that he'd missed his true vocation.

Dan started the tape up and made the introductions. Mrs. Allsop looked affronted at having to give her address.

'I just can't believe it,' she said with some anger. 'How dare you come into my place of work and drag me and all my staff out like that. What on earth is going on?'

Dan sat and looked at her without saying anything. Mac always thought that Dan had a good stare.

'I demand to know...' she said but stopped as Dan leant forward and glared at her.

'We know everything,' Dan said giving some stress the last word.

She now looked more nervous than angry.

'We've spoken to your friend Noor Farzan and it didn't take her long before she realised that telling the truth was the only way out. We know everything.'

Veronica Allsop went pale and sat back in her chair.

'We also set a little trap for you, I'm afraid. Take a look at this,' Dan said.

He started up a video up on his phone. It showed Jackie Hughes. He had a DNA swab in his hand and he was laughing. A disembodied voice was telling him what to do. He took the cover from the swab and rubbed it on the inside of Tommy's cheeks and then sealed it. The video zoomed in on the label. It said 'Jackie Hughes'.

'It wasn't his DNA!' she said in wonder. 'You tricked me.'

'Yes, we did. The DNA that you were so sure was present at both Chloe's and Ana's murders actually belonged to a young detective. We chose him because we could prove that he was some fifteen hundred miles away sunning himself on a beach in Southern Spain when the murders took place. We guessed that using some- one famous like Jackie might convince you that it was for real. After all someone like him would be unlikely to gamble with his reputation in such a way, would he? Luckily for us, he was willing to go along with it. We knew for certain that you were cooking the evidence when we got your report. It wasn't the first time either, was it?'

Mac could see that she was making a concerted effort to pull herself together.

'It was just a mistake that's all,' she said.

'It was definitely a mistake alright. Tell me, had you ever rigged any evidence before the night that Aaron came home and told you and Mrs. Farzan that he'd murdered Chloe?'

She remained tight lipped.

'Here, I'll play you something,' Dan said as he turned to Andy.

Andy put a tape in the recorder and played it back. It was the voice of Noor Farzan.

I could see when he came home that night that he was upset, I'd never seen him like that before. He'd been going

259

through a bad time, depression and so on, and he was taking all sorts of medication but now he was crying and banging his head off the wall. I was scared and I didn't know what to do so I called Veronica. She came straight over.'

'That's Veronica Allsopp who works at the forensics lab?' Andy asked.

'Yes, that's right.'

'And why would she do that?' Andy asked.

'Because she's his mother. I mean I'm his mother, I brought him up, but Veronica is his biological mother. My husband had an affair with her when she was a student. She became pregnant but she didn't want the child so my husband came to an arrangement with her...'

'Was that a financial arrangement?' Andy asked.

'Yes, she was at university and in debt, so my husband paid it all off for her. We were desperate for a child and so it seemed a good solution at the time. When Aaron was young, she didn't see that much of him, my husband didn't think it would be a good idea. Still, I felt sorry for her and I used to let her see him from time to time. I think she deeply regretted giving him up. She married but her husband didn't want children so Aaron was all she had. When my husband went back to Iran, she saw a lot more of Aaron and I could see that she'd become quite attached to him.'

'So, Veronica came over. What happened then?'

'She managed to convince Aaron that it was all just some sort of bad dream and she got him to take some medication that would help him sleep. At the time I thought that she was probably right, I mean Aaron is such a gentle soul that I just couldn't believe that he'd be capable of killing anyone. Then I heard about Chloe on the news the next day and I knew that he'd been right after all. He'd killed her. He said that he hadn't meant too but I knew that he'd done it.'

'So, what did you do the next day?' Andy asked.

'I didn't need to call Veronica. She came over as soon a she heard the news. She told Aaron that it would be okay and that she'd protect him. She'd make sure that any evidence that pointed towards him would disappear.'

Andy stopped the tape.

'She told us a lot more than that but I think you get the idea,' Dan said.

'You may think you're clever but I've deleted everything. You won't be able to prove anything as there aren't any records any more,' she said defiantly.

Dan smiled at this. This seemed to disconcert her more than anything.

'There's a young man who works for me. You'd never guess he's a policeman if you looked at him but he knows his stuff. He's a computer forensics specialist, you know what that is, don't you?' Dan asked.

She nodded and went a shade paler.

'They kind of do what you do except their crime scene is the inside of a computer. I had a word with him just before I came in here to interview you and he was in quite a good mood.' Dan paused and looked at her. 'Not going to ask me why?'

She said nothing.

'Okay, well I'll tell you then. I guess that you're aware that your lab has a back-up computer system? I mean it must be very important that everything is properly backed up when it comes to the sort of crucial evidence that your lab processes, don't you think?' Dan said.

Mac could see that she knew what was coming. Her shoulders slumped and her face actually turned grey.

'Well, you may have deleted or changed lots of things on the computer system but the way this particular back-up system works is that it just backs everything up, all the time. My specialist says that even quite powerful servers eventually get filled up and have to have data culled from it. However, luckily for us, the specification for your back up server is absolutely top notch and it's still got a bit of space left. That means that nothing has been culled yet and so every original record will be in there somewhere plus every single change that you made to the evidence. It's perfect really and you've made him a very happy man. It'll be a lot of work of course sorting through the data but then again he likes work.'

Dan gave her a smile. She looked like she was going to throw up.

'Now, I'd like some answers from you,' Dan said. 'Did you kill Ana Tomas?'

She didn't respond. Mac could see the answer in her face though.

Dan turned around, 'Mac do you want to tell her how she did it?'

'Sure,' Mac said. 'You met Ana when you turned up after the robbery at the hotel she worked at. I've asked the forensics team and they said that your lab helps them out from time to time if they have people off sick or if they've got too much work on. You were helping out that night. You were the lady that made Ana laugh when you took her fingerprints. I reckon that you'd seen her before as you had to drive past the hotel on your way home from the lab. When you needed another murder to conveniently happen while Aaron was in Iran you thought of her, didn't you? She'd met you before and she'd trust you, after all she probably thought that you were a policewoman. I'd bet that you borrowed one of the big forensic vans with the police markings that night too. That would convince her even more.

So, you pulled up alongside her that night as she walked home. I bet you said that you'd called by the hotel and just missed her. So, what was the excuse, another DNA test perhaps? I'd bet that you told her it was urgent and that the whole case might hang on it or something along those lines. You got her to sit in the front seat of the van while you opened the side door and got in behind her. Did you tell her that you were just getting a DNA kit?'

She didn't answer, she just sat there and stared at Mac as if he'd just grown a second head or something. Mac felt that what he'd said so far must have been fairly close to the truth.

'Anyway, what you really got was the scarf that Aaron had used to kill Chloe. You quickly looped it around her neck and then pulled on it with all your bodyweight. Ana would have been taken completely by surprise and there would have been nothing that she could have done to stop it. It would have only taken a few minutes to strangle her. Then you took her panties off and drove over to the football pitch. She was quite light and would have been easy enough to carry. It wouldn't have taken long to arrange her body to make it look identical to Chloe's. Then you drove off. However, you were upset or excited or both perhaps and you nearly hit a car when you went back onto the main road, didn't you?'

'How on earth…?' she said before quickly shutting up.

'They questioned a lot of people who were out and about that night and one man said that he was driving down that road at around the time of Ana's murder,' Mac continued. 'He said that a van had come out of the Police Headquarters and nearly hit him. He'd gotten it wrong though, hadn't he? You were coming out of the sports centre not the police headquarters which is the next entrance along. I dare say that he just assumed it was the police headquarters because it was clearly a police van.'

'You can't prove anything,' she eventually said.

'You may well be right when it comes to Ana's murder,' Dan said, 'but we can prove that you were an accessory to Chloe Alexander's murder and we'll be throwing in a charge of perverting the course of justice too. I'm sure that we could come up with quite a few

263

more once all the evidence is in. Meanwhile, you'll be held in custody until a hearing is arranged.'

Dan stood up and turned to face Mr. Himbury.

'If I were you, I wouldn't bother asking for bail.'

Dan looked quite delighted as he walked back towards the team room.

'It's a shame that we can't get her for Ana Tomas but I reckon that we'll get enough against her to send her down for at least fifteen years or so.'

'The only problem is that everyone who's had evidence against them that's been processed by the lab will be busy right now arranging for new appeals,' Andy said.

'Yes, we can only hope that Martin can identify all the evidence that's been doctored with some precision otherwise there'll be a lot of convicted criminals getting released early,' Mac said.

'We've come to rely on DNA evidence so much that we forget that it might be fallible as human beings are still involved in the process,' Dan said. 'She fooled us for five years and, if it hadn't been for you noticing that photo Mac, she might be fooling us still.'

'We got lucky,' Mac said.

'Lucky, we have you, you mean. In the end it's usually the little details that matter the most,' Dan said. 'And Andy, please thank Tommy for me. His suggestion of using his DNA was a good one and your idea of pretending that it was Jackie Hughes' DNA was absolutely brilliant. Having met her now, I'm not sure that she'd have bitten otherwise. We really should thank him in some way. Now, I know that we've all got a lot to do but if you're in the vicinity of the Magnets at around seven o'clock this evening then I'm buying.'

This was a date that Mac had every intention of keeping.

Chapter Thirty

Dan said that for consistency Andy should do the last press conference as he'd taken all the others. Mac thought that this was very generous of him as it was going to be one of the biggest that they had ever done. So, once again they drove to Stevenage and, once again, they were met by Zehra who had a look at their script and tidied it up for them.

'You're getting the hang of this now,' she said to Andy with a smile as she handed him a neatly typed copy. 'I haven't had to make many changes this time. I don't want to worry you but this is probably going to be the largest press conference that we've ever held. I've even had to get some policemen in to act as bouncers, can you believe that?'

Mac looked over at Andy. Thankfully, he thought that he looked more excited than worried. They all turned as they heard a noisy hubbub from outside.

'That'll be your special guest arriving. I'll go and rescue him,' Zehra said.

They all waited at the side of the stage for Zehra to return. She was looking at her watch as she walked towards them.

'He's in the toilet,' she said. 'I told him to wait by the side of the stage until we call him. Okay, are we all ready?'

Everyone nodded.

'Let's go then,' Zehra said.

The room was quite noisy as she walked out onto the stage but it quickly fell silent. No-one wanted to miss a word of what was going to be said.

'Thank you all for turning up this morning. There's quite a few more of you than we were expecting. Okay, the format today will consist of a short statement by DI Andy Reid after which you can ask some questions. As there is such obvious interest in this case, we've allowed a whole half an hour for questions. You should all have a good chance of getting your question in so please be patient.'

Zehra turned towards Andy and nodded. Tommy and Kate took the two seats furthest away then Andy took his seat and Mac was glad to be able to sit on the nearest one. He took it very carefully. There were cables all over the place and he didn't want to trip up in front of the TV cameras.

Andy looked out at the crowd but, as before, with so many lights it was hard to see who was out there.

It was probably just as well, he thought, as he readied himself.

Zehra gave him the nod and he began.

'Thank you all for coming today. As you're aware we've been looking into the murders of Chloe Alexander, Ana Tomas and Ruth Avaloe. As you're also aware, we've already arrested and charged a man in connection with the death of Ruth Avaloe. I'm now announcing that we have arrested two people in connection with the murder of Chloe Alexander. We have also issued an international arrest warrant in the name of Aaron Farzan for the murder of Chloe Alexander.'

Andy paused as lots of camera flashes went off.

'We believe that Aaron Farzan in currently residing in Iran, a country with which we have no agreed extradition arrangements. We will apply for his extradition but, of course, that does not mean that we will necessarily succeed. However, we are holding his mother, Noor Farzan, and a woman called Veronica Allsop who we now know to be his biological mother. We've had this confirmed by DNA tests.'

Mac noticed a little smile on Andy's face as he said this. He thought it was quite ironic too.

'We've charged Noor Farzan and Veronica Allsop with being accessories to murder and with perverting the course of justice. I'm sure that you are all aware that, until yesterday, Veronica Allsop managed the Foursight Forensics laboratory which carries out all forensic testing, including all the DNA testing, for the police services of Hertfordshire, Bedfordshire and Cambridge as well as others.'

Andy let this sink in for a moment. Even though the room was crowded it was totally silent.

'I'm sure that most of you have turned up here expecting us to announce that we were charging Jackie Hughes with something. However, Jackie was never a serious suspect in any of the cases that we were invest- igating. I want to repeat that, Jackie was never a serious suspect. I know that wasn't exactly what some of you have printed in your papers, indeed some of you had pronounced him guilty even before you knew what the evidence was. However, I'm not really complaining as it was DS Kate Grimsson here who leaked the story to a local journalist on my orders. I'm afraid that I can't go into all the details at the moment but the full story will come out at the trial.'

Andy glanced to the side and he could see Jackie Hughes waiting anxiously by the side of the stage.

'We talk about sporting heroes when all they've done is excelled at something they've chosen to do and, in most cases, something that they love doing. I'll admit that, like a lot of hopeful English supporters, Jackie Hughes was a hero of mine too. However, he's now proved himself to be a real hero in my eyes. When we explained what we needed and how his name would be dragged through the mud, he didn't hesitate. He's here this morning, Jackie Hughes.'

Jackie walked on the stage shielding his eyes from the flashlights that were going off all over the room. They hadn't planned it that way but Andy stood up and started applauding him. Mac, Kate and Tommy stood up and joined in. Mac was surprised to see that quite a lot of the press did so too. Jackie looked quite embarrassed as he sat down next to Andy.

'On behalf of all of the police forces of Hertfordshire, Bedfordshire and Cambridgeshire, I'd like to formally thank Jackie Hughes for his help with this case. So, there is one murder for which we've still not charged anyone and that is the murder of Ana Tomas. We'll keep looking for further evidence but it is unlikely that charges will be lodged at this time.'

Andy put down his script and looked out at the assembled journalists.

'We started this investigation with little hope of success. I was part of the original investigation that had consumed countless manhours and had gotten nowhere. The fact that a period of time had elapsed was certainly useful but I would mostly put our success down to the team that you see before you. Without their efforts all three of the Match of the Day murders might have gone unsolved. I'd like to thank all of them too. Okay, any questions?'

Zehra stood up and tried to impose some control as a barrage of questions was shouted out at them. Almost all of them seemed to be aimed at Jackie Hughes. Zehra ensured that the questions were reasonable and something that Jackie could answer. He'd been schooled on what he could say and what he couldn't so as not to prejudice any trial. He answered the questions simply and in good grace.

Mac thought back to the day or so he'd spent in the station when he'd been 'under arrest'. They'd all had quite a good time as Jackie was a good storyteller and he certainly had a lot of stories to tell. They all said that he should really try for some TV work again. Mac noticed a movement to his right and turned.

Alicia Hughes was standing there looking straight at her husband. She was smiling affectionately at him. It looked as if they'd gotten back together again and he wished them both all the luck in the world.

Mac then heard one of the reporters ask the very question that he'd have asked himself.

'Jackie, you took quite a risk there in helping the police but exactly why did you do it?'

Jackie took some time to think.

'Guilt,' he said. 'I knew that Chloe looked familiar when I saw her picture in the papers but it was only later that I realised that she'd been in the pub that I was trying to drink dry that night. I was also at the football field that Chloe was found dead in later on that night but I was so drunk that I couldn't remember anything. I might have actually seen the person who murdered Chloe or his car but I couldn't remember anything and that was all my fault. When the police called and asked me to help them, I jumped at the chance. I'd had enough of waking up in the night and wondering if I could have saved the lives of Ana Tomas and Ruth Avaloe if I hadn't been so selfish.'

Mac thought that it was a good answer. He was happy to sit there and listen to the to and fro of the questions but, towards the end, there was a question that was addressed directly to him. It was Bob Taunton again.

'Mr. Maguire, I know that you can't comment on the specifics of these cases but could you comment on the current state of the police forensics services? I've been hearing a lot lately about them cutting corners and basically providing a shoddy service. In fact, there was the recent case where over ten thousand cases had to be reviewed and we're also hearing of cases of bribery and duress involving forensics lab staff. I've been around a while and this was something that I never heard of in years gone by. I'm hoping that I might get an honest comment from you as you've now retired from the police.'

Mac turned and looked at Andy. He nodded at Mac.

269

He was going to give an honest comment alright.

'When all the forensic services were under our control we had some problems, I'll admit that, but, compared to the scale of the problems that we face nowadays, they were nothing. I remember when the government first started talking about cost-cutting and I was really surprised when they came up with the idea of privatising the forensics services. There were other areas where we might have saved more money with less impact but even with those the cost cutting exercises have now gone way too far. As a society if we want protection and we want justice it comes at a certain cost. Justice on the cheap will not guarantee justice for all and if it's not justice for all then it's not justice. It's not the politicians or the accountants in the Treasury who will have to pay the price. It's ordinary people like you who will pay with years of their lives, locked away because of faulty or manipulated evidence. I feel strongly that we need to bring the forensics services back under police control again. It will be slightly more expensive and it won't be perfect but it will be a vast improvement on the system as it now stands. The government seems to know the price of everything but the value of nothing. If justice for everyone isn't worth spending a little more on then I don't know what is.'

Mac was glad that Bob had asked the question. He felt that it need saying. He looked to his left and Andy was smiling. He gave Mac the thumbs up.

'Well, I don't think that could have gone any better,' Zehra said just after they'd walked off stage. 'Jackie, you were very good out there. Tell me have you thought of doing any TV work? I know someone who might be very interested.'

They left Jackie and Zehra talking and headed off down the corridor. They turned when they heard the sound of steps behind them. It was Alicia Hughes.

'I couldn't let you go without saying thanks. You know, for these past five years I've had this cloud hanging over me. One minute I'd be suspecting Jackie of murder and the next hating myself for thinking that it was even possible. Poor Jackie had no idea and I felt that I couldn't tell anyone. I know now that he felt guilty too. Allowing him to help you has helped him too. And me.'

'We all wish you both the best of luck,' Andy said. 'Jackie was really great today and I've got a feeling it won't be that long before we see him on TV again.'

They drove back to Letchworth most of the way in silence. It was a satisfied silence though.

'It's gone twelve already,' Andy said. 'I promised that I'd go shopping with the wife. I'm quite looking forward to doing something normal, if I'm being honest. I think I've had enough excitement for a while.'

Mac knew exactly what he meant. It had been quite an investigation, by turns utterly frustrating and utterly surprising. He too was looking forward to a quiet weekend. The thought of Nora's service on Tuesday sneaked into his head. He quickly pushed it back out again. He wanted to enjoy what was left of his weekend.

Back at the station Andy thanked them all once again before disappearing off to the supermarket.

'I'd better get going too,' Tommy said. 'I've got to help Bridget with... er... something. See you later.'

'What about you, Mac?' Kate asked.

'I've got a date with Tim to watch the Villa live on the TV and hopefully some refreshment will be involved. What about you, Kate? You can always join us if you're at a loose end?'

'Thanks Mac, but I'm meeting my brother this evening and I've got a few things to do before that,' she replied.

'See you soon then.'

Mac watched her go and wished her luck.

Chapter Thirty One

Kate had decided while they were driving back what she really wanted and she now knew exactly what she needed to do. She thought about it again on the train back to Welwyn. The flat was cold and silent when she walked in. It had always felt cold and unwelcoming and she had no good memories of living there. All she'd known within these four walls was the misery of a lonely life. She'd had more than enough of that.

Her old life had to end now.

She packed a large suitcase as quickly as she could and left the flat behind without a backward glance. She was only looking forward now. She felt a little nervous as the train neared Letchworth but the dominant emotion she felt was hope. As the train pulled into the station the sun came out and suddenly it was summer again.

She took this as a sign.

Toni was out so she was once again waiting outside her flat. She'd hidden her suitcase behind a bin as she wanted to see what Toni thought of her idea first. It was nearly three by the time a little car pulled up and Toni got out. She didn't see Kate at first, she seemed to be quite thoughtful as she went to the back of the car and started pulling out bags full of groceries.

'Need a hand?' Kate asked as she walked towards the car.

Toni turned and her look of surprise was immediately replaced by the warmest of smiles.

'Sure,' Toni replied.

'You've got a lot of food here,' Kate said as they carried the bags towards the door.

Toni stopped and opened the door. She picked up the bags and then turned to face Kate.

'I've bought enough for two,' she simply said.

Tears came to Kate's eyes. There was so much meaning, so much hope in that short sentence.

'I've brought a bag of my own,' Kate said.

She went to the side of the house and retrieved her suitcase.

Toni laughed when she saw it. She then said the most beautiful words that Kate would ever hear.

'Welcome home, Kate,' she said as she held open the door.

They went straight to bed, not to make love but just to hold each other. Kate found tears coming to her eyes again, tears of happiness. Without saying anything they knew that they had just laid the path that could only lead to a life together.

'I want you to come and meet my brother and his wife tonight, if you want to that is?' Kate asked.

'I'd love to but are you sure?' Toni asked.

'I've never been so sure of anything in my life,' Kate said as she caressed the side of Toni's face with her hand.

'Then I'd love to,' Toni said.

'I want to tell everyone else about us too. I don't want to keep it a secret or is that going too fast?'

'I was awake for most of last night, thinking about that, Kate. If I'm honest, I was miserable without you. I've waited thirty eight very long years before I met you so, as far as I'm concerned, go as fast as you like.'

'I was miserable last night too. I don't want to be without you ever again,' Kate said.

They hugged and kissed and, although the words 'I love you' hadn't yet been said, they both knew that they weren't too far away.

Magnus was both surprised and happy to see Toni turn up with his sister. Kate remembered what her brother had said about the shit they'd have to deal with after their father had died. For once he'd been wrong.

The mood that evening was light and happy and the talk never stopped.

Nobomi told them all about her impressions of London and had them laughing out loud at times about the things that had struck her as being strange. Kate had never realised that she could be so funny. Later, while she and Magnus were talking, she looked over to see that Toni and Nobomi seemed to be getting on very well indeed. Her heart had never been fuller.

Sundays for Kate had always been the black void between Saturday, when shopping and other things filled up the day, and the welcome return to work. That first Sunday with Toni though was wonderful. The sun shone down on them as they went out for breakfast. It felt so special to be out and about with Toni and seeing other couples didn't make her feel sad anymore. It was strange but just being with Toni made every little thing they did so special and so new.

That Monday she turned up for work early. She needed to talk to Dan Carter. However, he went straight on the phone as soon as he came in so she had to bide her time. The whole team was meeting at nine thirty as Dan had something to tell them. She was hoping to get in and see him before then.

She was delayed by the arrival of the honeymoon couple. Jo and Gerry entered the room and the whole team got up to greet them. Kate thought that they both looked wonderful. Gerry was bronzed and relaxed and looked years younger while Jo was Jo but even more so. Married life appeared to have done wonders for them both.

Kate said hello to both of them but kept an eye on Dan. As soon as he put the phone down, she slipped into his office.

'Kate, what do you need?' Dan asked as he looked up.

'A minute of your time that's all. There's something I need to tell you.'

Dan thought that she looked quite serious.

'You're not leaving us or anything?' he asked with some concern.

'No, no, well I hope not. It's something personal and, if I'm honest, I don't quite know where to start.'

'Is this about you and Toni?' Dan asked.

Kate's mouth fell open with surprise.

'You know?'

'Oh God, I should think that everyone knows about that. It's a small station Kate and news travels fast,' Dan said. 'I mean, the way you two have been mooning over each other there was no way that you'd be able to keep it a secret.'

'Is it okay? With you, I mean,' Kate asked.

She looked nervously at Dan as he gave this some thought.

'No, I wouldn't use the word okay,' he said giving her a mischievous look. 'No, ecstatic I think would just about cover it.'

Seeing Kate's puzzled look Dan carried on.

'There've been lots of times when I've had to ask the team to work late, sometimes very late, and then I get it in the neck from the wives and partners when birthday celebrations, school plays and shopping trips have to be missed or restaurant bookings cancelled. Toni's a copper, and a good one too, so I know that she won't moan when I dish out the overtime. So, it's a win-win situation for me as far as I can see,' he said with smile.

'Thanks, Dan,' Kate said as she leant forward and touched his hand.

'Is that it?' Dan said gruffly. 'Go on get back to work. I'd bet that Jo is showing everyone her photos by now.'

She got up to go.

'Kate, be careful,' Dan said. 'There are people in the station who don't think so kindly about you and Toni.'

'I know but, so long as you and the team are okay with it, then I couldn't care less about them.'

275

Kate walked back into the team room. They were all crowded around Jo as she showed them all her honeymoon photos on a big tablet. Even Mac was craning his neck to get a look.

The thought struck Kate that, apart from Jo and Gerry, they probably all knew about her and Toni and probably had for a while. As far as she could tell they were the same with her as they'd ever been. Her thoughts were interrupted by Jo.

'A penny for them, girl,' she said.

'I was just thinking how much being married suits the two of you. You both look absolutely wonderful. I take it that you had a good time?' Kate asked.

'Good? Oh, it was much better than that. He may not look much but that man's a devil when he gets going,' Jo said with a wink.

This made Kate laugh.

'How are you and Toni getting on?' Jo asked.

Kate's mouth fell open with surprise for the second time that morning.

'Oh, I kept up with all the station gossip. We have Twitter in Jamaica too you know,' she said.

'Well, we're getting on great, better than great actually, much better,' Kate replied feeling somewhat flustered.

'Look, we'll need a couple of weeks to recover but I'd like you and Toni to come visit us. We can have a drink and I'll do some nice food and then you'll really get to see all the honeymoon photos properly. What do you think?' Jo asked.

Kate found tears welling from her eyes and she gave Jo a big hug. She'd thought it would be so hard telling everyone about her and Toni. She hadn't expected this.

'I'll take that as a yes then,' Jo said before she went back to her husband.

Kate looked at the team around her as they all were talking excitedly together and especially at Mac. She thought of Toni and her little flat just down the road where she had only known happiness and she thought of their future life together. She had a very strange feeling, one that she'd never experienced before in her life.

When she'd been young she had never felt that she belonged anywhere; in Ireland, where her mother was from, they thought she was English; in England they thought she was Irish and strange with it too because of her red hair and in Iceland they didn't know what to make of her at all. Throughout her life she always been aware of being different and strange.

She didn't feel any of that now and she knew the strange feeling for what it was.

For the first time in her life she felt as if she belonged.

Chapter Thirty Two

Mac had seen Kate in Dan's office as he walked in and he had a good idea what they were talking about. She looked both relieved and radiant when she walked out. Things had obviously gone well between her and Toni over the weekend and Mac silently wished them both all the luck in the world.

After all the exertions of the week, and apart from a short session down the Magnets with Tim, Mac had a quiet Sunday. He had been hoping to spend some time with Bridget and Tommy but they both seemed to be mysteriously busy as they had been for some time. It was probably just as well as his back had started playing up anyway. Tomorrow was Nora's service and it was approaching fast like a big black cloud. He couldn't wait until it was over and done with.

His thoughts were interrupted by Dan.

'Well, the first piece of business this morning is to welcome back our honeymooners Jo and Gerry. Welcome back both of you. While you've been away, I can safely say that a few things have happened. In fact, it's been a really good few weeks for our team. Chris, Adil, Leigh and myself have finally nailed the nutter who stabbed three people in Hertford while Andy, Kate, Tommy and Mac have gone one better and only solved the 'Match of the Day' murders. I know that it's been a real team effort so I'd just like to thank you all. The reason I've asked you all to turn up together like this was partly, of course, to thank you and tell you how much your efforts are appreciated. I've also been told to pass on the thanks of all the Chief Constables. You've given the Three Counties policing efforts a really good reputation, not just nationwide but even internationally so I've been told.'

He stopped and looked around the team.

'One of the other reasons was to tell you that Jackie Hughes is being made an honorary policeman at a special ceremony that the bosses are cooking up. I'm not saying that he doesn't deserve it, and I suppose it's good PR for us, but I've heard that the main reason for the event is that the Chief Constable of Cambridgeshire is a mad fan and he's desperate to get some selfies with Jackie. Anyway, you'll all be invited and I'd attend if I were you as I've heard that there's going to be a free bar.'

This made the whole team smile.

'So, onto the main reason for this meeting. Chris will soon be leaving the team as he's had an offer to take over the local detective team in Cambridgeshire. It obviously makes sense for Chris as he lives in that neck of the woods and his first child is on the way so he won't be working so far from home. So, I'd like to take the opportunity to thank Chris for all the hard work he's put in since he joined the team. You'll be really missed.'

Dan shook Chris's hand. The rest of the team lined up to do the same.

'So, that means that there'll be a vacancy for a DI within the team. Anyone who's been a sergeant for at least two years can apply for a promotion,' Dan said as he looked meaningfully at Jo, Adil and Kate. 'I know this may not be the usual procedure but, as we're so popular with those upstairs at the moment, I've been told that I can award a promotion to whoever I like. You've only got four weeks to decide so get thinking. Thankfully, it looks like our local bad lads have finally had enough of the beach as over the weekend we've had an attempted ram raid on an ATM machine in Stevenage, a burglary with violence in Cottered and a mugging in Luton. That last one seems to be racially aggravated too. So, Andy if you can take the ram raid, Chris the burglary and Adil, Tommy and myself will take the mugging as we know the area well. Martin's got all the details for you so, enough of standing around looking at me, get on with it.'

279

Dan turned to Mac.

'Can I have a quick word in my office?' he asked.

Mac nodded. He went into Dan's office and waited patiently while Dan had a few words with the returning honeymooners.

'My God but they look well, don't they?' Dan said as he sat down.

Mac could only agree.

'I just wanted to say thanks again Mac for all your help. I also believe that it's the anniversary of your wife's death tomorrow, isn't it?'

Mac didn't need reminding.

'Yes. Yes, it is. We're having a small family service tomorrow evening at our local church to mark it.'

He noticed that Dan had given him a puzzled look after he'd said this.

'If I'm being honest, I'm not looking forward to it,' Mac continued. 'It's been a strange year but, thinking back, not all of it was bad. That's mainly down to you, Dan, in allowing me to get back to work again. I honestly don't know what I'd have done otherwise.'

'If I'm being honest Mac, my motives were entirely selfish. With such a new team I knew that your experience would really help. Not only that but I know that you've also helped some of the team with advice, like Kate for instance.'

'Well, she's had a tough time recently and I've been glad to help. She seems to be in a good place now thankfully,' Mac said.

'So, if anything big turns up in the near future, I take it that you'd be interested?' Dan asked.

'I must admit that I'm feeling a little tired at the moment but yes, after I get this service over with and I've had a few days rest I dare say that I'll be getting bored again. You've got my number, just call me.'

'I'll do that,' Dan said.

When he walked out of Dan's office everyone was huddled around their computers cramming the details of their new cases into their heads. No-one looked up so Mac left quietly. He felt sad to be leaving them. He knew that it was just a small pebble of sadness though when compared to the mountain of what was coming.

Once he'd gone, they all turned around as Dan came out of his office.

'Do you think he's twigged yet?' Tommy asked.

'No, I don't think he has,' Dan replied. 'He's trying really hard not to think about tomorrow so you and Bridget might just get away with it.'

Mac dawdled around town for a while and once again found himself in David's and not because it was raining this time. The sun was shining and it seemed to be bringing the best out of people. They were smiling and stopping to chat to friends or just sitting outside the cafes and pubs silently watching the world go by.

He started browsing the crime section and noticed a poster on the wall –

Coming soon - the true explosive story behind the 'Match of the Day' Murders. Completely rewritten and including exclusive first-hand interviews with the people involved.

It had a picture of Becky Ferrante at the bottom. She'd already contacted him about an interview and he was more than happy to help her. After all it was her 'gut feeling' about Aaron Farzan that had started them on the path to the truth in the first place.

He looked at his watch. He had a whole afternoon to get through before he was due to meet Tim in the Magnets. He took his time but he knew what he was going to buy. There was a new Wallander book that he saw straight away, well new to him anyway. He'd was looking forward to reading it and wondered if that was just because it was all about a quite sad middle-aged policeman. He looked at his watch, ten minutes had passed since the last time he looked. He paid for the book and went into the café.

He'd only been sat down for a few minutes when he noticed that someone had sat opposite him. He looked up and saw Mrs. Alexander.

'I'm getting a distinct feeling of déjà vu at this moment,' Mac said with a smile. 'How are you?'

'I'm okay, better than I have been for years. Well, for five years to be precise. I've just come from the police station as I wanted to thank you all personally for what you've done. They said that you'd just left and I guessed that you might come here.'

Mac looked at her closely as she spoke. She did indeed look better, even the shape of her face seemed to have changed a little. All those years of mourning her daughter had still left a mark but it was beginning to fade now.

'How's your husband and family?' Mac asked.

'We're good, it feels as if we're finally getting our lives back again. We've been on hold since Chloe left us, we've just been waiting for something to happen. Now at last it has,' she said with a smile.

Mac was curious.

'So, the fact that the person who killed Chloe has more or less gotten away with it doesn't hurt?'

She shook her head.

'No, not really. We now know how Chloe died and who did it and probably why. That's enough for now. I remember Aaron. He was a shy boy but I could see that he really liked Chloe. I also knew that he was a troubled boy too. It's my belief that it was a moment of madness on his part. He was on a cocktail of drugs from what I've heard and I doubt if that helped. I don't believe that there was any hate in his heart, Mr. Maguire, and that's what's important. It's my guess that he's suffering anyway. He can never come back to the country he was born in and Chloe's death will be hanging over him wherever he is.'

'Yes, I guess that you're probably right there,' Mac said thinking that she was very wise in letting her anger go.

They chatted for a while longer and, before she went, she gave him a smile. It was the first time that he'd seen a genuine smile on her face.

Alone again Mac looked out of the window at the people passing by. The shorts, sandals and the bright colours of their clothes made it look as if he'd just been transported to a holiday resort. He decided to join them. He started walking and, for some reason, he found himself outside the church. He stood looking at the building for a while before he decided to go in.

It was cool and quiet inside. He'd been wondering why he'd come this way and perhaps it was because he needed a little peace. He sat there enjoying the silence until the thought of tomorrow's service disturbed his thoughts. Father Pat Curran appeared out of a side door, genuflected in front of the altar and then walked towards him.

'Mac, you haven't got your dates wrong by any chance?' Father Pat said with a smile.

'No, Father. I just felt that a little peace might be good, that's all.'

'Shall I leave you then?'

'No, you don't have to. I was looking for peace but I'm afraid that I haven't found it.'

Father Pat sat down beside him.

'Is this about tomorrow then?' he asked.

'Yes, I'm afraid that this service has been hanging on my mind,' Mac replied. 'I want to get it over and done with but then, when I have, I know that it will have been a whole year that I'll have been without Nora. For some reason that scares me. Perhaps I'm scared that I might forget her.'

'You won't Mac, that I can promise you. Yes, some say that it's the hardest anniversary to bear but you're lucky Mac, you have friends who'll support you.'

Mac heard a loud bang from outside the church.

'What was that?' Mac asked.

'Oh, it's just them next door in the parish hall carrying in some tables,' Father Pat hastily replied. 'There's a party in there tomorrow. It's...er...someone's birthday, I believe, but don't worry, they won't be starting until seven thirty and the service will be well over by then.'

'Thanks Father, for the service. I'm sure that it means a lot to Bridget.'

'And I hope it might mean a lot to you too. Cheer up Mac, it might not be as bad as you think.'

He thought of Father Pat's words as he wandered around Letchworth. He couldn't think of any way that the service might be enjoyable. As far as he was concerned it was like a visit to the dentist's, just something to get out of the way. His thoughts were interrupted by his phone going off.

It was a text from Tim.

In Magnets now. Where are you?

He looked at the clock on the phone. Tim was early for once and Mac was truly glad for it.

Chapter Thirty Three

The dreaded Tuesday arrived. It was sunny out as Mac watched the birds feeding as he ate breakfast. He felt the loss of his wife even more than usual. He could sometimes feel her presence and even hear her voice in his head but today there was just a black void. He knew that half of him had died when she had gone.

The better half too, he thought.

Mac looked at the clock. He still had a few hours to kill as Bridget was picking him up around twelve. She was going to take him out for a drive and lunch somewhere. Mac supposed that it would be something to do while they both waited for six thirty to arrive.

Mac stopped himself. He was starting to feel sorry for himself again. He disliked self-pity in others but truly hated it in himself. Bridget and everyone else were trying to do their best for him so he told himself to buck up. He got the dog lead and Terry immediately started jumping up and down in a frenzy. Mac would take him out for the longest walk that he could. After that he'd visit Nora's grave, make sure that it was clean and tidy and then have a chat with her. It would be something to do.

Bridget was quite surprised to find her father being so positive and guessed that he was putting it on for her sake. She knew that he hadn't been looking forward to today. She drove him out towards Cambridge and stopped at a little town called St. Ives. They parked up and Bridget took him to a pub that overlooked the river. It was one that Mac had been to several times before. There were lots of brightly dressed people out and about even though it was a weekday. The sight of the people out walking, the river and the swans floating effortlessly by cheered Mac up as did the warm sun that shone down on all of them.

'This was one of your mother's favourite drives and she loved sitting here watching the river go by,' Mac said.

'I know dad,' Bridget said. 'If I'm honest, I wasn't totally sure if it would be the right place to take you today of all days.'

'It's the right place Bridget. I just needed reminding that I should be thinking about all the good times that I had with your mother rather than just feeling sorry for myself. After lunch, do you fancy a stroll up the river? There was this place that used to do the most wonderful ice cream.'

'Yes, it's still there too. I drove up last weekend and checked it out,' Bridget said.

The afternoon went well and he enjoyed being able to spend some time with his daughter. If the service only went half as well, he would be very thankful.

He thought that they were quite lucky to find a parking space right outside the church when they arrived as cars seemed to be parked everywhere. He thought that it must be down to the birthday party in the parish hall next door.

'Just hang on a second, dad,' Bridget said as she took out her phone. 'I just want to check that Tommy's here.'

She texted something and then smiled when the reply came.

'It's okay, he's here. Do you want to go in?' she asked.

Mac gave his daughter a strained smile, girded his loins and opened the church's door.

He stopped dead with shock. The church was packed and he wondered if he'd blundered into someone else's service by mistake. Then he noticed some familiar faces. Everyone from Dan's team was there and he especially noticed Kate and Toni who were smiling at him and holding hands. His old sergeant, now Detective Inspector Peter Harper, was also there with a contingent from his old station. Old friends and neighbours were all there and, best of all, his sisters and his oldest friends Blue and Liam from Birmingham were there too.

As he walked up the aisle, he realised that just about everyone he would have liked to have been there was there.

Bridget led him up to the front where two seats were free. Tim stepped out and let Bridget sit beside Tommy. Mac now knew what it was that had kept them both so busy lately. Mac sat down next to his friend.

'Are you okay, Mac?' Tim asked as he touched the back of Mac's hand.

'I am, Tim. Yes, I am now.'

Father Pat started the service off.

'This will not be a normal service. We'll of course have some prayers at the beginning and end of the service but this will mostly be about celebrating a life and not mourning a death.'

After a few short prayers, friends stood up one by one and told stories about Nora. Some were very funny too and Mac reminded himself that his wife had loved to laugh.

She'd have loved this, he thought as he looked around.

Then Bridget got up and talked about how wonderful she'd been as a mother. Mac nearly cried at that point but he somehow managed to keep the tears at bay.

There were more prayers before Father Pat said, 'There's just one more item and then the service will be over. Afterwards, if you all want to go into the parish hall there will be food and music and also a bar or so I've been told.'

Father Pat winked at Mac.

'Now, Bridget has asked for this particular hymn to be sung as it was her mother's favourite. Thanks to Jo, one of Mac's colleagues, we've been able to get someone really special to sing it.'

He pointed towards the back of the church. In the choir stalls looking down on them were a half a dozen

287

or so of the choir that Mac had heard at Jo's wedding. The woman at the front started singing by herself...

'Amazing Grace, How sweet the sound
That saved a wretch like me
I once was lost, but now am found
T'was blind but now I see'

Mac thought it the most wonderful version of the song that he'd ever heard. When the rest of the choir joined in on the second verse Mac could no longer help himself and the tears came pouring out. Bridget held him but, although they were tears of emotion, they weren't tears of sadness. Tears of gratitude perhaps for the lengths that his family and friends had gone to in order to make this happen for him.

The evening went by in a flash as he was busy all night going from person to person, thanking them for turning up and catching up with them as best he could. Luckily, his sisters and friends from Birmingham were staying for a few days so he'd have plenty of time to catch up with them later. He was really looking forward to that, they had a lot of catching up to do.

Afterwards, as he drove back home in the taxi with Bridget and Tommy, he felt a sense of peace descend on him. He sincerely hoped that the worst times were now behind him. He wanted to stop being sad and remember his wife for what she had been in life.

A simple and beautiful woman and his Nora.

The End

I hope that you've enjoyed this story. If you have please leave a review and let me know what you think.
PCW

Also in the Mac Maguire series

The Body in the Boot

The Dead Squirrel

The Weeping Women

The Blackness

23 Cold Cases

Two Dogs

The Chancer

The Tiger's Back

The Eight Bench Walk

https://patrickcwalshauthor.wordpress.com/

Made in the USA
Las Vegas, NV
30 April 2022

48225860R00173